The C

D0539914

FREE GIFTS FROM
THE ARMADA COLLECTORS' CLUB

Look out for these tokens in your favourite Armada series! All
you need to do to receive a special FREE GIFT is collect 6 tokens in
the same series and send them off to the address below with a
postcard marked with your name and address including postcode.
Start collecting today!

The Chalet School series by Elinor M. Brent-Dyer

Jo of the Chalet School

Elinor M. Brent-Dyer

Armada
An Imprint of HarperCollins*Publishers*

First published in 1925 by W. & R. Chambers Ltd
First published in paperback in 1967 by
William Collins Sons & Co. Ltd.
This impression 1993

Armada is an imprint of HarperCollins Children's Books,
a division of HarperCollins Publishers Ltd,
77–85 Fulham Palace Road, Hammersmith,
London W6 8JB

Printed and bound in Great Britain by
HarperCollins Manufacturing, Glasgow

CHAPTER ONE

The Three

"Charlie's neat, and Charlie's sweet, and Charlie
is a dandy;
Charlie, he's a nice young man, and feeds the
girls on candy."

"OH JO! Do stop that awful thing! I'm sick of it!"

Joey Bettany kicked her heels against the fence on which she was sitting, and gave a chuckle. "I think it's jolly nice."

"Well, *I* don't; and I just wish you'd stop it!" retorted Grizel Cochrane, frowning.

"Poor old thing! You *are* in a bad way!" laughed Joey teasingly.

"I just wish term would begin, and the others come back!" declared Grizel.

She looked round at the lake beside which she was standing, Ringed in by big mountains, with a long, narrow valley stretching away to the west, and water-meadows at its southern extremity the Tiernsee in the North Tyrol is surely one of the loveliest places in the world, and an ideal spot for such a school as the Chalet School. Here Joey Bettany's sister, Madge, had established herself at the end of the previous April, beginning with nine pupils—Joey, Grizel, and Simone Lecoutier (niece of the French lady who had joined in the enterprise), and six Tyrolean girls who came from the summer chalets which have grown up round the lake—and ending the first term with just twice that number.

The new term would begin in ten days' time. Meanwhile,

Joey, Grizel, and one other pupil, Juliet Carrick, an orphan and the ward of Miss Bettany, were finding time hang rather heavily on their hands. They missed their other friends, especially Grizel, who was a gregarious little soul, and, unlike the other two, had no resources of her own.

Grizel was an active tomboyish person, who was happiest when she was rushing about, climbing the steep mountain-paths, or rowing over the blue lake in one of the clumsy but serviceable boats which were kept there, largely for the use of the many tourists who came there during the summer months.

To make matters worse, Miss Maynard, the mathematics mistress, had brought back for Joey a copy of *The Appalachian Nursery Song-Book*, and Joey had sung them in season and out of season, till even the donor of the gift was beginning to regret that she had ever brought it. Grizel was not musical—Herr Anserl, the music-master who came every week to the Chalet from Spärtz, declared that she had as much soul as a machine, and played like one—and before many days were over she hated those nursery songs, a fact of which naughty Jo was not slow to take advantage.

Now, the songstress swung herself down from her precarious position on the top of the fence that divided Briesau, the little village where the Chalet School was, from the rough pathway that leads round the lake to Geisalm, the next hamlet, and demanded briskly, "What are you so humpy about?"

"It's all so slow," returned Grizel. "You and Juliet are always reading—unless you're reading, and she's working. I wish we could have an expedition somewhere!"

"P'r'aps we can." Joey considered for a moment. "Where'd you like to go?"

"D'you think Miss Bettany would take us into Innsbruck the next time she goes? If we wrote to the Maranis they might meet us. Gisela said in her last letter that she and Maria would be staying there till term began."

"That's rather an idea. I'd love to see Gisela again; I think she's a splendid girl."

"Some of the others might be there too!" Grizel was

growing enthusiastic over her own plan. "Wouldn't it be lovely if we could all meet and do something together?"

"Splendiferous!" Joey gave a little leap into the air. "Let's go and hunt up my sister, and ask her at once!"

"We can't this minute. She's gone down to Spärtz to see Herr Anserl about the new people, and to buy some more china."

"How do you know?" demanded Joey, her face falling.

"I went as far as the top of the mountain-path with her and Miss Maynard. Never mind! Let's go as far as Seespitz and see the train come in. We can get some apples from old Grete, too."

"All right," agreed Joey. "But it's no fun meeting the trains now; everyone's going away—not coming."

"It does seem lonely, now all the visitors are going," sighed Grizel.

Joey glanced at her. "It'll be all right when the others come back," she said. "What crowds of us there'll be! All the old girls, and Wanda and Marie, and their cousin Paula, and Rosalie Dene, and that American girl Evadne Lannis, and Vanna di Ricci."

"It's gorgeous to think we're growing like this. Why, Madge thinks we may get up to thirty by Christmas—and it's only our second term!"

"I know. And I thought your sister said you weren't to use her Christian name in school," put in Grizel a trifle maliciously.

"I know she did; and I don't! 'Tisn't term yet!" retorted Jo.—"I say, there's the smoke of the train! We'll have to hurry!"

They set off running at their best pace, but the train with its procession of funny little open cars got there before them, and, when they had reached it, its small load of passengers were already making their way to the boat-landing where the little white steamer awaited them. There were only ten visitors. The remainder were dwellers in the valleys round about. Some might even have come from Tiernkirche, a large village some four or five miles away from Scholastika, the hamlet at the head of the lake.

Many of those who lived on the lakeside recognised the

girls in their short brown gym tunics and brown blazers, and called out a friendly *"Grüss Gott!"* as they passed.

The strangers looked curiously at the two children, so obviously not Tyrolean, and commented on them. Grizel, with floating brown curls, tanned rosy cheeks, and dancing eyes, was typically English; and Jo Bettany of the pointed face with straight black hair, neatly bobbed, and eyes like pools of ink, was apt to attract notice wherever she went. Years of delicacy had left her with hollowed cheeks which had not yet filled out; and even a summer spent in the life-giving atmosphere of the mountains and at an altitude of some three thousand feet had not altogether taken away the fragility of her appearance, though she was stronger and healthier than she had been since she was a very small child.

Of these inquisitive visitors, none showed greater interest than two Italian girls of fifteen and twelve. They turned and stared at the pair with such concentration that the younger one tripped over some wood that happened to be lying in the path. Joey and Grizel promptly made a rush, and hauled her to her feet, Joey chattering the whole time.

"Are you hurt?—*Etes-vous blessée?*" she demanded, dropping rapidly from English into French as the other child looked at her blankly. "Oh, bother! She doesn't understand! *Haben Sie sich weh getan?*"

The little Italian shook her head and smiled. She had no idea what Joey was saying, as she spoke only Italian. Her sister, however, understood French, and caught at the word *blessée*.

"She asks if you are hurt," she said to the younger child in their own tongue.

At the sound of the musical syllables Jo's face lightened. She knew very little Italian, although her French and German were both fluent. She hastily recast her sentence.

"*Nuocete?*" she demanded.

The two girls laughed; and at that moment a gentleman, obviously their father, called them imperatively, "Bianca! Luigia! *Venite—adesso!*"

They went immediately, the elder pausing to say, *"Addio; e grazie!"*

"Goodbye; and thank you," translated Joey for the benefit of the less learned Grizel.

"They're rather jolly, aren't they?"

"Yes. But their father is a bossy old thing," commented Grizel.

"Here's Grete," cried Joey. *"Grüss Gott*, Grete!"

Grete, an old shrivelled apple woman, greeted them with an outburst of Tyrolean German, to which Jo responded with much fluency, and Grizel with a few somewhat halting sentences. She was very slow at picking up languages, and often had to think before she got the word she wanted. Jo, on the other hand, never had the smallest difficulty, and chattered away as rapidly and as gaily as the old woman.

"There is snow on the mountains," she remarked presently, as old Grete picked out her best apples for them.

"Yes, *mein Fräulein*. The winter will come quickly now. Soon the snow will descend from the skies; the lake will freeze; and then we shall sit all day by the stove, and shiver—shiver, and long for the spring to come again."

"I shan't," observed Grizel in her own language after she had got the sense of this. "I shall go for walks, and skate."

"Rather! Heaps of skating here, I should think!" agreed Joey. She turned to the old woman. "One skates, *nicht wahr?*"

"Oh yes; one skates. But it is not always safe. There are springs in the lake, and the ice is thin, there. Then, one day, someone more daring or more foolish rushes over, and—there is a crack—a cry! And it is finished! One recovers the bodies in the spring!"

"B-r-r-r-r!" shivered Grizel. "How horrid!"

"We shan't smash in," said Joey confidently. "Herr Mensch and Herr Marani will show us where to go, and they will take care of us!"

"They won't be here all the time," Grizel reminded her.

"Oh well! Herr Braun will, and he will show us where the springs are.—How much, *meine Frau?*"

Grete told her; and when they had paid they strolled slowly homewards, eating the apples. At the little gate they were met by Juliet, who had got tired of her sewing, and come to find them.

"You mean creatures! How dare you go off like that and leave me! " she demanded, laughing. "What have you got? Apples?"

Joey nodded and held out the big paper bag and said "Have one?" Juliet accepted the invitation, and they went on to the Chalet, munching happily.

The Chalet was a very large wooden building which had been designed for a hotel. Miss Bettany had rented it from Herr Braun, the proprietor of the big white-washed hotel which stood near the boat-landing, and had converted it into her school. Up to the present it had proved quite large enough; but now, with the prospect of additional pupils and another mistress, she had been obliged to take the smaller chalet that stood a little way from it, and was making it into a junior house, with a couple of class-rooms, so that she could keep the little ones entirely by themselves. There had been six of them in the previous term, but now their numbers were to be enlarged by four, and the young head-mistress had decided to let the "babies" have their own department this term.

"Won't they be *thrilled*?" said Joey, nodding her head towards this building.

"They certainly will," laughed Grizel. "Heigh-ho! I *shall* be glad when we start school again! I'm longing to see the others! "

"So am I! " said Joey. "I say! I'm hungry. Let's go and see if *Mittagessen* is ready."

They all went in to find Marie Pfeifen, the head of the domestic staff, awaiting them in the *Speisesaal* with bowls of delicious soup, such as she only knew the secret of making.

"I'm glad of a hot dinner! " said Joey. "It's cold today! "

"No wonder! There's snow on the mountains," returned Juliet.

"Two new girls came on the train," Joey remarked presently as she laid down her spoon. "Italians! And they can't speak a word of English! "

10

"Or German," supplemented Grizel. "And the little one didn't seem to understand French either."

"How do you know?" asked Juliet.

"Oh; the little one fell down and we helped her up, and Jo asked if she was hurt. She looked rather silly, and Jo tried her in German, and then the older one spoke to her in Italian; so, of course, we knew they were Italians."

"Surely it's awfully late for visitors? There are only the Kron Prinz Karl and the Post open. I wonder why they've come?"

"They didn't say, and we didn't ask them. Their father called them away. They've got jolly names—Luigia and Bianca."

"Perhaps they're new pupils," suggested Joey as she turned her attention to the *Kalbsbraten* Marie had just placed in front of her.

"Perhaps they aren't! I think they're just tourists come up for a few days," was Grizel's answer to this—"I wonder why it is the things always taste so nice here? I used to loathe veal at home! "

"Something to do with the cooking," said Juliet wisely. "Marie's a jolly good cook! —*Sehr gut*, Marie." This last to Marie, who stood watching them with a smile on her pleasant face.

Marie nodded, well pleased. She liked all the girls at the Chalet, and adored Miss Bettany, who was such a kind mistress, and took such an interest in her younger brothers and sisters. It was worth while working one's hardest for anyone so good, thought Marie. What made it seem better was the fact that Madame also made Fräulein speak politely to her always, and they followed the headmistress's example, and were interested, as well as polite. Marie's conversation sometimes made her less fortunate friends quite green with envy.

When *Mittagessen* was over, the three girls made for the railway once more. They knew that Madame—as they called Miss Bettany—and Miss Maynard, the mathematics mistress, would be coming back that way, and, as they would be laden with parcels, Juliet suggested that a little help in carrying them would be appreciated.

11

When the train arrived the two mistresses looked out of the window and the first thing they saw was the three girls waiting for them.

CHAPTER TWO

The Robin Arrives

"GOOD GIRLS!" said Miss Bettany as she descended. "Yes; you can take those two baskets, Grizel, but carry them carefully—they are full of china. Will you take this suit-case, Juliet? And, Joey, here's a parcel for you—can you manage it? It's rather on the large side!"

"Rather!" said Joey cheerfully. "I say! What heaps of things you must have bought! Is there much more?"

Miss Bettany smiled rather queerly. "Only two suitcases, and I'll manage those. Miss Maynard is going back to Spärtz, and then she's going on to Innsbruck; so we must do without her."

The three gasped. Miss Maynard going to Innsbruck? *Now?*

Their head-mistress knew what was in their minds, but she said nothing, though her dark eyes twinkled with fun. She sent Joey across to the little ticket-office to buy the new ticket for Miss Maynard, and stood with them until the train had vanished round a curve. Then she bade them pick up their burdens and come home.

"But—but what's the joke?" demanded Joey as they set out. "Why have you got all these things? What is Miss Maynard going back to Innsbruck for? What's it all about? Why——"

"Stop—stop, Joey!" cried her sister in laughing protest. "Let me answer those questions before you ask any more!

12

Now, let me see. There's no joke at all—not the faintest shadow of one. We've got all these things because they had to be brought up, and we guessed that you would meet us. As to why Miss Maynard has gone to Innsbruck and what it's all about, that is a story which can wait until we get home. It's rather a long one, and I'm too chilly to tell stories just now. It's much warmer in the valley than it is up here."

Joey said, "Won't you really tell us anything?"

"Not until we're at home," said Miss Bettany decidedly. "Tell me what you've been doing instead."

"Oh, just the usual things! We went down to meet the last train, and there were two Italian girls on it," began Grizel. "I thought they looked awfully jolly."

Miss Bettany nodded. "Yes; I saw them in Spärtz. Did Marie give you a good dinner?"

"Topping—I mean very nice," said Jo, correcting herself hastily. Her sister had inaugurated a crusade against slang, declaring that she would not allow the foreigners to pick up the appalling expressions that the English girls very frequently used. All three felt this edict. Perhaps Grizel came off the worst. But, young as she was, Madge Bettany always made herself obeyed, and they were doing their best to speak good English only.

"Miss Bettany," said Grizel at this point, "whatever will Evadne Lannis do about not talking slang when she comes?"

"My dear girl, why should you imagine that it will be worse for her than it is for you? I shall be sorry for the rest of us if it *is*! "

"But Americans do use a great deal of slang, don't they?" queried Juliet.

"Not at all," replied Miss Bettany. "I have known Americans who used as pure English as anyone could wish. Quite possibly Evadne will; and, if she doesn't, then you people must try to remember not to pick up any of her expressions."

"Hurrah! Here comes Marie and Eigen!" cried Jo suddenly, as Marie and her little brother who helped with the rough work came running towards them.

Eigen was a sturdy little fellow of eleven, and quite accustomed to carrying loads, so he took two of the cases with a cheerful grin, and Marie commandeered the other as well as Joey's big parcel, and they were soon inside the *Speisesaal*, with its green-washed walls, and long dark wood tables with their cloths of blue and white checked material.

"Coffee, Marie, as hot as ever you can! *Auch Brötchen*," ordered Miss Bettany as she threw aside her coat and hat and warmed her hands at the great white porcelain stove that stood in one corner of the room. "Get chairs, girls, and come and sit down. I know you're all aching to hear my story."

"Aching? I shall expire from sheer curiosity if I don't hear soon!" Jo declared as she hauled up a couple of wooden stools for herself and her sister, and collapsed on one of them.

Madge laughed. "Poor old thing! I hope you won't do that! Here's the coffee, thank goodness! It's positively wintry up here today! Just look at the lake!" Three pairs of eyes glanced casually at the Tiernsee, which had a cold grey look, and then everyone turned imploringly to the Head. "Take your coffee," she said. "Thank you, Marie. We shan't need anything now till sixteen o'clock. Fräulein Juliet will bring the bowls along to the kitchen when we have finished."

Marie curtsied and trotted off to her own domains, and Jo, Grizel, and Juliet turned eagerly to Miss Bettany, who was drinking her coffee slowly and with a meditative air. "Joey," she said, "do you remember a Captain Humphries who stayed with us in Cornwall some years ago?"

Joey shook her head. "No; I'm sorry, but I don't."

"I suppose you wouldn't really." Miss Bettany set down her bowl. "It was years and years ago. He was a great friend of our father's." Madge Bettany paused a moment. "He came to see us in the summer holidays, and he took us all over—Dick and me. He was very good to us, and Dick adored him. When he went back to France—he was home on leave—he used to write at first. Then, when peace was signed, he was sent up the Rhine: he was in the army of

14

occupation, you see. Then, somehow, we drifted apart. I had you," she smiled at her small sister, "to look after, and Dick was training for his forestry work. I've often thought of him, because he was so good to us, but I've never seen or heard of him till I met him in Spärtz today."

"In Spärtz? Did you meet him there? What's he like? Is he coming here? Why did he stop writing?" Needless to say, it was Joey who poured forth these questions. The other two sat deeply thrilled, but silent.

"For asking questions, I'd back you against anyone, Joey Bettany!" declared her sister. "Yes; it was in Spärtz. I was bargaining with an old lady for some crocks, and he saw me. He is on his way to Vienna, really, and from there he is going to Russia. He recognised me at once, and came over and spoke to me. He's had a very bad time, poor fellow! He married a Polish girl whom he met in Cologne, and they were very happy, I believe. They had a little girl whom they both worshipped, and, after the Rhine was evacuated and he was demobilised, they stayed on in Germany, living in Munich, where he had got some post or other—I didn't quite gather *what*. Mrs Humphries taught the baby, and kept house, and made all her own and the child's clothes, and seems to have done pretty well everything. They were poor, you see; but there was always enough, and she—Marya, he called her—was a good manager. Then, eleven months ago, Captain Humphries noticed that his wife was looking thin and poorly, and that she was easily tired. But she only laughed at him when he worried. Well, things went on like this for another fortnight, and then he insisted on having the doctor, and she gave in."

Here Madge made a pause so long that Joey gave her a little shove, asking plaintively, "That isn't all, is it? Go on; what was wrong with her?"

"It was what people used to call 'rapid decline'," replied her sister gravely. "She had suffered terribly during the war, of course, and the doctor said it was a wonder the trouble hadn't shown itself sooner. He thought that probably her great happiness and the quiet life they had led had helped to keep the disease back. There was nothing they could do for her, of course. That sort of thing can't be cured when it is like that. They could only keep her as happy as possible, and see that things were made easy for her. Captain Humphries did everything he could; but she died in six weeks. Up to the very end she was hopeful, always talking about what they would do when she was strong again, and making heaps of plans for the baby. He told me that it was only the evening before she died that she realised what was going to happen."

"Oh, Madge!" Joey choked.

Madge flung an arm round her little sister. "Joey! Don't cry! Even then she was happy, for they had had seven perfect years together. She died; and for months he has been just looking after the baby, and doing his work, and trying to get used to doing without Marya. Then someone who knew him got him this post in Russia, and, as he can't take the baby with him and has no one with whom he can leave her at Munich, he remembered that his old friend, Herr Anserl, had talked about this English school at Briesau. Funnily enough, dear old Herr Anserl had never mentioned our name. He just talked about 'Madame' and 'Fräulein Joey', as far as I can gather. Captain Humphries decided to bring the baby here if we would take her, and brought her as far as Innsbruck. He was just going to hunt up Herr Anserl and get our proper address from him, when he saw me."

"Then is she coming here tonight?" queried Grizel, who had listened to the story with wide-eyed sympathy.

"Yes; he got a wire this morning, saying that he must be in Petrograd by next Friday, and as he has some business to attend to in Vienna, he must get it done before he goes on to Russia. He will have to set out at once, so I've undertaken the care of the Robin, and Miss Maynard has gone into Innsbruck to fetch her."

"*What* did you say she was called?" demanded Joey.

"Her real name is Cecilia Marya, but they have always called her the Robin."

"How old is she, Madame?" asked Juliet.

"Just six. He says she is a happy little soul and accustomed to living with older people, so we shan't find her too much of a baby. I have told you three her story because
16

I want you to be very kind to her. Captain Humphries will be away for at least a year, so she will have to spend all her holidays with us, and this will have to be her home."

"Where will she sleep?" Grizel wanted to know.

"In your dormitory for the present. In term-time she will be with the other little ones, over at Le Petit Chalet, of course."

"What time is she coming?" asked Joey.

"They will be here by the eighteen o'clock boat, I expect," replied Madge. "And that reminds me, I must go and see about having her bed made properly. Joey, it's your turn to help. Coming?"

"Rather!" Joey jumped up and followed her sister out of the room, leaving the other two alone together.

There was a little silence; then Grizel spoke. "Isn't it weird how everyone seems to come to Madame for help?"

Juliet shook her head. "I don't think so. She's the sort of person people *do* come to. She's a dear, and I adore her!"

"Oh, so do I," agreed Grizel.

Juliet opened her book, and then there was a silence, which remained unbroken until Marie brought in *Kaffee und Kuchen*, and the two Bettanys joined them. After that, they got into their coats, and rushed wildly to the boat-landing, for the steamer was already stopping at Buchau on the other side of the lake. From the windows of the Kron Prinz Karl the two little Italians of the afternoon watched them go racing past and envied them. Neither Joey nor Grizel remembered them. Miss Bettany's story had driven everything else out of their minds. They were literally dancing with excitement as the boat neared the landing-place, and they saw Miss Maynard with a bundle in her arms, standing at the side.

Madge met her as she came off the boat. "Asleep?" she queried in low tones.

"Yes—poor little dear! She's tired out with the travelling and the good-byes," replied Miss Maynard in the same key. "Here's Fritzi with the little trunk.—*Danke sehr, Fritzi.*"

"The girls can take that between them," said Miss Bettany. "Give the baby to me. Your arms must be aching by this time if you've carried her the whole way."

17

"She was so upset at parting from her father," explained Miss Maynard as she gave up her burden. "Hullo, you people! Can you manage that trunk?"

"Oh, rather! But we want to see the Robin!"

"Please let us see the Robin, Madame!"

"Just turn back a tiny bit of the rug, and let us see her! Please do."

The three exclamations came simultaneously.

Miss Bettany shook her head. "You must wait till we get indoors. I don't want her to be out in this awful wind any longer than can be helped. Remember, she's not accustomed to it as you are, and she's not very strong."

They hurried back to the Chalet. In the warm *Speisesaal* Miss Bettany sat down and carefully drew back the rug in which the Robin had been wrapped. The girls pressed forward eagerly.

Such a lovely baby-face! With curly black hair clustering over the small head, and long black lashes resting on the rosy cheeks, which were tear-stained. She was very fast asleep—so fast, that the two mistresses were able to undress her and put her to bed all without waking her, and the upcurling lashes never even fluttered. They lighted the night-light to which she was accustomed and they crept out of the room and ran downstairs to join the others.

The Robin had arrived!

CHAPTER THREE

The Chalet School Grows

THE WHOLE of the next day was devoted by the girls to the Robin, with whom they all fell in love at once. She was a dear little girl, very happy and sunshiny, as her father had said, and not at all shy. The very first morning of her coming, when she awoke, she sat up in bed, looking curiously round at the little curtained-off cubicle with its dainty yellow curtains and pretty touches, rubbed her eyes, and said, "But where am I now?" in the prettiest French.

Joey, who had been lying reading, tumbled out of bed and trotted in to her. "Hullo, Robin!" she said. "Can you speak English?"

"A ver' leetle," replied the Robin. Then she went back to her French. "Who are you? Where am I? And where is papa?" she asked.

"I am Joey Bettany," replied the owner of the name. "You are in Briesau, at the Chalet School; but I don't know where your father is."

"Joey?" The baby made a valiant effort at pronouncing the word, but it failed, and came out something like "Zhoey".

Grizel, in her dressing-gown, appeared. "Hullo," she said. "I'm Grizel—Grizel Cochrane."

"Grizelle," repeated the Robin.—They found that it was a trick of hers to repeat the names of people she met for the first time.—"Zat is easy to say. And ze ozzer demoiselle —what does she call herself?"

"Her name's Juliet," replied Joey in French. "You'll have to buck up and learn to speak English, you know."

"I understand him verree well," replied the Robin with dignity. "It is but zat I do not speak him well. At home, wiz mamma, we speak ze French. Mamma has gone a long way," she went on, dropping into the more familiar language, "and papa is going a long way too, and I cannot go with him, so I must stay with you. Who will give me my bath and dress me and brush my hair?"

"I will," responded Juliet, who had just come out of her cubicle and into the one where the Robin was holding her little court. "Will you get up now, Robin, please? It is time we *began* to get up.—Joey and Grizel, you must hurry up, or you will be late as usual."

The Robin turned her great dark eyes on the tall girl with the long fair hair, who was standing smiling down at her. "Are you Juliet?" she asked.

"Yes, I'm Juliet. Will you get up now?"

19

The Robin clambered out of bed, and dropped on to the floor with a bump. "I can't bath myself," she informed the older girl.

"Never mind." Juliet's French was by no means as fluent as Joey's, and she often had to pause before she got the right words. "I'll do the bathing for you. See, here comes Marie with your tub."

Marie, with a broad smile, appeared between the curtains, carrying a wooden tub and a large jug of hot water. "*Grüss Gott, mein Fräulein,*" she said to Juliet Then, as she looked at the baby, "*Ah, das Engelkind! Grüss Gott, mein Liebling!*"

"*Guten Morgen,*" replied the Robin politely.

She was not at all overcome by being called an angel-child, and Juliet gathered from her chatter as she was tubbed and dressed that pet-names and tender words had been a matter of course in her little life. Just as the little frock of pink woollen material was slipped over her head there came a tap at the door, followed by the entry of Miss Bettany, come to see how her new pupil was faring. "Good morning, girls," she said as she came into the room. "Well, Robin, so you are dressed?—That was kind of you, Juliet. Run along and finish your own dressing now, dear, or you will be late. Robin can come downstairs with me."

The Robin slid her hand into the slender one held out to her. "Good morning, Mademoiselle. Juliet had been so good to me, and Zoë and Grizelle are kind too."

Miss Bettany nodded her head. "Of course! Come along now, dear."

She led the child away, and presently Joey, helping to hang out the *plumeaux* over the balcony railings so that they might be aired, saw them going down to the lake together, the Robin chattering at breathless speed.

"She'll be baby now," she said. "Won't Amy be thankful?"

"Shriek for joy, I should think," laughed Grizel. "It's just as well. She might have been jealous. I say, Joey! Look! There's those girls we saw yesterday. They're staring at the Chalet like anything! See them, Juliet? Don't they look topping—I mean jolly?"

20

"Awfully jolly," agreed Juliet. "I wonder if they're thinking of coming here to school? They're staring hard enough."

The three hung out the *plumeaux*, watching the two Italian girls with such interest that they never heard the bell ring, and Miss Maynard had to come to fetch them. "Now then, you people," she observed cheerfully from the door, "don't you want any breakfast this morning? Whatever are you doing?"

They turned round, all very red at being caught like this. "Miss Maynard, I'm so sorry!" cried Juliet. "We never heard the bell."

"So it seems," returned Miss Maynard dryly. "Well, are you coming?"

They followed her meekly downstairs, and into the *Speisesaal*, where the Robin was making short work of a bowl of hot milk before she attacked her roll and honey.

"Why are you three so late?" demanded Miss Bettany as they came in.

"We were watching those girls," explained Joey as she slid into her seat.

"Which girls? Do you mean those two you talked about yesterday?"

"Yes. They were standing on the lake-path, by the bushes, and staring at the Chalet."

Madge Bettany was interested. "Really?"

"Yes. Oh, *do* you think they might be coming here?" implored Grizel.

Her head-mistress laughed. "My dear girl, I have no idea! They would hear about us, of course, at the Kron Prinz Karl, and that would probably account for their interest."

"It would be gorgeous if they did!" Juliet contributed her share to the conversation. "How many would it make us, Madame?"

"Over thirty."

"Oo-oh, how decent! I do hope they come."

"Wouldn't it be magnificent?"

Miss Bettany laughed again. "You're startling the

Robin. She won't understand such wild enthusiasm.—Do you like honey, Robin? Will you have some more?"

The Robin accepted some more honey and another roll. She was very quiet, watching everything with big eyes, and listening to everything that was said.

"What are you people going to do?" asked the young head-mistress as they finished their *Frühstück*. "I'm going down to Innsbruck tomorrow, and I'll take you all with me to help to carry the parcels, and so on. What do you want to do today?"

They considered. "May we take the boat to Buchau and walk to Seehof?" asked Joey finally. "We can carry the Robin if she gets tired. We might go directly after *Mittagessen*, and get tea there, and then come back by the boat. They give you such gorgeous cakes at the Seehof hotel! "

"Very well; you may do that. This morning, I think you had better show the Robin Briesau. Don't tire her, though!" Miss Bettany smiled at the small eager face under the black curls which was raised to hers. "Do you like walking, Robin?"

"Veree much, t'ank you," replied the Robin promptly.

"Very well, then. That's arranged. Now trot along and make your beds. Do you want to go with them, *Bübchen*?"

The Robin nodded, and slipped down from her chair, and trotted happily out of the room with them.

Miss Maynard stood looking after them. "Poor little soul! " she murmured.

Miss Bettany nodded. "Yes, indeed! I don't like the idea of Captain Humphries going to Russia! One hears such dreadful stories about happenings there."

"She's such a baby," said her colleague. "Well, talking won't alter things. What shall we do today?"

"I want the new dormitory over here put right," replied Miss Bettany. "We can put the curtains up, now that the beds are in place. Then, there's Mademoiselle's at Le Petit Chalet, and yours here to put in order. Shall we go up and do the long dormitory first?"

Miss Maynard agreed, and they were soon busy with the pretty pale-green curtains of the big dormitory that ran right across the house from back to front. It was under the roof, so that in the middle it was quite lofty, and at the sides it was very low. A long window ran across the wall at each end, and the door was in the middle at one side. There was room here for four cubicles, and Madge had planned to put Gisela Marani, the head girl here, also Bernhilda Mensch, Grizel Cochrane, and Bette Rincini, the other senior boarders. Juliet Carrick was to remain head of the big dormitory immediately beneath, which had eight beds in it.

The room which Miss Maynard had occupied during the previous term was to be made into a bedroom for two, and Mademoiselle's old room would hold three. Over at Le Petit Chalet there would be nine small girls, with Mademoiselle in charge.

"And," said Miss Bettany as she finished draping the last pretty curtain, "if we get any more older girls as boarders, I must send Simone Lecoutier and Margia Stevens over as well. That will mean arranging another dormitory."

"Who will be in the lower one?" queried Miss Maynard.

"Oh, Juliet, Joey, Gertrud, and the four new girls, Paula von Rothenfels, Rosalie Dene, Vanna di Ricci, and Evadne Lannis. The Hamels have taken that little chalet near the Post; and Anita and Giovanna Rincini may come, or they may not!"

"Are the Merciers going to Le Petit Chalet?"

Miss Bettany stopped short. "My dear! I had absolutely forgotten about the Merciers!"

"And you haven't given Simone and Margia a place yet. Are you putting them in Mademoiselle's old room?"

"Yes. They're about the same age; and for Joey's sake I think it better to separate her and Simone. Well, Suzanne can go with them, and Yvette will, of course, go over to Le Petit Chalet!" She sat down on the nearest bed. "Well, I never for one moment imagined we should grow like this. Of course, people like the Maranis and the Steinbrückes and the Mensches are only boarders for the winter. Still, it's extraordinary; isn't it?"

Miss Maynard nodded. "In a way, I suppose it is, but

they all like you enormously; and, after all, you are doing a lot for their girls, you know."

"It's easy," replied Miss Bettany, as she pencilled her dormitory list. "They're all such dears, and the girls are so keen on the school! Then, they've recommended us to their friends as well. The Maranis spoke to the von Eschenaus, and, of course, Paula is coming because her cousins are. The Eriksens are coming through the Stevens; and so it goes."

"And there goes the bell for *Mittagessen*!" laughed Miss Maynard.

They went downstairs, and presently the six were sitting round the table eating *Nudelsuppe*, followed by chicken, cooked in some delicious way which was Marie's own secret, and *Apfeltorte*, a kind of cake with baked apples on the top. When it was over, the two mistresses accompanied their charges to the boat-landing, and saw them on to the boat. It was a lovely day. Once more the September sun was shining, and the Tiernsee was blue with the blueness which adds so much to its beauty. The Robin was delightfully happy over everything, and she shrieked with joy at "*Le lac si bleu!*" as she danced along the path. The bright day had tempted out the few visitors that still remained, and among them they saw once more the two Italian girls and their father.

Joey nudged her sister. "Look! Those are the girls we saw yesterday," she said.

Madge looked at them with interest. She approved of the pair. They had a fresh, well-groomed appearance, and they seemed nice girls. They, on their part, gazed at the group, which had reached the landing and stood waiting for the little steamer, with more than ordinary gazing.

Miss Maynard noticed it too. "I believe the girls are right," she said. "I shouldn't be a bit surprised if you received a visit from their father, or whoever he is, before very long."

"Here's the boat!" said Grizel ecstatically. "Oh, isn't it a topping day?"

Miss Bettany raised her eyebrows at the forbidden slang, but she felt that she couldn't be continually nagging at

24

them, though she wished that Grizel would try to remember. Juliet saw, though the culprit didn't, and determined to say something if she got the chance later on. Meanwhile, she turned her attention to the passengers coming off the boat.

The next minute Joey uttered a shriek: "Gisela! Gisela Marani!"

A tall dark girl, who was walking sedately down the gangway, turned her head. "Joey!" she cried.—"Papa! Here is Joey!"

"Oh, Gisela!" exclaimed Grizel. "How lovely! I thought you weren't coming till next week. We are going over to Seehof for tea. Can't you come too?"

Gisela glanced at her father for permission. "Certainly," he said, smiling, as he raised his hat.

"Thank you, papa," said Gisela. "That will be so nice.— All right, Joey; I'm coming."

She ran round to join the others, while Herr Marani moved over to where Miss Bettany stood waving to them.

"*Grüss Gott, Fräulein Bettany!*" he said, greeting her with the pretty Tyrolean greeting. "How goes it with you?"

"It goes well, Herr Marani," she replied, giving him her hand. "How good of you to let Gisela go! Now I shall feel quite happy, as our head girl is with them. You see we have a very small new pupil?"

"Yes; she is indeed a baby one," returned Herr Marani with a smile.

"And how goes it with you? Is Frau Marani well? And where is Maria?"

"My wife is very well," he said. "She and Maria are still in Wien, where they will stay until Wednesday of next week. Then they will come home to Innsbruck. I am sorry," he went on, "that we cannot use our summer home up here for the winter months as I had arranged; but my mother has been very ill, and wishes us to be with her this winter. I am glad you can make room for my girls as boarders. They are very happy with you."

"I am glad," said Miss Bettany simply. "I am very pleased to have them—especially Gisela. She makes a splendid head girl."

There was a little more conversation, and then Herr Marani took his departure.

The two English girls went back to the Chalet School, and there set to work on the other dormitories. They were still very busy when Marie appeared with a card in her hand.

"Signor di Ferrara," repeated Miss Bettany. "Who on earth can he be?"

"Better go down and see," suggested Miss Maynard. "I can finish this quite well by myself. Perhaps it is the father of those two girls come to arrange with you for them to be boarders."

"Very well, Marie; I will come at once."

The Head vanished, and Miss Maynard went on with the task of hanging up the pretty mauve curtains that divided the cubicles of the three-bed dormitory. Half-an-hour later, just as she was sitting down to her *Tee mit Citron* and cream and honey-cakes from Innsbruck, Miss Bettany came into the *Speisesaal*.

"Well?" said Miss Maynard.

Madge Bettany nodded. "Yes; Luigia and Bianca di Ferrara are coming here; and, my dear, we shall start this term with thirty-three pupils! "

CHAPTER FOUR

Term Begins

"GRIZEL! I'm going to meet the boat! Are you coming?" shouted Joey, outside the Chalet School.

Grizel poked her curly head out of the east window in her new dormitory, and looked across the lake to Buchau, where the little lake steamer was lying. "All right! Wait a tick, and I'll come! "

She hunted madly for her blazer, struggled into it, and fled downstairs and out to the path where Joey was waiting for her.

"At last! Thought you were never coming! Come on; we must buck up!"

They tore along the path to the landing, where the nine o'clock steamer was just tying up.

"There's Mademoiselle!" shrieked Joey. "Simone's beside her. I s'pose the other kid's her sister Renée!"

"I can see Bernhilda!" proclaimed Grizel. "The von Eschenaus are over there! See them? Cooo-eeee!"

The excitement of the pair sent a smile round the people standing near, but they cared nothing for that. From the boat the other girls were waving and calling, and when at last they all met on the path the noise they made was simply terrific. Mademoiselle was quite as bad as anybody; and there were so many questions to be asked and answered, that the boat was well on its way to Seehof before any of them moved on.

"How many are we this term?" inquired Bernhilda Mensch of Joey as they set off for the Chalet.

"Heaps more than last term, anyway," replied Joey. "Thirty-three."

"Thirty-three? But how delightful! Who are there?"

"Well—Wanda and Marie von Eschenau and their cousin," began Joey.

"Yes—yes! I know that!" replied Bernhilda with an impatient movement of her hands. "Also that Gertrud brings her little sister. But who else?"

Joey thought. "There's the Robin. You won't know about her, of course. Her father was a friend of my father's years ago. She's six, and a darling, and her mother is dead. Her father is in Vienna just now, but he is going to Russia. You'll love her, Bernhilda."

"I am sorry for her." Bernhilda's blue eyes were very soft. She was a tall, pretty girl of the fair German type, with long fair plaits and an apple-blossom skin. Her younger sister, Frieda, was very like her, but there was much less character in her face, and she was a quiet little mouse, while Bernhilda was quite a leader in the school.

Simone Lecoutier, the little French girl who clung closely to Joey's other side, was as typically of France as Bernhilda was of the North Tyrol, with big dark eyes set in a little sallow face, black hair, and very neat hands and feet. She was intensely sentimental, and cherished a tremendous admiration for unsentimental Jo, who was thoroughly bored by it, but was too kind to say so. The von Eschenau girls, Wanda and Marie, who followed with Grizel, and their own cousin, Paula von Rothenfels, were a lovely pair, with thick golden hair, violet eyes, and skins of roses and cream. Grizel was pretty, and so were the two Mensches, but Wanda and Marie von Eschenau made them quite commonplace. As for Paula, she was dark and very ordinary; and Renée Lecoutier, Simone's little sister, who was a second edition of Simone.

Meanwhile, Grizel was pouring forth much the same information as Joey had given, with the added news that Gisela and Maria Marani had already arrived, and that the new mistress, Miss Durrant, was also at school. "She's sleeping over at Le Petit Chalet," chattered Grizel. "*We* shan't have much to do with her—only drawing. She seems quite jolly, and she's keen on hockey. Miss Maynard told me she had played for her county."

"Where is Juliet?" asked Bernhilda, as they reached the Kron Prinz Karl.

"My sister wouldn't let us all come," explained Joey. "She said we'd deafen the whole lake if we did. So we drew lots to see who should come first, and it came to Grizel and me. Juliet and Gisela are going to meet the eleven o'clock boat; crowds of people are coming by that— the Stevens, and the Merciers, and the Rincinis, and some others."

"Have the English and American girls of whom we heard last term arrived yet?" asked Bernhilda.

"Gracious! What a sentence! Oh, it's correct English all right, but it's so—so *correct*! " complained Jo, who often found the English of her foreign friends very boring. "You mean Rosalie Dene and Evadne Lannis, don't you? No; they aren't here yet. I don't think they're coming till the sixteen o'clock boat, as a matter of fact."

28

"Then, are Gisela and Maria the only early ones?"

"M'm," was Jo's reply. "Unless the new Italian girls have turned up, of course."

"*What* Italian girls, Joey?" asked Simone, speaking for almost the first time.

"Oh, two quite new ones. They came up last week, and their father landed the next day to make arrangements. He's Italian consul somewhere, and he heard of this school through someone—I forget who—and came up to see it. He's quite mad on English things 'cos he went to an English public school himself, and he liked the Chalet awfully, so they're coming. One's fifteen, and the other's twelve, and their names are Bianca and Luigia."

At that moment Miss Bettany appeared with Miss Maynard, and everyone promptly surrounded the two mistresses.

"Madame, it is so nice to see you again! You are well, I hope?"

"Yes, thank you, Bernhilda; I am very well. No need to ask how *you* are! You look splendid, all of you. Have you had pleasant holidays? Where is Mademoiselle, by the way? I thought she was coming by this boat."

"She went round to Le Petit Chalet, Madame," explained Grizel. "She said she would see you afterwards."

"Oh, I see! Wanda, I am so glad to see you and Marie. Is this your cousin? Welcome to the Chalet, all of you! Now come along and see our new arrangements. Grizel will take you up to your dormitory, Bernhilda; and, Frieda and Paula, go with Joey. Wanda, I've put you and Marie together for the present, as you asked for it until Marie gets accustomed to school. And, Simone, we've moved you into a new dormitory with Margia and Suzanne. Renée is over at Le Petit Chalet with the other small folk, and you shall take her over when you've seen your new quarters. Ah, here come Juliet and Gisela! Come along, you two! I want you to take these people to their dormitories, and then you can all go over to Le Petit Chalet and inspect it thoroughly. Now hurry up, for there's still heaps to be done."

They scattered, laughing. Bernhilda and Grizel ran up

to the top dormitory, where Bernhilda was introduced to one of the lake-window cubicles.

"Gisela has the other," explained Grizel. "Bette and I have the valley windows between us. Aren't they decent? Gisela is head here, and we are to have some privileges, as we are the oldest. Juliet is head of the yellow room—this is the green room—and she is to share our privileges."

In the room below Jo was explaining to Frieda and Paula where they were to keep their possessions, and all about dormitory rules. Shy Frieda listened in silence, and Paula was rather too much overawed to say anything. In any case, Jo's English was distinctly difficult for her to follow since that young lady forgot all about rules against slang in her excitement, and "topping—ripping—vile—absolutely *It*!" and other forbidden expressions freely sprinkled her speech. Miss Bettany, coming in to see that all was well, stood in the doorway, smiling grimly as the unconscious Jo informed the new members of the dormitory that "It's simply ripping having such crowds this term! Even if the kids don't play hockey, we'll have enough for two teams, which is top-hole luck!"

"Josephine!" said her sister's voice at that moment.

Joey swung round, and turned beetroot colour. "I forgot," she said lamely.

"It sounds like it," said Miss Bettany, a twinkle in her eyes. "Please don't forget again." Then she turned and left them to go to the blue room, where Gisela, Wanda, and Marie were all standing by the window, chattering.

"Here is Madame," said Gisela as she entered.

Wanda turned with a smile. "Oh, Madame! It is such a charming room! And the colour is de-light-ful!"

She spoke slowly and carefully, for English was still a difficulty to her.

"You like it?" said Madge. "That's splendid! Has Gisela shown you the form rooms yet? Show them all over, Gisela. You old girls will have to look after the new ones."

She withdrew, and went to the last dormitory with a little quaking sensation. She was not at all sure how Simone would take this separation from her beloved Jo. She and Mademoiselle, who was a distant cousin of Simone's, had talked it over at the end of the previous term, and had decided that it would be better for both children if they were parted. Simone must learn to make other friends besides Joey; and Joey ought to have a little freedom sometimes. She was one of the most unsentimental of schoolgirls, and the French child's adoration had often been trying to her during the past term.

"All the same," thought Miss Bettany, "I *do* hope Simone won't spend all her spare time in tears, or I shall regret our decision."

She went into the room, but it was empty. Evidently Simone had taken her small sister over to Le Petit Chalet. Miss Bettany heaved a sigh of relief, and went off to her own quarters. It was now half-past ten, and in half-an-hour there would be a fresh inflow of pupils. She had barely settled herself down to copying the time-table before Miss Maynard appeared, waving a dormitory list at her.

"What *is* the matter?" demanded the Head.

"We've forgotten those new Italian children!" gasped Miss Maynard.

"Goodness! How awful! Let me have the list." Miss Bettany took the neatly-written list and skimmed it through. "Yes; I have it! Simone can go over to Le Petit Chalet as I said, and Frieda Mensch too. Then Bianca can have Simone's cubicle, and Luigia, Frieda's. What a good thing we got that extra dorm. ready in case of need! Go and tell Frieda, will you? and send Joey to take Simone's things over. I'll run across and settle it with Mademoiselle. We must fly."

Fly they did; and, as Bernhilda and Gisela came to the rescue, the two cubicles were soon rearranged, and Simone and Frieda were settled.

"In a way," said Miss Maynard, "it ought to be a good thing. They're a colourless pair, and they would certainly never have had a chance in those other rooms. Now, one of them will be bound to take the lead, which will be just as well."

The two people concerned didn't think so. Simone promptly dissolved into tears at the thought, and Frieda wondered unhappily how she would get on so far away from Bernhilda. However, when they all assembled for *Mittagessen* at thirteen o'clock they were as cheery as anyone.

Miss Bettany glanced down the two long tablefuls of girls with pride. They all looked so fresh and trim in their brown tunics with tussore tops. The people with long hair had it fastened with ribbons to match, and, as she afterwards said to Mademoiselle, the Chalet *Speisesaal* really looked like a school dining-room. Twenty of the boarders had now arrived. The others would be arriving during the afternoon, and on the morrow work would begin. The girls were all together today, but, except at the week-ends, the juniors would in future have all their meals in the little *Speisesaal* at Le Petit Chalet. As far as possible they would be kept there, having their own class-rooms over there, and their own music-room and play-room. Yvette Mercier, the oldest of them, was nine, and the others were mainly eight-year-olds, so it had been decided that it would be best for them to have their own quarters away from the elder girls.

Yvette, who had just been informed that she would be head of the Junior School, was very proud of herself. She was a quick, clever child, with any amount of personality, and her mistresses felt fairly sure that under her the juniors would soon grow in unity of spirit, and later on, would be able to make themselves felt in school affairs.

After *Mittagessen* they scattered to unpack, and the rest of the day was spent in getting their books ready for the morrow, settling about seats in the form-rooms, and racing about in the bright September sunshine, and *talking*—any amount of talking. On the morrow they would have to speak in English most of the time; but today they might use their own languages, and the effect was reminiscent of the Tower of Babel. German and French predominated, naturally, but there was a good deal of Italian; and two new juniors, Thyra and Ingeborg Eriksen, could speak very little but their native Norwegian.

Joey chattered a polyglot mixture, for she was as much at home in French and German as in English, and Juliet and Grizel stuck to their own language as much as possible;

while Rosalie Dene, the new English girl, felt literally tongue-tied with most of the others.

When twenty-one o'clock brought the bedtime of the senior dormitory, and Juliet and Luigia, Miss Bettany drew a sigh of relief.

"I feel," she said to her three colleagues—Marie Pfeifen was in charge at Le Petit Chalet for the moment—"just as though no one had stopped talking *once* today! Thank goodness for a little peace! "

"Hear, hear! " laughed Miss Maynard. "And I'm off to bed if you will all excuse me! "

"I think we'll all go," said her Head.

Mademoiselle assented. "I too. Come, Mademoiselle," to Miss Durrant, "let us seek our own chalet."

They all went to the door.

"Good-night," said Miss Bettany; "I think it's going to be a good term."

"Tophole! " said Miss Maynard wickedly.

And with that they retired for the night.

CHAPTER FIVE

New Interests

"GISELA—GISELA! Do stop a minute! I want to speak to you! "

Gisela Marani halted and turned round to see Joey Bettany racing after her. "I am sorry, Joey," she said as the younger girl reached her. "I did not know you were following me."

" 'Course you didn't! I say, are you in a hurry? 'Cos if not, I want to speak to you."

"Yes? What is it? Some important event you wish to celebrate?"

"No fear! It's nothing like *that*! Only, do you remember that book you showed me last term—'Somebody or other of the Fourth'?"

"Yes," said Gisela. "It was from that that we took our idea of celebrating Madame's birthday."

"So it was! I'd forgotten that. By the way, what *was* the name of the girl?"

"Her name was Denise. But do you wish to read it? I will ask mamma to post it if you would like it."

"Thanks awfully, but I'd rather not. It looked awful tosh, really! No; all I meant was about the school magazine. What about it?"

Gisela had frowned at the word "tosh", which sounded to her uncommonly like forbidden slang, but now her frown vanished as she exclaimed, "Of course, I had not forgotten; but we are always so busy!"

"I know we are. The bell will ring for *Mittagessen* in a minute! Oh, Gisela, *do* get started! There's a gem!"

"I should like a magazine," said Gisela thoughtfully. "How shall we begin?"

"I should call a meeting and ask the others," said Joey promptly. "My idea is, ask the day-girls to come tomorrow morning at nine, just like ordinary school-days, and hold a meeting in the dining-room. I'm sure my sister would agree."

"She said we might have a magazine last term," said Gisela. "I will ask her if we may call the meeting, and, if she gives permission, we will do as you suggest, and perhaps we may begin this term."

"Good! That's splendid of you, Gisela! You *are* a gem! And there goes the bell. Come on! I'll race you back!"

Gisela, however, as head girl, had a certain amount of dignity to uphold, and she refused the challenge, so Joey set off by herself, and arrived at the Chalet, panting for breath. Her sister was standing at the lakeside, looking at the grey waters, and raised startled eyes as she dashed up.

"Jo! Why are you racing about like that? It's enough to start you coughing again!"

"But it hasn't," retorted Jo with perfect truth. "I say! Do you think there's going to be a storm?"

"I don't know. The lake looks rather like it. I've a good mind to send the Hamels and the Rincinis home now. They all have to get to Torteswald, since the Hamels have had to turn out of the chalet by the Post; and, if the wind comes, it will blow from the north-east, and that means waves breaking on the path if it's a strong wind."

"Well, before you *do* send them home, Gisela wants to know if we may have a meeting tomorrow to discuss the magazine," said Jo eagerly.—"Don't you, Gisela?"

Gisela, who had come up in time to hear the last sentence, smiled. "If we may, Madame, it might be well. See, it is now October, and we should begin at once, *nicht wahr?*"

Miss Bettany nodded. "Yes. If you want a magazine this year you certainly ought to begin now. Have the meeting tomorrow by all means. I am going to send the Hamels and the Rincinis home now, as I think we are going to have a storm, so come along and tell them."

The second bell sounded at that moment; so Gisela, flinging her dignity to the winds, raced into the house to find the four day-girls who lived at Torteswald, a little village beyond Seespitz, and bid them come next morning for the meeting. Her head-mistress followed to send them home.

The news of the meeting thrilled the girls enormously, and they could talk of nothing else. Even the rising of the storm scarcely distracted their attention. After *Mittagessen*, Gisela ran across to Le Petit Chalet to let the juniors know about it. Coming back, she could scarcely keep her feet. In these narrow valleys the wind roars down as through a funnel, and its violence is doubled. The lake was already covered with white-capped waves that dashed themselves against the shore, bespattering the path with spray and foam.

"Isn't it a good thing," said Joey as she struggled with her sewing, "that the Hamels have left Scholastika? It would have been an awful walk."

"They couldn't have come every day," replied Juliet. "Either they'd have had to be boarders, or they'd have had to have a governess, now the steamers have stopped."

"The railway will have closed in a fortnight's time," put in Gisela. "After that we shall have to take the mountain-path when we want to go to Spärtz."

"Coo! Won't it be cheery when the snow comes?" commented Joey.

"You know what the winter is like here, Gisela. You'd better write an article on it for the magazine," suggested Juliet. "Lots of us have no idea."

"You will know when this term has reached its end," laughed Gisela as she laid aside her own beautifully-done work to see what Jo was doing. "*Joey!*"

"Why, what's wrong?" demanded the owner of the work. "It's quite neat, and the stitches are *nearly* all the same size."

"But it is the wrong stitch!" wailed Gisela. "Give me your scissors."

"Oh, I say!" protested Jo. "You're not going to take it out, are you?"

"But it cannot remain like that! It is all wrong! It will spoil the garment!"

"Well, I don't mind that. I'd rather it was spoilt altogether as have to do the horrid thing all over again! I simply *loathe* sewing!" returned Jo, who, till last term, had scarcely ever touched a needle.

To the foreign girls this was a shocking state of affairs. They could all do exquisite plain sewing themselves, and the older ones, at least, embroidered beautifully. Juliet Carrick, Margia Stevens, and Rosalie Dene were the only ones among the English girls whose work would pass muster with Mademoiselle. Jo Bettany and Grizel Cochrane were considered worse than the juniors, and the American child, Evadne Lannis, had scarcely known one end of a needle from the other when she first came. Some of the elder girls had promptly constituted themselves teachers to Grizel and Joey in the previous term, and Bernhilda Mensch did her best for Evadne, who hated sewing even worse than Joey did, and did everything she could to get out of it.

On Mondays and Wednesdays a book was read; but on Fridays discipline was somewhat relaxed, and the girls were allowed to talk, so long as they spoke English and did not make too much noise over it.

"I must send a copy of the *Chaletian* to England to my old school." said Joey, as she resignedly watched Gisela snipping out her stitches. "They'll be awfully interested. I wonder who'll be editor?"

"It ought to be one of you English," replied Gisela, re-threading Jo's needle and beginning the work again. "See, Joey. I have begun for you. Make your stitches thus, and keep them very even."

"Well, I'll try," sighed Joey, "but I shall never sew like that."

"You will if you try," returned her friend. "See, I have made them a little larger than usual, so that you may keep yours the same size."

Joey took her work, and stitched slowly; while Gisela, who was doing elaborate smocking on a frock intended for her little sister, went on with her own.

"We must have a page for correspondence," observed Juliet presently.

"Oh, rather! And I think someone ought to write a description of that picnic to the Mondscheinspitze last term," added Joey. "Herr Mensch told us some jolly legends about the mountains, too. I should think someone might write out at least one of them. Bernhilda could do that."

"Please fold up your work," Mademoiselle said at this juncture.

"What are we going to do, Mademoiselle?" asked Joey eagerly. "We can't go out today."

"Miss Durrant is coming to teach you a new dance," replied Mademoiselle. "Please carry all the chairs into the little class-room, and leave this one empty."

In less than ten minutes the big double form-room was cleared of all chairs save the one at the piano, and the girls stood ready, wondering what this new dance might be. They knew very little of Miss Durrant, really. She came over to the Chalet two afternoons in the week, and taught them drawing; but otherwise they rarely saw her. They looked at her with interest as she came into the room, followed by Miss Bettany, who was carrying some music.

"All ready? That's right," said Miss Durrant briskly. "Will you please get partners, and then form in two lines down the room. One over, is there? Well, never mind, Rosalie. I'll come in a minute. Now, girls, I'm going to teach you some of the old English folk-dances. We'll learn two very simple ones today, and I'll teach you the movements, and then another time we'll learn more. One thing let me impress on you now. You must never dance on your toes or point them, because that's not folk-dancing. I'll tell you more about it when we've done some, and then you'll see why. All face me."

They turned and faced her in two long files. They were all interested, and one or two people were thrilling with excitement.

"Take hands," said Miss Durrant. "Now run three steps forward, and then three back. Begin with your right foot always, *and don't bend your knees*; give at the ankles."

With shrieks of laughter they began, and soon they were running backwards and forwards as lightly as they could, while Miss Durrant walked up and down, criticising them.

"Don't point your toes, Wanda!—Grizel! Stop jumping —*run*!—Joey, you aren't an elephant; so don't try to be one!—Straighter knees, Gisela! That's better!—Come along, Rosalie; try with me."

Two minutes later she stopped them. "That's called 'leading up a double'," she explained. "If you do it without holding hands, it's called 'running up a double'. Heaps of the dances begin in that way. Now join hands with your partners, and I'll teach you slipping step."

This was easier, and before long they were all slipping, first up, then down, while Miss Bettany played for them. Finally, they learned "setting to partners" and "turning single", and this last movement proved full of pitfalls for them.

"Joey! You aren't a spider!" cried Miss Durrant. "And you'll certainly kick your next-door neighbour if you do it like that. Make your steps as neat as possible.—You ought to be able to turn single in—in a soup-plate!"

"Turn to your right, child! " This was to Evadne. "*Never* turn single to your left unless you're definitely told to do so.—*Four* steps, Grizel; not two.—Now let's begin again, and go straight through them."

When, finally, they were all sure of those five movements, Miss Durrant turned her attention to skipping, and had them all skipping round the room till they were breathless. Then she let them rest for a few minutes while she told them of Cecil Sharp, and his great work for English folk-dancing, and England.

"You all know *some* of the folk-songs," she concluded with a twinkle. "I have even heard some of you objecting to the constant repetition of a few of them. Joey's Appalachian nursery songs are very 'folk'. Now form your lines again, and I'll teach you 'Gallopede' and 'We Won't Go Home Till Morning'."

When four o'clock came, they were all rosy and breathless with exercise, and, when Miss Durrant give the order to dismiss, they all crowded round her, begging for more.

She laughed at them. "Oh, you'll have a good deal of folk-dancing," she assured them. "I hear that the weather is often very violent here in the winter; so, whenever you can't have walks or games, you will dance, and by next spring I hope you'll all know at least twenty dances! "

"Coo! " said Jo. "That'll take some learning! But I like this. It's heaps more sensible than foxtrots and onesteps! I say, Gisela! Something more for the mag."

Gisela nodded. "Yes. We must also teach the others what we have learned today."

They all trooped off to tidy themselves for *Kaffee*.

CHAPTER SIX

The "Chaletian"

THE WHOLE SCHOOL was waiting in the big double form-room by nine o'clock the next morning. The wind was still blowing hard, but it had veered to the north; so the lake-path, though wet from its bath of the previous day, was not continually washed by the waves now, though the water meadows which lay between Seespitz and Torteswald were, to quote Jo, "thoroughly squelchy". The four day-girls who lived in the latter place had, therefore, managed to come, and Lisa Bernaldi, the other one, was living at the Post Hotel, and had been at school on the Friday afternoon. The wind had stopped blowing continuously, too, and only came in great gusts now. Between these, the juniors were rushed across to the Chalet, even the Robin arriving without mishap.

"I'm thankful to know the mountains protect us from east winds," said Miss Bettany as she stood at the window watching the angry waves tossing madly to and fro. "If it were not for them, I should be afraid that some day we should be washed away. We are very near the shore here, and the water is never more than a few inches below the path."

"Mercifully, *ma chère*, it is an impossibility," said Mademoiselle, to whom she had been speaking. "What are the children to do today?"

"I hope the storm will have gone down by this afternoon," replied her Head. "If it does, they shall have a long walk to the head of the valley. This morning they will have their meeting, and mending, and home-letters. Tonight, they shall dance and play games."

40

"They are very much interested in this magazine," said Mademoiselle pensively.

"Yes—thank goodness! It will give them something to think about! "

The school had no idea of the interest the staff were taking in their latest venture. They assembled in the greatest excitement, and, as usual, when they were in their places, Grizel's was the first voice to be heard, though what she said had nothing to do with the magazine."

"Joey Bettany! " she cried. "For goodness sake stop that *wretched* humming! "

"What for? I can hum if I like! " protested Joey in injured tones.

"No, you can't! You've got to think of other people a little. I'm sick to death of those ghastly Appalachian things! I wish Miss Maynard had never brought them for you! "

" 'Twasn't one of the Appalachian songs! " retorted Jo triumphantly.

"Well, whatever it was, dry up! It's enough to make anyone ill! "

Luckily, Gisela saw fit to interfere, or the squabble might have become serious. "Grizel, will you please sit down," she said. "And, Joey, we are going to discuss our magazine now."

The pair subsided at once. Gisela was an excellent head girl, and knew how to make her authority felt. She gave the meeting no time to ponder on the wrangle, but plunged straight into the cause for its being held.

"We wish, some of us, to have a school magazine," she began. "We shall arrange it for ourselves, and we shall have in it accounts of our concerts, and picnics, and school-work. We also hope that there may be stories and poems, and letters to the editor. Before we go any further, we should like to know that you all wish such a thing; so will any who do not, please hold up their hands?"

Needless to say, not a hand was raised.

"It goes well," said Gisela. "Then we must now elect our editor."

Joey rose to her feet. "I beg to propose Gisela Marani as editor," she said.

"I'll second that!" said Juliet, following up the proposal.

Gisela shook her head. "It is very good of you—I am grateful. But, indeed, I should prefer that someone else had the position. I do not know enough about it, and I already have much to do."

The members of the assembly looked at each other blankly. They had quite taken it for granted that Gisela would fill the post, and they had not troubled to think of anyone else. There was a silence.

"What about Bernhilda?" asked Juliet at length, somewhat doubtfully.

The shy colour flooded Bernhilda's face. "Oh, no! Please no! I could not!"

"What about yourself?" demanded Grizel of Juliet.

"If I was any use at English, I might," replied that young lady. "As it is, you might as well have the Robin for editor. She'd be as much use!"

There were giggles over this at the idea of the Robin wielding the editorial pen, but they soon died as the girls once more faced the problem of the editorship. A suggestion put forward by Wanda that Grizel might manage it was promptly squashed by Joey.

"Grizel? She hasn't any more imagination than a—a cheese!"

"I've got common-sense, anyway!" retorted Grizel hotly. "That's better than——"

"Stop it, you two!" interrupted Juliet. "If you want to scrap, you can do it outside!"

Once more the pair desisted, but there seemed a good deal of truth in Bette Rincini's remark to Bernhilda that Joey and Grizel were simply spoiling for a fight, and it would come off before the day was over.

Then, no less a person than Simone Lecoutier addressed the meeting. "Will not Joey do?" she said shyly. "She speaks the English; she has the imagination; she is not a prefect, as are Gisela, and Bernhilda, and Juliet, and Bette, and Gertrud; so she is not busy."

There was a dubious pause. The idea certainly had its

42

points; but to set against them was the fact that Jo was not thirteen for a month yet, and she had no experience.

Then Wanda spoke once more. "I think it is a good idea," she said. "Would not Miss Maynard help with it, so that Joey shall not have too big trouble to worry her?"

"A bit muddled," remarked Joey genially, "but I see what you mean. I don't mind taking it on if Miss Maynard will give a hand with it. But I've never run a magazine before, any more than anyone else here, and I can't do it off my own bat, that's certain."

Then Juliet had an inspiration. "Look here, why not divide it into pages and give various people a page each to be responsible for? Then Joey would only have to collect the pages in, and write her editorial, and arrange the thing!" They jumped at the suggestion, for there was common-sense in this. It solved all their difficulties at one blow; for people who might feel too busy to tackle the whole magazine would scarcely grumble at having one page to look after.

"Then, shall we appoint Joey as the editor?" inquired Gisela. "Will you hold up your hands if you agree?"

A forest of hands was promptly waved in the air, and the motion was carried.

The next thing was to decide on the pages. At the invitation of the prefects, Joey joined them on the little dais, and was called on to make suggestions.

She screwed up her eyes, ran her fingers through her hair till it got into the wildest confusion, and then said, "Well, who will do the School Notes? That's the first thing."

"Gisela will, of course," said Juliet. "Grizel must do the Sports Page, and I propose that Bernhilda does a page on the folklore of the district. She must know heaps about it, because her father knows so many legends."

"Oh, jolly good!" declared the editor joyfully. "That's three pages settled, then. Who's going to do the stories?"

"Oh, has only one person to do the stories?" said little Amy Stevens disappointedly.

"Oh no! Anyone can; but there must be someone to choose them," explained Joey.

"Miss Maynard might do that," suggested Gisela; "and ought we not to ask the mistresses to contribute to it?"

"Yes, of course. And, if any of you have interesting things to write about, you can write me a letter, and I'll put it in if it's decent enough," promised the editor kindly.

"What about poetry?" someone wanted to know.

"If we get any that's good enough, we'll put it in."

"And everything must, of course, be in English," added Gisela. "I think we ought to have all our—our——"

"Contributions? Is that what you are driving at?" asked Joey.

"Thank you, Joey. Yes; that is what I want. I think they ought to be in by the end of the month."

"That's a fortnight," pondered the editor. "All right. October the thirty-first is the last day for sending things in.—And they must be decently written!"

A tap at the door interrupted proceedings. The Robin ran to open it. Miss Bettany was there.

"Do you people know that it's nearly eleven o'clock?" she said. "Haven't you finished?"

"Yes, thank you, Madame," replied Gisela. "All is prepared, and Joey is to be editor."

"Joey?" The Head had not expected this. "My dear girls, I don't want to interfere, but surely it would be better to have someone a little older?"

"I'm almost thirteen," said Joey, a little resentfully.

"Also, Madame, Joey has read so much; and we thought if Fräulein Maynard would help her. We are to have Pages, you see."

"I don't quite understand. Explain, please."

Gisela explained, and Joey and Grizel supplemented her remarks. "Don't you think we can manage?" asked the latter anxiously when they had finished.

The Head nodded slowly. "Yes; I think you can. It is a good idea to have the Pages. I should think it would answer very well. Now come for your milk to the *Speisesaal*, and then, if you seniors like to walk back with the Torteswald people as far as Seespitz, you may—all except Grizel; she has a cold, and will be better indoors today."

Grizel made no attempt to question this decision. She

44

knew a certain tone in Miss Bettany's voice, and there was no argument possible when it was heard.

"Us too?" questioned Margia.

"No; it's getting very wild now. If you people want a walk, you may go up the valley a little way; but you'll have to keep very tightly hold of each other. I think the wind must be veering round to the north-east, to judge by the lake and the trees. The juniors can't go at all, I'm afraid; and, if the rest of you are going, you must hurry up about it, and get ready."

They ran off at full speed, and presently they were all standing ready in long brown coats, brown tam-o'-shanters, and stout boots. Miss Maynard and Miss Durrant were waiting for them, and, as the former joined the lakeside walk, Gisela turned an imploring face to her Head, who had come to see them start off.

"Oh, Madame! May Joey come with us? We can then talk about the magazine."

Miss Bettany nodded. "Very well. Don't get any wetter than you can help, though." Then they set off.

The wind was blowing steadily again, and, as Miss Bettany said, was coming from the north-east. Out on the lake the waves were big, considering that the Tiernsee is only three miles in length, and never more than a mile wide. They formed a choppy sea, battling with the strong current that flows about due north to become the Tiern River below Scholastika at the northern end. The path, barely ten inches above the water's surface, was drenched with spray, and every now and then a wave, larger than the rest, would roll up, and actually break on it, so that it was well under water.

As long as they were in the Briesau triangle this did not really matter, as they were able to get away from it on to the grass. But once they had passed the fence, which divides the lake-path from the peninsula, the mountain-side rose steeply up from the path, and the most they could do under the circumstances was to dash wildly to one side and wait there until the water had retreated, when they tore along again at full speed. As Miss Maynard afterwards said, whatever else you called it, it wasn't a walk.

"Ow! Here's a *huge* one coming!" shrieked Jo, as a rather larger wave than usual swept towards them. "Ow—ow!"

Crash! Down it came. The water swirled over the road, then receded, and they all fled along in the direction of Seespitz.

"Quick, girls!" called Miss Maynard. "Here's another! Climb up on to those stones!"

They scrambled up, clinging to the rock wall, as another wave sent its volume over the way. Then, down again, and another wild scamper, this time finishing by the boat-landing, where the mountain curved round, and they were able to rush out of reach. Jo declared afterwards that it was the maddest walk she had ever taken, save one.

"Which was that?" asked Grizel with interest.

"Never you mind!" Joey told her.

But Grizel was in a teasing mood, and worried until her friend told her.

"One I took last term."

Grizel went crimson. Last term, she had run away and tried to climb the great Tiernjoch, with results that were very nearly disastrous; for a mist had come down, and she had found herself on the verge of a precipice. Joey had come after her, and had succeeded in keeping her quiet until help came, but Grizel herself had gone down with bronchitis, and for three days they had feared brain-fever for Joey. It was not an exploit of which Grizel was proud, and she would have liked to forget it.

Jo had had no thought of unkindness when she had referred to it, and, at the sight of Grizel's face, she promptly declared herself to be a beast.

"It is all over," said Gisela, who had overheard their conversation. "But, Joey, we have still not talked with Miss Maynard about the magazine."

"Well, how could we?" demanded the editor. "Going was bad enough; but coming back was the limit! We had the wind against us the whole time, and the lake got wilder and wilder!"

"Shall we go to her now?" asked the head girl.

"Righto!" agreed Jo easily.

They went to the little music-room where they knew Miss Maynard was to be found, and tapped at the door.

"Come in," she called. Then, as they entered, "Well! What can I do for you?"

"It's the magazine," explained Jo. "Will you help us?"

"Yes, of course! What do you want? Sit down and let us discuss it."

They sat down, and Joey poured out their plans, Gisela explaining here and there—rather a necessary thing, for Joey, enthusiastic, was very apt to be incoherent.

When they had finished, Miss Maynard nodded. "I see," she said thoughtfully. "You really want me to act as a final court of appeal."

"Ye—yes, I suppose so." But Joey looked rather crest-fallen.

"Well, what else *did* you want me to do?" demanded the young mistress. "It's your magazine, and you've got to manage it. I'll be there when I'm needed, but you must do the work yourselves."

Joey got to her feet. "Thank you, Miss Maynard," she said.—"Come on, Gisela. I'm going to begin *now*!"

CHAPTER SEVEN

Rufus is Adopted

"GIRLS," said Miss Bettany in worried tones as she came into the big school-room early on the following Saturday, "have you any idea where Joey is?"

The fourteen people variously employed in the room at the moment looked up in surprise at her question. They had supposed—those of them who had thought about it at all—that Joey was either practising, or else in the little form-room, struggling with her editorial. For the past week

—in fact, ever since the preceding Saturday—she had thought of little else. She had managed to control herself during lessons, her sister's threat of putting a stop to the whole thing having settled *that*; but, out of them, she thought, talked, and, the others declared, *dreamed* magazine.

"Is she not in the little room, Madame?" asked Gisela.

"No; I have looked there. She isn't practising, and she's not in her cubicle. She seems to be nowhere in the house. Have any of you any idea as to her whereabouts?"

"Perhaps she's over at Le Petit Chalet," suggested Grizel. "She *did* say something at *Frühstück* about finding a quiet place to write her editorial."

But Miss Bettany shook her head. "No. She isn't there either. I knew she wanted a quiet spot, because she told me so herself. That is why I came here last. Don't any of you know where she would be likely to be?"

Nobody did.

"Who is practising?" asked the Head.

Gisela glanced at the list nearby. "Simone Lecoutier, Vanna di Ricci, and Marie von Eschenau, Madame," she replied. "Simone might know, perhaps."

"Grizel, please go and fetch Simone here," said Miss Bettany. "It really is extraordinary where Joey can be. You're all *sure* you haven't seen her?"

No one had, however, and just then Grizel returned, bringing Simone with her. Simone looked badly scared, for Grizel had simply said, "You're to come to the schoolroom; Madame wants you! " and left it at that.

Miss Bettany nearly laughed at her big startled eyes, for she looked *all* eyes. As it was, she merely said, "Simone, have you any idea where Joey is?"

"*Mais non, Madame!*" replied Simone. "*Est ce qu'on ne peut pas la trouver?*"

"No," replied the Head, too worried to notice that the little French girl was not speaking the regulation English. "When did you last see her?"

Simone thought hard for a minute. "*Je ne l'ai pas vu dépuis neuf heures,*" she said finally.

"Has anyone seen her since nine this morning?"

No; no one had. They had had school prayers as usual at nine o'clock, and since then Miss Joey seemed to have vanished.

"Perhaps the Tzigane have been here and have stolen her," suggested Simone.

"Nonsense, Simone! " Miss Bettany spoke sharply. "It's the last thing the Tzigane would be likely to do! They have children enough of their own! Please try to control your imagination, and don't make silly suggestions! "

"Has she perhaps gone to Torteswald?" This was Gisela.

"Did she say anything about going?" demanded Miss Bettany.

"No, Madame. Indeed, I thought her here with us until you came in."

"Have you others heard her speak of it?"

"No, Madame," they choruses.

"Shall we look everywhere for her once again?" proposed Bernhilda.

Miss Bettany assented. "Yes; you might do that. Two of you go to Le Petit Chalet, and the rest of you hunt through the house. Please report to me in the study when you have finished. If you find her before that send her there to me at once."

With this she withdrew, and the girls started their search. Gisela and Bernhilda went over to Le Petit Chalet; Juliet and Grizel tackled the dormitories, and the others hunted all over the lower part of the house. They dived into the stationery cupboard; they looked behind the book-lockers; they moved all the desks—though how they thought even Robin, much less Joey, could have hidden in them was beyond anyone with any common-sense! They peered under the tables in the *Speisesaal*, and took down every coat hanging up in the cloak-rooms; they invaded the *Küche*, to Marie's disgust, and insisted on opening every single cupboard and poking about it. Margia Stevens even peeped inquiringly into the great jar where the flour was kept. Needless to state, no Jo was there. Simone climbed on to the music-stool and looked down into the piano, undeterred by Bette Rincini's suggestion that, thin as Joey Bettany was, she was not thin enough to be there. When,

49

finally, they had driven neary everyone distracted, and Simone and one or two of the babies were quite convinced that something awful must have happened to their missing friend, and had accordingly dissolved into tears, they went to inform Miss Bettany that, wherever else her small sister was, she was not in the lower part of the house.

At the study door they met Grizel and Juliet, bound on the same errand, and ten minutes later Gisela and Bernhilda came back from Le Petit Chalet, knowing as much of Jo's whereabouts as they did. No one seemed to have seen anything of her since prayers that morning, and she had certainly not been over to the juniors' quarters.

A kind of eloquent silence fell on the school after Gisela had finished speaking, even Simone choking down her sobs. The general attitude was one of surprise. Had it been Grizel, who could be thoroughly wrong-headed when she chose, or Simone, who was quite famous for doing silly things, it would not have come with quite such a shock. But Joey was a level-headed young person as a rule. Mademoiselle, who came fussing over from Le Petit Chalet, said as much to Miss Bettany, who was standing looking thoroughly puzzled and worried.

"Joey has common-sense!" cried the Frenchwoman in her own tongue. "She will not have run to climb mountains, or to cut off her hair!"

Grizel and Simone both went crimson at this allusion to their exploits of the previous term. They felt that Mademoiselle was not playing fair in raking up past events, and their faces said as much.

"Can she have gone to Torteswald?" pondered Miss Bettany aloud.

Mademoiselle glanced out of the window. "But regard you the rain, *ma chère*! It pours like a torrent!"

"I can't imagine her doing such a thing without telling me first!" went on her sister. "Still, she might have done so! Or she may have gone to see the Brauns. She is very fond of them.—Gisela, go and ring up the Villa Maurach and—where is it your cousins are staying, Bette? Wald Villa?—Well, ring them up, Gisela; and also Die Rosen, the Brauns' chalet at Buchau, and ask if any of them know anything about her."

Gisela went off to the telephone, but presently returned, saying that nobody had seen Jo that day.

Miss Bettany frowned as she turned away, after thanking the head girl. It was so totally unlike Jo to go off by herself in this fashion. She was a gregarious little soul, and was generally to be found with crowds. Where she could be now was a mystery, and the girls, streaming back to their own quarters, were thoroughly curious. Some of them inclined to Simone's suggestion that the Tzigane had carried her off; the others declared that she must have gone for a stroll somewhere.

"But it isn't the weather *for* strolls!" Grizel pointed out, with an eloquent wave of her hand towards the window. "The rain's simply *emptying* down! Just look at it!"

"Well, anyway, there's no truth in that idiotic Tzigane idea!" declared Juliet. "I think you ought to be ashamed of yourself for saying anything about it, Simone! Madame's worried enough without your suggesting such ghastly things!"

"I d—didn't!" sobbed Simone in her own language. "I love Madame!"

"It looks like it, I must say!" retorted Juliet grimly. "Well, Robin? What do *you* want?"

The Robin, who had been tugging at her sleeve, said, "I don't think you ought to speak so unkindly to Simone, Julie!" (Her name for Juliet.) "I think also that Zoë is with Eigen."

"Eigen?" The big girls crowded round her at once.

"But why do you think that, Robin?" asked Gisela.

"Eigen isn't here," returned the mite. "He was talking this morning with Zoë, and perhaps they went somewhere."

"Come and tell Madame," said Gisela. "She will like to know."

Accordingly, as Madge Bettany was pacing up and down her study, trying to puzzle out where Joey could have gone, she heard a tap at her door, and then the head girl and the school baby entered.

"Robin thinks Joey may be with Marie's little brother

51

Eigen, Madame," explained Gisela as she made her little regulation curtsy.

The Head stared at that. "Joey with Eigen! But why?"

"She was talking with Eigen this morning, Madame," said the Robin in her pretty French.

Miss Bettany sat down and held out her hand. "Come here, Robin. Now, tell me just when you saw Joey and Eigen together, and where."

The Robin leaned up against her knee, and looked up at her with confident brown eyes. "It was when we came from Le Petit Chalet, Madame. They were standing by the stationery cupboard, and Zoë"—she still could not manage the English J—"was looking very angry—but *very* angry, and she stamped her foot and said, 'Oh—ze—brutal—*beasts!*'"

The Robin repeated the English words with great care and a distinctness which would have been laughable under any other circumstances. But nobody felt very much like laughing just then.

"You're sure that is what she said?" asked the young head-mistress.

The curly head was nodded emphatically. "But yes, Madame. I heard her."

"Gisela, would you ring for Marie?" asked Miss Bettany.

Gisela rang, and presently Marie appeared. At first when she was questioned, she declared that she had no idea as to what the two missing children could have been talking about. She was very angry with Eigen, for he should have been in the kitchen, helping her, and she had seen nothing of him all the morning. Then, after a little more urging from her mistress, she suddenly remembered that the dog of a neighbour of theirs had had a litter of pups, and she had heard that the little things were to be drowned that day.

"If that is what Eigen was telling Joey," said Miss Bettany with great decision, "then that is where they are! But she had no right to go off without telling me!" Then a sudden thought struck her. "Is it that beautiful St. Bernard dog?"

"Yes, *mein Fräulein*," replied Marie. "They are too poor

to keep the pups, for they eat much; and, indeed, they spoke of shooting Zita."

"Oh, what a shame!" The Bettanys all adored animals, and the same spirit which must have sent Jo off in an attempt to save the puppies boiled up in her sister now. "Poor Zita! If they can't afford to keep her, why don't they sell her to someone who can?"

Marie stood respectfully silent. It was not for her to speak, but she thought that if Madame had seven children to clothe and feed, and a husband who could earn money only during the summer, since he was a cowherd, she would not have been so indignant over the proposed shooting of a mere big dog who ate far more than she ought to do. Of course, if the pups had arrived during the tourist season, they would most likely have sold, in which case there would have been plenty to buy food for all. But Zita had not done what was expected of her, and so they must go. That was a matter of course.

Madge, looking up, guessed what was passing through the girl's mind. "Are they very poor, Marie?" she asked gently.

"They can live, *mein Fräulein*," replied Marie dryly.

A wild shriek of "Joey! Joey!" broke across the conversation, and Madge, running to the window, beheld her small sister and Eigen racing madly along. Eigen looked much as usual, but Joey was a sight to behold. She was soaking, and her hair was on end. Her face was splashed with mud; her gym tunic was torn so that a great triangular piece hung down in front. She was crying, too—an unusual thing for her; and in her arms was a soft little roly-poly ball, which she cuddled to her.

Leaving the people in the study to do as they chose, Madge fled to the door, and caught the child in her arms. "Joey! How could you?" she cried reproachfully.

"Oh, Madge! Oh, Madge!" sobbed Joey exhaustedly; "I could only save him! The rest were all drowned! Oh, Madge! Such little *young* things! But I pulled him out and saved him! And, oh! the poor old mother! If you'd seen her eyes! Oh. I *can* keep him, can't I?" She thrust the little wet bundle against her sister. "He's such a baby!"

53

"Hush, Joey! Don't cry so, darling! Yes; of course you shall keep him! —Eigen! Go and change at once, and tell Marie to give you some hot coffee! —Come, Joey! Come and have a bath! "

An hour later, Joey, cleansed and in her right mind, with her new possession cuddled up to her, told her story to an attentive audience.

Eigen had told her about the two-week-old pups, and their destiny, and she had torn off with him as soon as prayers were over. They had arrived too late to do anything but save this last pup, even though they had scrambled over rocks and through thorns to do it. Joey, clutching the poor baby-thing to her, had harangued the man fiercely in a mixture of French, German, and English, which luckily he had not understood. She had cried all the way home over the memory of poor Zita's frantic grief; and Eigen had cried too—mainly out of sympathy, Madge suspected.

"I can keep him, can't I?" wound up Joey passionately.

"Yes; you may keep him," said her sister. "He must go back to his mother for a few weeks, and I will pay for him, so that they can keep her. I'm going now, to see about it. If things are very bad, Zita had better come here for the present. We can feed her better than they can, I imagine, and that will be my birthday present to you, Joey. Until I come back, you can give him some warm milk and water with a very little sugar in it."

She set off, and on reaching the little hut found that things were as Marie had said. The people had enough to do to feed themselves, and there was no margin for keeping such a huge animal as Zita. The herdsman at once fell in with her suggestion that the poor brute should go to the Chalet for the winter. He also agreed to accept some money for the pup, and his wife wept for joy when the kroner notes were laid on the table. The money would make all the difference to them. Then Zita was unchained and handed over to her temporary owner, and Madge arrived back at the Chalet with her.

The joy of the poor mother over her restored baby made Joey cry again. Zita washed her puppy thoroughly, and then lay down with him snuggled up to her, thumping the floor ecstatically with her big tail, and looking her gratitude out of her pathetic eyes. She had reached a dog-paradise. For the first time in months she had had a good meal. She was in a warm place, with plenty of fresh, sweet hay for her bed, and she had got back one of the babies they had taken away from her. What more could a sensible dog ask?

"I shall call him Rufus," said Joey, as she reluctantly shut the door of the shed where they were, and went in to *Kaffee*. "I love him, and it's the nicest birthday present I ever had!"

CHAPTER EIGHT

The New Singing-Master

HAVING DISTINGUISHED herself by scaring everybody and rescuing Rufus from a watery grave, and Zita from an untimely end, Joey "lay low" for a while. As a matter of fact, nobody did anything specially striking for the next week or two; little things, such as Amy Stevens tilting her chair over backwards during *Mittagessen*, or Grizel Cochrane handing in her diary instead of her composition-book, not being sufficiently important to count. True, Grizel was fearfully teased over her exploit, but that was to be expected. Things jogged along very comfortably and quietly, till one break, when Margia Stevens, who had been having a music-lesson with Herr Anserl, the master who came up twice a week from Spärtz, rushed into the little form-room where the middles were, obviously bursting with news.

"Guess what!"

"What is it to do with?" asked Rosalie Dene ungrammatically.

"Oh, school, of course! Go on! Give you three guesses!"

55

"We're going to the theatre at Innsbruck!" suggested Joey.

"No!"

"Madame has arranged for a dance on Saturday," volunteered Frieda Mensch.

"No—no! Nothing like that! You've only one more guess!"

"Someone has given us more new books for ze librairie!" This was Simone's idea.

"No! Not that at all!"

"Then what is it, please?" asked Paula von Rothenfels.

Margia drew a deep breath. "We're to have a singing-master! He's an Englishman, and—— Oh bother! There's the bell for silence!"

The others echoed her exclamation, but, as they had had a long lecture—much needed—on the necessity of keeping the few rules of the school only that morning, they dared not speak after the silence-bell had gone. In the meantime, Mademoiselle and Miss Maynard couldn't imagine what had happened to make them so stupid this morning.

When finally the bell rang and Mademoiselle had left the room, they all thronged round Margia demanding to know all details of the new singing-master.

"I don't know *much*," she said, "but he's come to live at the Villa Adalbert for the winter. His sister is with him, and he's very good, and awfully keen. He wants to teach singing here because he likes to have something to do; so he came and asked Madame if he might."

"I wonder why he has come?" said Simone thoughtfully. "He is ill, perhaps?"

"I wonder what kind of songs he teaches," said Joey.

"Let's hope it's not those awful folk-songs you're for ever shrieking!" observed Margia with point.

"I hope it isn't beastly tuneless things like the rubbish you play!" retaliated Joey.

"Jo Bettany!" said Gisela's horrified voice. "You must pay a slang fine."

Jo grumbled under her breath; but after all, as the others assured her when Gisela had gone, she had simply *asked* for it. "Topping" and "ripping" and kindred expressions were banned to them, but most people were a little lenient about their use; but nobody showed any lenience over such words as "beastly", and she knew it. The crusade against unpleasant slang was being carried on thoroughly, and already the girls were improving in that direction. Luckily for everyone, the bell rang for *Mittagessen* at this point, and they all had to stop talking until they were seated at the table. When the meal was over, and before she said grace, Miss Bettany informed the school of the new arrangements she had made for their singing-classes.

"Mr. Denny," she said, "is spending the winter here for his health. He is a singing-master in England, and loves his work, so he came to see if I would allow him to take you. I have agreed, and he is coming this afternoon to have the first classes. You will be divided into three divisions as you are for lessons, and I hope you will show Mr. Denny that you can sing, and also behave well."

At half-past two punctually Mr. Denny came, and the whole school was assembled at his request in the big school-room. When they were all in their places, with Mademoiselle at the piano, Miss Bettany appeared, and following her was one of the weirdest creatures the girls had ever seen. He was tall and gaunt, with long brown hair falling wildly into his eyes and on to the wide collar of his shirt. His suit was of brown velveteen, and he wore an enormous brown bow at his open shirt-throat. There was something untamed about him, and his vivid pink-and-white skin added to his unusual looks.

"These are my girls," said Miss Bettany with a very grave face. "Girls, this is Mr. Denny. Please sing your best for him."

Then she turned and left the room abruptly, and Mr. Denny and the school faced each other. "Will you sit down?" he said in a deep musical voice.

They sat down and waited to hear what he had to say. He put an arm on the music-stand that had been set on the dais for him, and surveyed them solemnly. "Years ago," he began, "in the time of the Greeks, music was considered to be one of the necessary foundations of a good education. Read Plato's *Republic*, and you will see that it is so.

Nowadays, music is *not* so regarded. In many schools it is taken as an 'extra'. Music! The gift of the gods to this earth!"

"Quite mad!" murmured Joey to her next-door neighbour, Simone. Then she stopped, for Mademoiselle was regarding her with a baleful glare.

"Fortunately for you girls, your mistress knows better. A lover herself of good music—I do not speak of the appalling amount of syncopated trash that is now flooding the world!—she has resolved to see that your knowledge of the heavenly art shall be a full one. She is right—very right!"

"More than he is!" decided Grizel. "He looks absolutely touched!"

The lecturer was concluding his remarks. "I am here to act, not as a teacher—I, who am only a learner myself, would not presume to that rank! No! but, as a *guide*, I will do my best for you. Will you all please stand and sing to me?"

The school rose to its feet, vaguely wondering what it was to sing. Mademoiselle promptly settled that question by playing the opening bars of "Where'er You Walk", which had been one of their last term's songs. Those who knew it sang with all their might, and Mr. Denny listened with a beaming face. "Excellent!" he said, when it was over. "But now we will sing a song we can *all* learn. Will you, little maiden, distribute these to your compeers?"

He held out a sheaf of songs to the Robin, who took them and gazed wonderingly at him. She didn't understand him in the least. Luckily, Joey held out her hand for a few and passed them along, so the school baby guessed what he wanted and gave out the rest in her usual composed little way.

The girls looked at their copies eagerly. They were a setting of Henry Maughan's "Song of St. Francis":

There was a Knight of Bethlehem
   Whose wealth was tears and sorrows;
His men-at-arms were little lambs,
   His trumpeters were sparrows.

His castle was a wooden Cross
  On which He hung so high;
His Helmet was a crown of thorns
  Whose crest did touch the sky.

It was new to all of them—even Joey had never seen it before. Mr. Denny gave them a minute or two to look at it; then he tapped on the stand with his baton.

"If Mademoiselle will be so kind as to give us the keynote, we will begin."

Mademoiselle meekly sounded the note, and the school made an effort at humming the air. It was easy to read, and they did it well. Once they had got the notes, they were switched on to the words. Finally, Mr. Denny made them sit down, and sang it to them himself in a sweet baritone, and with the utmost simplicity, as the music demanded.

When it was over, the master looked across at Gisela. "What do you think of the song?" he demanded embarrassingly.

"It is a beautiful song," said the head girl thoughtfully.

"Why is it beautiful?" He turned to Joey, who could think of nothing to say, and just gaped at him.

Margia answered for her. "It is beautiful because the words are simple, and so is the music."

"Right!" he said promptly. "We will now sing it again, and then we will turn our attention to another kind of song. Attend, little maidens!"

They sang it straight through once more, and he nodded his satisfaction.

"That went well. Now if the tiny maiden"—he indicated the Robin again—"will bring me the first song, we will ask this next little elf to distribute these!"

He waved a second bunch of papers at Amy Stevens, and presently the girls found themselves looking at another song they did not know at all—one entitled "Brittany".

Once again they were given the keynote, and then had to read the melody. This was more difficult than the last, though, again, it was perfectly simple. The girls liked it. These two songs, both by the same composer—an Englishman who, they learned later, had fallen in the war—were

59

totally unlike anything they had ever done. They wound up with another song of very much the same type, "A Page's Road Song", and then the first lesson was over.

"We will have three divisions next lesson," explained Mr. Denny, tossing back his long hair out of his eyes. "The elder maidens will sing first; then, we will have the little lasses; and, finally, our small elves. I wish you adieu until then."

He bowed deeply to Mademoiselle, smiled at the girls, and strode out, leaving a gasping class behind him. Miss Maynard appeared almost at once.

"Be quick and tidy up the room, girls," she said. "Then go and get ready for a walk. No talking until you are outside!"

That last command was a rather necessary one. The girls were bursting to discuss their new master, and, as he was only in the study across the passage, he would probably have heard every word that they said. So they cleared the room, and scrambled into their coats and hats without a word; but, once they were safely round the lake, the comments came thick and furious.

"What a weird soul!" exclaimed Grizel.

"He is—unusual," said Gisela hesitatingly. "I liked the songs."

"Yes, so did I. Thank goodness he kept off folk-songs!"

Joey was too far behind to hear this comment, which was, perhaps, just as well. She and Simone were chattering in French about Mr. Denny. Simone considered that he looked "romantic".

"He looked an ass!" returned Joey briskly. "I loathe men who have their hair bobbed! And why couldn't he wear a decent collar and tie like other folks?" which put a complete stopper on the one thing Madge had feared when she had finally agreed to letting him have the singing.

It was Margia who sealed it. "Who was that Greek man he talked about who said music was education?" she inquired when they had broken ranks.

"Plato," replied the omniscient Jo. "Why?"

"It would be a jolly good name for *him*! Don't you think so?"

"Fine! We'll call him that!"

And "Plato" he remained from then onwards.

As the Head said when she came to hear of it, "It would be rather difficult to be sentimental over Plato!"

CHAPTER NINE

Shakespeariana

"I'M FED UP!" observed Evadne one day, shortly after Mr. Denny had made his début at the Chalet School. "I think Gisela is right-down mean!"

"Why!" demanded Margia, who was sitting on the top of her desk, swinging her legs. "What's she done to you?"

"Fined me!"

"Oh! Why? Was it slang?"

"You know real well it was! I think she's a—a rubber-necked four-flusher!"

"Those prefects are getting very trying about slang," said Joey Bettany thoughtfully. "I think it's about time we choked them off a bit! Bette actually fined me for saying something was awfully decent!"

"Juliet's just as bad as the rest," put in Rosalie Dene. "I'm sure Madame never meant we were to stop saying 'jolly' and 'decent'. Why, *Shakespeare* used them—'jolly', at any rate!"

A gleam lit up Joey's eyes. "What is it, Joey?" asked Simone, who noticed it.

"An idea," replied her friend laconically.

"What *sort* of an idea? Something to down the prefects?"

"Goodness, Margia! What English! If Gisela heard you now, she *would* have a fit."

"Oh, let her! Tell us your idea, Joey! Go on!"

"Can't! 'Tisn't ready, yet! I'll tell you when it is!"

And Jo slipped off to visit Zita and Rufus, who by this time had his eyes open, and was beginning to stagger about on four unsteady legs, while his proud mother looked on.

After *Kaffee* that afternoon she condescended to reveal her idea to the others, and they listened with breathless interest.

"Won't it mean an awful lot of work?" said Margia doubtfully.

"Well, we'll have to read it up a bit, of course," conceded Joey; "but it's quite easy, really! Don't do it if you'd rather not, though!"

"Jo! Don't be an ass! Of course I will! We *all* will!"

While this was going on, Miss Bettany had opened the fines box and was frowning over the amount in it.

"It's really disgraceful!" she said. "The number of fines the middles have is simply appalling! We must do something to stop this silly slang. Put it away with the rest, Gisela, please; and then we must think of some other punishment, I think."

"Perhaps if you were to speak to them, Madame," suggested Gisela. "It is Evadne who is worst. She speaks so much that seems ugly."

"All slang is ugly," said the Head absently. "Some is worse than the rest, of course. I've no wish for you all to talk like the heroines of goody-goody books, but at the same time there is a line to be drawn somewhere, and I draw it at expressions like 'gumswizzled', and 'jim-dandy'!"

"Yes," said Gisela. Then she added unexpectedly, "Madame, what is a rubber-neck?"

Miss Bettany gasped. "My dear Gisela?"

"I heard one of the juniors talking—ah, no, *saying* it to another!"

The Head got to her feet. "I am going to put a stop to this, once for all! I will not have the babies using such expressions! Please go and assemble the seniors and the middles in the big school-room at once!"

Gisela fled; and ten minutes later the school was assembled, and waiting to know what it was Miss Bettany had to say to them. They hadn't long to wait.

Three minutes after the last of the middles had been hauled away from her private affairs, and hunted into the big school-room, the Head appeared and read them all a lecture on the iniquities of slang that left them gasping and breathless.

"I will not allow it!" she wound up. "You can surely speak English without descending to these ugly, meaningless, slang phrases. At any rate, they are strictly forbidden! Please understand that I shall punish most severely any girl who is reported to me for using slang!"

Then she left them, and went over to Le Petit Chalet to impress on the juniors the evils of such expressions as "rubber-neck".

The middles clustered together in a corner to discuss the affair, while the prefects went off to their own room, and the other seniors retreated to the little form-room. It had taken the younger members of what was unofficially known as "the big school" nearly all the term to become a united body. The difference of their nationalities had had something to do with it; also their want of a common tongue. Many of the new girls found English terribly difficult, and Rosalie Dene and Evadne Lannis were still unable to carry on a conversation of any length in either French or German. Jo Bettany's facility and fluency in all three tongues were the envy of the others. She could even chatter in Italian now, for she had persuaded Vanna di Ricci and Bianca di Ferrara to talk to her whenever it was permissible. It was natural, therefore, that she should be the leader of the middles. Now they gathered round her to hear what she proposed doing.

"We've got to speak good English," she said slowly. "Well, I don't see any reason why we shouldn't! *Shakespeare* spoke very good English. Of course, lots of it is rather out of date now, still we can't go wrong if we copy him!"

The English girls saw the point of her remarks at once, and as soon as it had been carefully explained to the others they saw too.

"But, Joey, how shall we do it?" asked Simone. "I only know so little of Shakespeare."

"We'll read all we can," said Joey. "Whenever we get a chance, we'll talk to each other; but mind, no one's to say a word till I tell you. We don't want to let the others know before we're ready. I want it to burst on them like—like—a hurricane, sort of!"

For the rest of that week the middles were surprisingly quiet and studious for them. Gisela, under the impression that this was the result of the Head's lecture, was quite jubilant about it. There were very few fines, and all seemed to be going well. Saturday was a wild stormy day, with a tearing gale from the north-west, and a heavy grey sky. Bernhilda, the weather-wise, declared that if the wind shifted to the north the snow would come. It was later this year than it had been last, and when it came it would probably be a regular blizzard. The wind was blowing too heavily for anyone to go out; and mistresses and prefects prepared for a strenuous day. They need not have worried. Every one of the eleven people who were responsible for most of the mischief going on in the school read nearly the whole day, and Sunday was the same. The great surprise was to begin on Monday, and everyone wanted to know as much Shakespearian English as possible before then.

In the yellow room Joey Bettany still had one of the window cubicles; Juliet, as head of the dormitory, had the other. Paula von Rothenfels and Luigia di Ferrara had their little domains at the other end of the room. In between came Evadne and Gertrud, Rosalie and Vanna. It was the usual thing for one of the "door" people to ask Joey what the weather was like, when they first woke, and Juliet had got so accustomed to the query that she never paid any heed to it. So this morning, when she heard a rustling from Paula's cubicle, she merely snuggled sleepily down under the *plumeau* after a glance at her watch. The next minute she was widely awake, for, instead of the usual "Joey—Joey! *Quel temps fait-il?*" Paula had remarked, slowly and distinctly, "Joey! Prithee tell me, wench, doth it yet snow?" And Joey had replied, "Nay! But I'll warrant me 'twill come down yet ere the nightfall!"

A smothered giggle came from Luigia's direction, followed by, "Mayhap 'tis time we were arising!"

Then, Joey, "Prithee, fair Juliet, shall we not arise?"

Just then the bell rang, and five separate mumps told her that her dormitory was up—a fact which gave her further cause for wonder, since, as a rule, there were groans when getting-up time came.

"Marry, how dark 'tis!" observed Rosalie. "In sooth, the night hath not given place to day! Lights, ho!"

In response, Paula switched on the electric lights, and then a scurry of feet told the senior that the first two girls were making for the bathroom. She was longing to get down to the other prefects to discuss things with them, but she had to wait until the last junior had flung up her curtains over the rod and stripped her bed. Then, leaving them, to wedge open the door, she sped down to the big school-room, where Gisela, Bernhilda, and Wanda von Eschenau were standing round the huge porcelain stove, warming themselves. She poured out her tale to them amid their exclamations, and then demanded their opinion.

"I think we will wait and see what they will do," said Gisela in her careful English. "At least, it is not slang!"

"No; it isn't slang," agreed Juliet, "but it sounds so odd!"

The door banged open at that moment, and Frieda and Simone, who slept over at Le Petit Chalet, came racing in.

"Good-morning!" said Gisela pleasantly.

"Good—good-morrow, sweeting!" replied Simone rather nervously.

Gisela could scarcely believe her ears, and she received a further shock; for just then the members of the yellow room, with Mari von Eschenau, entered, and Joey, who was a little in advance of the rest, cried, "Well met, Gisela! How is't with thee, sweet chuck?"

Juliet gurgled. She really couldn't help it.

"Joey!" exclaimed Gisela. "You must not use slang!"

"Nor did I, pretty mistress!" replied Jo, her black eyes dancing wickedly.

"Surely 'sweet ch—chuck' is slang!" exclaimed Gisela, stumbling slightly over the unusual term.

"Nay; 'tis the English of Will Shakespeare," responded naughty Jo.

Gisela had nothing to reply to that, and, as the bell for *Frühstück* rang just then, they all filed into the *Speisesaal* in silence.

When they had sat down, Simone passed Frieda the rolls, saying, "Come! Fall to!" and Frieda accepted, saying with a giggle, "I thank ye; and be blessed for your good comfort!"

Miss Maynard, who was at the head of the table, raised her eyebrows, but said nothing. Meanwhile, Evadne, at the other table, turned to Bernhilda, and said, "How thinkest thou, gentle Bernhilda; will it snow?"

Bernhilda, dumbfounded at this unusual mode of address, said nothing. There really was little that could be said. Miss Bettany had told them to read the classics and see how little slang was used there, and to try to model their own speech rather more on them than on that of cheap magazines filled with Americanese and language which might be suitable for boys, but was not allowable for girls.

The middles had taken her at her word, and *were* modelling their language on the classics. They had only gone rather further back than she had intended.

Miss Maynard was thoughtful throughout the meal. The head-mistress was not there. She had wakened up with a violent headache, and had had to stay in bed for the present. Jo, glancing round, had just realised that her sister was absent, and was wondering uneasily what was wrong. She was recalled to herself by Margia, who leant across the table, remarking sweetly, "How now! Thou dreamst! Where lies your grief?"

"Margia, sit up!" said Miss Maynard authoritatively. "You must not lean forward like that!"

"I crave pardon, Madam," replied Margia.

A gasp went round the table, but the mistress took no further notice of it than to say, "Go on with your meal!"

Conversation rather languished after that. The others wanted Jo to give them a lead; but Jo was worrying over her sister's absence, and never opened her mouth. As soon as *Frühstück* was over, she dashed off upstairs to the little room on the second landing where Madge slept, and tapped gently at the door.

"Is that you, Joey?" said Miss Bettany. "You can come in for a minute."

Joey stole in, and came over to the bed. "What's wrong, Madge?"

"Just a headache," replied her sister wearily. "Oh, it's better than it was, so you needn't look so scared."

"Would you like some tea?" Joey asked softly.

"No; nothing, thanks! I've had some, and some aspirin, and I shall go to sleep, I think. Run downstairs now, Joey," she murmured. "Tell Miss Maynard not to worry; I shall be quite all right. You can come up and see if I am awake at eleven if you like. Don't tap; just come straight in. Bye-bye for the present! " She stretched out a slender hand and squeezed Joey's, then she settled back, and her small sister went quietly out of the room to find Miss Maynard and give her message.

The other middles found her decidedly quiet and dull. It was such an unusual thing for Madge to be poorly, that Jo felt scared. She adored her sister, though wild horses wouldn't have dragged it out of her, and she felt rather miserable. Bernhilda and Gisela, understanding, took her off with them when they went over to Le Petit Chalet to explain things to Mademoiselle, so that the others might not bother her with questions.

Luckily, when eleven o'clock came, Jo found her sister sleeping quietly, and went downstairs, much relieved; and *Kaffee* at sixteen o'clock brought a message to her from the study, where Madge, her headache completely gone, sat waiting for her. Jo went into the room rather apprehensively.

"You goose! " laughed Miss Bettany. "You look scared out of your existence! "

"I was! " returned Joey truthfully. "It isn't often *you're* ill, you know! "

"No; I know that! But I can't help having a headache now and then! Now, you know how I feel when there's anything wrong with *you*; so perhaps you'll try to avoid doing mad things that give you cold! "

"I haven't had *one* cold all this year! " cried Joey in injured tones.

"I know! I'm only warning you! Now sit down and pour out the tea, will you?"

"Well, rather! "

Joey had a joyful hour with her sister, and then went back to the others in high spirits.

Gisela came over to her at once. "How is Madame?" she asked.

"Nearly all right, thanks awfully! " replied Jo. "She's not coming into school at all today, but she'll be there tomorrow."

"I am so glad," returned Gisela. "We do not like it when Madame is ill! "

Then she sent the middle back to her own quarters, where she was promptly seized on by the others, who demanded to know how Madame was.

"I am glad she is better," said Simone. "It has been so *triste* all day!"

"In sooth it hath been a weary length," returned Joey, suddenly remembering their plans. "I pray you, tell me, doth it yet snow?"

"Nay, damsel, but the wind is howling much! " replied Evadne promptly.

The spirits of all the middles had gone up with a bound. How they managed to get through prep without any trouble was a mystery.

After prep Bernhilda appeared to say that there would be no dancing that night, but that they were all to get their sewing, and Miss Durrant had offered to read aloud to them.

"Woe is me! " sighed Jo. "I cannot stomach sewing! "

Bernhilda gasped. "Will you all please hurry," she said, when she had recovered her breath. Then she left them.

"I'll warrant me I startled her full sore! " laughed Joey, as she got out her much-abused petticoat. "Oh dear! How I hate sewing! "

Work in hand, they trotted off to the big school-room, where they found the others ready, waiting for Miss Durrant, who happened to be late.

"Here's snip, and nip, and cut, and slish, and slash! " quoted Margia as she shook out her sewing.

"Away, thou rag!" retorted Jo as she sat down. Then she turned to Bernhilda: "What sweeting; all amort?"

"Joey, be quiet," said Gisela. "And please do not use such language! I am sure Madame would not like it!"

"Nay; this to me!" retorted Jo. "Thou very paltry knave——"

"Josephine," said a quiet voice behind her.

Jo turned round in dismay. There stood her sister.

"When I told you to model your language on that of the classics," said Madge, "I never meant you to use Shakespearian expressions, and you knew it!"

Eleven people looked down, their cheeks scarlet. Miss Bettany surveyed them, a little smile twitching at the corners of her mouth.

"Please don't do it again," she said, and then left them.

"I suppose it was your plan, Joey?" she said later to her small sister, who had come to say "Good-night" to her.

"Oh, don't be cross!" pleaded Joey. "We spent *ages* reading Shakespeare, and now it's been nearly all wasted!"

"And serve you right!" was the answer.

Joey looked at her doubtfully. "We know a lot more about him, anyway," she said irrelevantly. "And it's awfully hard not to be able to say 'jolly', and 'decent', and 'awful'! Really, it is, Madge! And Shakespeare used such *gorgeous* words!"

Madge gave it up and laughed. "Go to bed," she said.

"I won't use Shakespeare's expressions any more," promised Joey. "And we *may* say 'jolly', and things like that, mayn't we?"

"Good-night, you baby!" was the only reply she got.

However, as the prefects relaxed their vigilance a little, the middles thought it was fairly safe to take it for granted that Miss Bettany did not mind a *little* slang; so their Shakespearian studies had not been in vain.

CHAPTER TEN

"It was all my own Fault!"

NEXT DAY the snow came, and with it the winter. All that day and the next it snowed, a huge whirling blizzard, and the clouds were so heavy with it that they seemed to be lying on the mountain-tops, and still the snow fell. On the Thursday there was a lull which lasted for two hours, and the girls, well wrapped up, played about the Chalet during the whole time. As Miss Bettany said, they would have to take advantage of fine weather when they could. So from ten o'clock until twelve they rushed about in the dry, powdery white, which was so unlike English snow, and had a glorious time. Just before twelve the great flakes began drifting down again, and they had to go in, and then once more everything was veiled in whirling white, and the blizzard raged until the Sunday. When the girls got up in the morning the wind had gone down, the snow had ceased to fall, and it was freezing hard.

Joey, sitting up in bed gazing out of the window, gave a cry of ecstasy as she saw the beauty before her. Mountains, path, and level grass were thickly covered with a white mantle against which the lake lay, still and black beneath its veiling of thin ice.

"Oh, wonderful!" gasped Joey. "Juliet! Wake up! Isn't it glorious?"

There was a groan from the other occupants of the dormitory.

"Joey, *do* be quiet! It's Sunday—the only day we get a really decent time in bed!" complained Juliet. "I can see it's stopped snowing without sitting up. It's going to come down again, though! Just look at that sky!"

"How it is cold!" shuddered Gertrud in her own language. "Joey! Does it freeze?"

"I should think it did! The lake's absolutely black, and the snow looks so white!"

The members of the yellow room hopped out of bed, and dressed as quickly as possible.

Downstairs, Simone was waiting in the passage; and Marie von Eschenau, who was noted for being a quick dresser, came racing down too. The three little girls ran to the door and opened it, letting in a rush of icy-cold air that made them shiver.

"B-r-r-r! Isn't it *cold*?" gasped Joey. "We'll be able to have a walk today!"

"Yes—if it does not snow again," said Simone pessimistically. "Here is Frieda!"

Frieda, with her long blue cloak pulled tightly round her, and her pretty flaxen hair waving loosely over her shoulders, came flying across from Le Petit Chalet. "*Grüss Gott!*" she smiled as she reached them. "How it freezes!"

"*Grüss Gott*, Frieda!" said Joey. Then, eagerly, "I say! *You* know the weather about here. Do you think it will snow again today? Or do you think it'll hold off till tonight?"

Frieda looked seriously at the sullen sky above them. "I cannot tell," she replied. "The sky is very full of snow, but it freezes, and so no more may fall until the night. There is no wind, of course. If a south or a west wind should rise, then I think we should have much more snow —wet snow. A north wind might bring hail. As long as it does not blow, there will be frost. If the lake freezes, will Madame give permission for skating, Joey?"

"Sure to," replied Jo. "How long will it be before the lake bears, Frieda?"

Frieda shook her head. "I do not know. It depends on how long the frost holds, and how keen it is. Shall I go and put my cloak away? The bell will be ringing for *Frühstück*."

"And we shall be rowed for standing here without any coats on!" supplemented Jo.

They went in, shutting the door behind them, and ran into the cloak-room just as Miss Bettany came downstairs.

"Just in time!" murmured Joey under her breath. "Coo! It was cold standing there! Let's go and get warm at the stove!"

They went into the big school-room where some of the others were, and presently the bell summoned them to the *Speisesaal*. After breakfast Miss Bettany told them that she intended arranging for walks that morning. In the meantime, no one was to go outside without a coat, as there was an icy wind getting up. Everyone was overjoyed at the idea of getting out after two days' imprisonment.

There was a service in the little white-washed chapel today, so all the Roman Catholics—which meant the greater part of the school—would attend. The remainder, eight girls, Miss Bettany herself, and Miss Maynard, would have a little service of their own. Then they would have a kind of scratch meal and a long walk, having *Kaffee* at the usual time, and a semi-dinner at seven in the evening.

"Splendid scheme!" declared Margia. "Isn't it, Joey?"

"Awfully jolly!" agreed Jo, suppressing with difficulty a shiver.

She cast a little rueful glance at her sister, who was laughing at something Gisela had been saying. No one knew better than Jo what was going to happen. Oh, how bitterly she regretted those few minutes at the open door! She had been standing there such a little time, but she had felt the icy cold grip her, and she hadn't been warm since. There was nothing for it but to tell Madge, and all the laughter would vanish from her face, and the old anxious expression would come back into her brown eyes, and Jo hadn't seen it since April.

She shivered violently; and Grizel, standing near, noticed it. "Joey! You're shivering!" she cried. "Whatever's the matter? You can't be cold!"

The words reached Miss Bettany, and she swung round at once. "Jo! Aren't you well?"

"I—I'm sorry," said Jo limply. "I—I was standing at the door before *Frühstück*——"

"Joey! How could you! You must go to bed at once! —

72

Grizel—no, Gisela, run to Marie and ask her for two hot-water bottles! Grizel, you can turn on the bath.—Come, Joey! Come *at once*!—Miss Maynard, please look after the girls!"

Joey was hurried away and into a hot bath. Then she was put into pyjamas heated at the stove, and rolled in a blanket and carried up to Madge's room, where she was tucked into bed with two hot-water bottles and sundry pillows to lift her up to help the breathing that was already becoming difficult. Nearly all her life her colds had been serious matters, to be dealt with immediately and given no chance to get any hold. The old bronchitis kettle was routed out and set going, and then Madge went over to the window and stood looking out with compressed lips. A croak from the bed brought her to it.

"What is it, Joey? Don't try to talk! You will only tire yourself. Would you like a drink?"

"Yes, please," croaked Joey. But when it came she gripped her sister's hand. "Madge—I'm sorry! "

Madge held the glass to her lips before answering. "All right," she said curtly as she set it down. Then she sat down on the side of the bed, and lifted the child up against her shoulder. "That easier, old lady? Mademoiselle is hunting up some medicine."

"Shall I ring up Doctor Erckhardt?" Mademoiselle asked her young head-mistress. "It might be well to have him. He would come, for he loves *la petite*."

Madge nodded. "Yes; better send. We can't afford to take risks where Jo is concerned."

Later came the sound of voices as the girls returned from High Mass, and then the bell ringing them to *Mittagessen*. Miss Bettany ran down for this, leaving Mademoiselle in charge of the invalid. Joey's breathing was quick and hard, and her cheeks were flushed with the rising fever. An unpleasant little cough had developed too. Mademoiselle readjusted the bronchitis kettle, and saw that the hot-water bottles were all they ought to be, then she went off in charge of the senior walk.

Miss Bettany had brought back with her some calves-foot jelly, and she fed her small sister with it, forbidding her to put her arms out of bed. "Try to sleep a little, Joey," she said, when the jelly had vanished. "Are you comfortable? Like another pillow?"

"No, thanks!" croaked Joey.

She closed her eyes obediently, but sleep wouldn't come. Her chest felt as though there were tight iron bands round it, and a little sharp pain kept stabbing her in the side. She had a queer idea that the walls of the room were closing in on her, and she cried out in sudden fear. Madge, sitting at the window watching for the doctor, was with her in an instant.

"All right, Joey—it's quite all right!" said the low, sweet voice that Joey loved. "Drink this, honey!"

Joey drank it—cool water with orange-juice in it, and then the kettle was attended to again, and breathing became a little easier for a while. Presently she raised her eyes. "It's the pain in my side," she said weakly.

An hour later, the doctor arrived.

After that, Jo had no very clear idea what happened during the next day or two. She came to herself late on Tuesday night, to find that the horrid tightness in her chest and the pain in her side had vanished, and she was lying down comfortably with only one pillow under her head. A night-light was burning on the little table by the window, and on a camp-bedstead lay her sister. Jo lay for a minute or two, pondering matters; then she made a slight movement, and at once Madge sat up, shaking the dark-brown curls out of her eyes.

"Hallo!" said Joey. "What's up? Have I been ill?"

"No; just a warning not to do silly things," replied Madge as she got up and slipped into her dressing-gown. "Drink this, Joey, and then go to sleep again."

Joey obediently drank what was given her, and then snuggled down; the long lashes fell on her cheeks almost at once. Madge stood for a minute, looking down at her. It had been a narrow shave. Not until that afternoon had the doctor told her that all fear of pleuro-pneumonia was at an end, and that, given ordinary care, Joey would be herself in another week. It was a tremendous relief, and not the least part of it was that the doctor had assured her that her small sister was much stronger than she had been in the summer, and that he quite thought she would outgrow her childish delicacy.

"That's something pleasant to write to Dick!" she murmured, her thoughts going to her twin-brother who was in the Forestry Department in India. "He will be pleased!"

She leaned over the child again, listening to the soft, even breathing. Then she pulled up the *plumeau*, tucking it in more closely round her, and retired to her own bed, where she speedily fell asleep, only awaking when the rising-bell sounded.

Joey slept through it, and through her sister's dressing. Indeed she only woke up when her breakfast tray appeared at nine o'clock. Her eyes went to the window. It was a gloriously sunny day, and she could see the mountains opposite arrayed in sparkling robes of snowy white. "Isn't it gorgeous!" she said. "When can I get up, please?"

"Not for a day or two yet," replied her sister, as she wrapped her in a thick woolly shawl, and banked her up with pillows. "That's what you get for doing mad things!"

Joey chuckled; then she turned wistful eyes to the delicate face above her. "It was all my own fault," she said humbly.

Madge nodded gravely as she laid the tray on her knees. "Yes—I know! Joey, do you remember Monday of last week when I had a headache?"

Jo paused in the act of peeling the top of her egg. "Yes, of course! why?"

"You told me that you were worried."

"I *was*! Horribly worried."

"How do you think I've felt since Sunday?"

Joey's eyes fell. "I didn't think," she murmured.

"Exactly! I'm not going to preach; but if you could realise all I've suffered since then, I think you'd do all you could to remember!"

Madge's lips twitched as she spoke. She had had a bad fright, and still had not recovered from it. Tender-hearted Joey saw it, and, at imminent danger of upsetting her tray,

75

she flung her arms round her sister. "Madge, I'm a pig! I'll try—honest injun, I will! "

Madge returned the hug heartily. "Yes, *do*, Joey! I shall feel happier about you now you've made that promise! I must go now; but I'll look in about eleven."

"Can I see any of the others later on?" demanded Jo, still clinging to her sister.

"Oh yes; so long as you don't get excited."

"You—you've forgiven me?"

"Yes! Haven't I said so?" Madge paused a moment, then she bent down and kissed the little white face.

Joey sat back contentedly. "*That's* all right! " she said happily. "Oh, Madge, I do love you so! And please couldn't the Robin come and see me a bit?"

Madge laughed. "Yes; I don't think *she* will excite you. Eat your breakfast, and she shall come up about ten."

At ten sharp the Robin arrived, carrying carefully some jigsaw puzzles, and when Miss Bettany came shortly after eleven, bringing with her the doctor, she found them disputing about the pieces, and wrangling joyfully.

The doctor smiled when he saw them. "I shan't keep my patient much longer," he said in his big rumbling voice. "We shall have you back into school next week, Fräulein Joey! "

"Good! " said Jo contentedly. "And please, when may I get up?"

He looked at Miss Bettany with a twinkle in his eye. "She is impatient, *gnädiges Fräulein, nicht wahr*? However, it is well, and *das Mädchen* may arise on Thursday for a few hours. I shall see her on Saturday, and perhaps she may be skating to Buchau on the following Saturday."

"Oh, tophole! " said Jo. "I'm sorry, Madge, but honour bright it *is*."

And what could Madge do but laugh?

CHAPTER ELEVEN

The First Issue of the "Chaletian"

Jo WAS RECEIVED with enthusiasm when she appeared in school on the Monday. She had been kept right away from the others until then, so that she might have a thorough rest, for she was growing very quickly, and Dr. Erckhardt had said it was a good thing that the holidays were coming so soon. Not that they were long holidays. Miss Bettany had decided to break up five days before Christmas, and start again on the seventh of January.

"Easter comes at the end of March," she said; "so we'll have only the fortnight or so at Christmas, and then I shall give the whole of April at Easter, when the weather will be better."

"What about Simone and Renée and the Merciers?" asked Joey. "Will they go home?"

"Mademoiselle is going to take them to Vienna, and Miss Maynard will take the three Italian girls up to Munich. You and I, Joey, are going to Innsbruck."

"To a hotel?" demanded Jo eagerly.

Madge shook her head. "Not for worlds! No; we're going to stay a week with the Mensches, and the rest of the time with the Maranis. The von Eschenaus have invited Juliet to go to them, and the Robin will come with us."

"What about Grizel?" asked Joey.

"Grizel is going home to England," replied Madge. "Her grandmother is very ill, and has asked for her; so she is going, and will not return till the end of January. Mr. and Mrs. Stevens are coming to Salzburg; so Amy and Margia will go to them. There'll only be the Robin with us, and you won't mind her?"

"Oh no! I love the Robin!" said Jo gaily. "What will

the Robin call you in the holidays?" said Joey.

"She told me quite seriously this morning that when it wasn't school time, she would like to call me *Tante Marguerite*, as she hadn't any aunts, and would like one! "

"Shall you let her?" asked Jo curiously.

"Yes. The poor baby hasn't any people of her own near her. If she wants to think of me as *ma tante*, I don't mind in the least! "

"It'll seem *weird*," commented Joey. "It must be *horrid* for her! "

There the conversation had ceased, and today Joey was back in school once more, and was received with acclamation, which she certainly didn't deserve.

"But it is so delightful to have you back, my Jo! " said Simone wistfully.

"Splendid to see you again, old thing! " was Grizel's cheery greeting.

"We have missed you, *mein Liebling*," observed Gisela.

It snowed all next day, making yet deeper the deep mantle which lay on the land; but towards evening it ceased, and Bernhilda the weatherwise proclaimed that it was going to freeze, and that soon the lake would be fit for skating, provided no wind got up to ruffle the ice.

She was right. When they tumbled out of bed the next morning, every single liquid that was not near a stove was frozen like a stone. The lake lay black against the snow, and the snow itself was hard as a rock. There was no wind, and the sky above was a clear pale blue, and almost cloudless. The girls were overjoyed, especially the English girls, for they had never known a winter like this. In the houses the great porcelain stoves were kept at full pitch, and the windows were covered with marvellous fairy designs, through which it was impossible to see. Jo, with a vivid remembrance of Hans Andersen's fairy-tales, warmed a penny and made little round holes on the panes, just as Kay and Gerda did, and the middles gazed out entranced on what she insisted on calling "Storybook-land".

At twelve o'clock everyone wrapped up warmly, and they went out and raced about, shouting and laughing. Even Jo, with "two of everything on, and one over, for luck, of some things!" to quote herself, trotted forth to enjoy the fresh, icy air. The glare of the snow under the December sun was terrific, so they all wore coloured spectacles, and shrieked with laughter at each other.

"We shall skate tomorrow," said Gisela, looking at the lake. "See! There are people on it already!" And she pointed to the Seespitz end of the Tiernsee, where two or three figures were to be seen circling about on the ice.

"Gorgeous!" cried Joey ecstatically. "I've never really skated in my life!"

"Have you not?" asked Wanda von Eschenau with wonder in her eyes. "But how strange!"

"Not at all," replied Jo. "We lived in the south of England, and there was never a long enough frost for the ice to reach the bearing stage—not that *I* can remember, anyway! Is it *frightfully* difficult to get your balance?"

The girls who were accustomed to skating every winter, and had been so from their earliest days, were rather nonplussed by this question, which they did not know how to answer.

"I do not think it is so very hard," said Bernhilda at length. "I do not remember."

"Here is Madame," said Gisela. "She comes to call you into the house, Joey!"

"Blow!" said Joey. "It's quite warm in the sun!"

However, when Madge called her, she went obediently.

"Sorry, Joey," said Miss Bettany, "but it's too soon after your last cold to take any risks!"

"It's hard luck, all the same!" sighed Jo. "Yes; I know it's my own fault, but it doesn't make it any nicer! Can I skate tomorrow if the ice holds?"

"We'll see what you're like after today," replied Madge cautiously.

Jo ran into the Chalet, and was met by Marie, bearing a large parcel. "For you, Fräulein Joey," she smiled.

"For me?" Joey stared. "Whatever is it?" She examined the label. "'*Gebrüder Hertzing, Drucker*'! Oh! *It's the magazines!*" She snatched the precious bundle from Marie. "How gorgeous! I didn't think they'd be here so soon! Marie, *bringen Sie Fräulein Bettany! Beeilen Sie sich!*"

Marie dashed out into the snow, to return presently with an anxious-looking Madge. "Joey! What is it? Don't you feel well?" she demanded.

"Goodness, yes! But look! The *Chaletian* has come! That's why I wanted you!"

Miss Bettany drew a long breath of relief. "Oh, what a fright I got! Marie simply said you wanted me at once! I quite thought you must be feeling ill again!"

"Well, I'm not! Come on! Let's go into the study and look at them! I'm dying to see it—the first magazine I've ever edited in my life!"

They went into the study, Jo hugging the big parcel affectionately to her, and presently the brown paper covering was off, and there, before them, lay the first number of the *Chaletian*. She picked up a copy and held it out to her sister. "There you are, Madame, the head-mistress! With the editor's compliments!"

"Jo, you *are* an idiot!" declared Madge. "Don't let the others see you like this!"

"Let's call them in to see it," suggested Jo.

"The people responsible for Pages, if you like! I don't want the whole school!"

Jo flew to the window and banged on it, till Gisela saw her frantic gestures and came to see if Madame had had a fit, or Marie had upset the dinner all over the floor. *"Was ist es?"* she demanded.

For answer Jo held up the *Chaletian*. The head girl's eyes widened. Then she vanished, and they could hear her calling, "Bernhilda! Grizel! Bette! *Kommen sie! Das Chaletian ist hier!"*

There was a wild rush as everyone surrounded her. The two people in the study couldn't hear what was going on, but the rapid gestures and shrill voices were sufficient signs of their excitement. It was fairly obvious that they all wanted to come, and that Gisela was having hard work to prevent them. Miss Bettany decided to take a hand herself. "Run and find Miss Maynard and tell her, Joey," she said. "Ask her to come to the study, and I'll fetch the others."

Joey dashed off in the direction of the little music-room, and the Head strolled out to the excited girls.

"Madame! When may we see the *Chaletian*, please?" asked Amy Stevens.

"You shall all see it this afternoon," said Miss Bettany. "In the meantime, I want the magazine committee to come to see it now in my study. Oh, and while I remember, will you all please try to remember the rule about speaking English? I heard a good deal that was *not* English as I came up."

She turned back to the Chalet, followed by the committee. Gisela left them, and ran on to join her headmistress. "Madame, I have spoken in German all the while! I am so sorry; please pardon me! "

"I heard you," said Miss Bettany dryly. "Of course, if the head girl doesn't remember, Gisela, I can scarcely expect the others to do so, can I?"

Gisela coloured. "I know! Indeed, Madame, I am very sorry! Shall I enter my name in the Order Book?"

Miss Bettany shook her head. "No; don't do that. It would be very bad for the juniors and the middles to see the head girl's name there. But do remember that your position makes carelessness a serious matter. Now go and get your things off and come along to my study."

Gisela went off to do as she was told, while the young head-mistress marched into the study, to find Miss Maynard already there.

"It looks very well, doesn't it?" said the mathematics mistress as she turned over a copy. "I think the girls are to be congratulated."

"So do I," smiled Miss Bettany.—"Come in! " as a tap sounded at the door.

In response, the members of the magazine committee solemnly filed into the room and sat down at her invitation. Then Joey doled out one copy each of the *Chaletian*, and there was silence while they all looked through it.

It was a very well-arranged little magazine, and, for a first number, quite good. Jo's Editorial, setting forth the aims and ideas of the *Chaletian*, was well written for a girl of thirteen, and very original. The School Notes, attended to by Gisela, were accurate, and their English would have shamed that of many English girls' efforts—

did shame Grizel's Sports Notes. That young lady, in her attempt to avoid slanginess, had gone to the other extreme, and become almost unbearably stilted. The two mistresses were hard put to it to keep straight faces over such statements as, "Tennis has been most enjoyable during the past season," "All have endeavoured to do well in cricket," and the like, from slangy Grizel. Bernhilda's narratives of how the Tiernsee became a lake, and the origin of the Wolfenkopf, a grim, dark mountain peak at the northern extremity of the lake, were interesting, but no one save Jo gave them more than a passing glance. Miss Durrant had contributed a delightful account of a summer school held by the English Folk Dance Society at Cambridge, and Mademoiselle had written a description of her own first term as a pupil in a big convent school in the south of France. But it was the Fiction Page which most interested the committee. At least ten girls had sent in contributions to this page, and four had been chosen by Joey for Miss Maynard to select from. As this had been done at the last minute, no one but she knew whose had been taken, so they were all agog to know. A groan of dismay went up as they discovered that the contributions had been printed unsigned, and only Jo and the authors themselves could know whose they were.

" 'The Wooden Bowl of Hans Sneeman'," read Gisela. "But who, then, wrote that? It is a story of Kobolds." She glanced up in time to catch the expression on Jo's face. That young lady was staring at Miss Maynard with startled eyes and wide-open mouth. "Jo! " exclaimed the head girl. "*You* have written it! "

"But it is charming! " cried Bernhilda, who had been eagerly reading it. "Joey, I make you my compliments! "

"But—but——" gasped Joey. "I never *gave* it to you, Miss Maynard. I didn't give *any*thing! "

"I know you didn't," replied Miss Maynard calmly. "I found it lying on the floor under your desk one day, and liked it so much, I decided to use it."

"Splendid! " Grizel put her word in. "It's simply gorgeous, Jo! I can't think how you did it! "

Jo remained dumbfounded. It was so unexpected that,

for once, she hadn't a word to say for herself, while the rest exclaimed delightedly over it.

It was a very simple little tale, following well-known lines. A poor forester met an old woman, who begged food and shelter from him. He had only a little log hut, and a wooden bowl he himself had made. In the bowl was a very little vegetable stew, which formed his one daily meal. Nevertheless, he gave it up to the stranger, who ate it, and then suddenly vanished. The next morning, as Hans Sneeman the forester was working, hungry and somewhat disheartened, a radiant angel appeared to him, who informed him that it was she whom he had helped the night before, and for his generosity and unselfishness the help he had given should always be his, and he should never be in want again so long as he lived. Then the angel vanished; but, from that time forth, everything went well with Hans Sneeman, who remained always humble-minded, generous, and unselfish; and to remind him of his days of poverty, and to keep himself from becoming proud, always ate his meals out of his old wooden bowl, which was buried with him when he died.

It was slender enough, but it was gracefully written, with a certain sense of humour to flavour it. All things considered, it was a remarkable thing for a schoolgirl to have produced. Madge Bettany read it with wonder. She had always known that her little sister was gifted in this way, but she had had no idea that the gift was so unusual. In the years to come Jo Bettany was to astonish those who knew her, again and again, with her writings; but her sister never forgot that icy winter's day at the Tiernsee when she first discovered that the family baby was going to write.

The other story, an account of the adventures of an old trunk, had been written by Bette Rincini, and was quite well done, though there was nothing to distinguish it from similar work by most clever schoolgirls. Bette had a marvellous command over the English language, and the little tale ran easily, and was told with a humour and freshness which made it very readable.

The Poetry Corner came next, and the *Chaletian* discovered the interesting fact that the Chalet School contained quite a number of would-be poets. Like the stories, all the verses were unsigned, but it was a comparatively easy matter to name the writers.

Rosalie Dene, an otherwise undistinguished member of the school, had sent in some pretty lines on "Roses"; Gisela had contributed a couple of stanzas on Spring; and Gertrud had given a very charming word picture of the lake. The surprise of this page lay in four lines entitled "A Rime".

Lilies in the garden; roses on the wall;
Apples in the orchard—there's plenty for us all.
Some prefer the apples, and some prefer the rose;
But I always think the lily is the fairest flower
    that grows.

"Who wrote that, Joey?" queried her sister. "It's rather pretty."

"Which is?" demanded Joey, rousing up from her rapture at first seeing herself in print with some difficulty.

"The little verse called 'A Rime'," replied Miss Bettany.

"That? Oh, Amy Stevens sent it in."

"*Amy!* Jo! Are you *sure*?"

"Of course I am! " Jo sounded distinctly injured.

Miss Bettany made haste to apologise for her seeming doubt. "I'm sorry, Joey; but—well—it's very good for such a little girl. She's only eight! "

"Yes; it *is* decent, isn't it?" observed the editor complacently as she turned to the Correspondence Page, and then, finally, the Head's letter. "I say. I don't want to buck, but don't you think it's a good mag. for our first, everyone?"

A chorus of assent answered her. They were all agreed; it *was* a good magazine for the first.

"And," said Miss Maynard later on when she and Miss Bettany were alone, "it looks to me as though *two* of the contributors to the first number of the *Chaletian* will be writers some day."

The head-mistress nodded. "Yes; at least I hope so. At any rate, we must see that they have every help and every encouragement."

Miss Maynard collected her possessions and turned to leave the room. "When we are old women," she observed as she opened the door, "I expect we shall be proud to say that we helped with the education of Amy Stevens the poetess, and Josephine Bettany, the well-known novelist! There are a good many consolations in our profession! "

Then she went out, and left the sister of the future "well-known novelist" to groan over a map of that young person's and wonder why Joey never seemed able to put in contour lines correctly.

CHAPTER TWELVE

The Hobbies Club

"Ow! You've upset my cards! You *are* mean, Grizel Cochrane! "

"Well, you shouldn't have them all over the place, then! " retorted Grizel as she hastily stooped and began sweeping the postcards together.

She was stopped by a wild shriek from Margia. "Leave them alone! You're muddling them up. *Oh!* and I'd just got them all sorted out! "

"Well, I'm sorry," said Grizel impatiently, "but I couldn't help it! "

"Why don't you pick them up in their sets?" suggested Joey Bettany, looking up for a minute from her collection of crests. "It would save trouble later. I'll help, shall I?"

She dropped on to all fours, and began gathering up views of Italy with great goodwill, while Margia, adopting her suggestion, collected Germany, and Grizel sorted out "pretty" ones.

It was Saturday afternoon. All day, a fierce wind had blown from the icy north, and it had been impossible for any of them to go out. In England it is difficult to realise just how furious the great winds *can* be that in the winter sweep across the central plains of Europe from the Arctic regions. Even in the Tyrol, with its mountain-ranges to protect it from the worst, the gales swirl down with devastating fury, and, of course, up in the mountains at the Tiernsee, three thousand feet and more above sea-level, there was no such protection.

Marie Pfeifen, who ruled in the kitchen at the Chalet, shook her head as she listened to the howling of the wind round the house, and prophesied a hard winter. Even—it was possible—the wolves might come! Certainly they would appear on the plains.

With the weather like this, the girls had to content themselves indoors as best they might. They had done country-dancing in the morning under Miss Durrant's instruction, going through all they had learned, and then joyfully making the acquaintance of two new ones—"Pop Goes the Weasel," a longways dance for as many as will, and going on to "If All the World were Paper," with its sung chorus and pretty figures in between the "arms to the centre," "siding," and "arming."

In the afternoon Miss Bettany, with an eye to the needs of her staff, had suggested that the girls should bring their hobbies into the big double school-room, and amuse themselves quietly, while the mistresses retired to their own rooms for a well-earned rest. Nearly everyone "collected" —in fact, there was quite a craze for it this term. Most of the younger girls went in for postcards or stamps. Jo's crests were unique, and so was her other craze— "Napoleoniana", to coin an expression to fit it. She begged postcards, cuttings and photographs of the famous man, also of his possessions, his battles, and his family.

Grizel collected photographs of notable sportsmen, and also owned forty-seven postcards of the Prince of Wales and other members of Britain's Royal Family. The elder girls went in for autographs, pressed leaves, and flowers; and Gisela collected feathers of various kinds of birds. Pretty Bette was quite a keen geologist, and was very proud of her "rocks". Wanda von Eschenau possessed a very good collection of copies of famous pictures; and Bernhilda Mensch had a large exercise-book into which she copied all her favourite quotations and extracts, a hobby in which her younger sister, Frieda, shared. Marie von Eschenau collected tiny models of animals, and at the present moment her corner of the huge trestle-table, at which most of them were sitting, looked rather like a zoo and a farmyard combined. The Robin, who adored these playthings, was curled up beside her, helping to arrange them.

It was left to Simone, in many ways the most colourless and unoriginal of them all, to have the funniest collection. *Her* craze was for paper dolls. She had over one hundred of these: some, the variety bought in boxes with their various garments all ready to slip on; others, figures cut out of magazines and books, and pasted on to cardboard. Many of these were celebrities, and Simone's favourite game was to pretend that one was holding a reception, to which the others came.

These, with Marie's animals, were decidedly the most popular of all the collections with the juniors, who would listen for hours to Simone's plays if she would only let them.

Grizel suddenly made a suggestion which thrilled them all. "I say," she remarked, "why don't we have a Hobbies Club?"

A Hobbies Club!

There was an instant hubbub, for everyone wanted to give her views on this magnificent idea, and nobody was at all disposed to listen to anyone else.

"What a tophole scheme! " cried Joey, her good resolutions with regard to slang completely forgotten.

"Grizel! But how charming! " remarked Bernhilda.

"Splendid!" "Wunderschön!" "Epatant!" "Magnifico!" The various exclamations rose in a perfect babel of languages.

Grizel stood trying to look modest, and failing utterly. It really was a good idea, and she knew it.

They made so much noise that Miss Bettany came across to them from the study to inquire what it was all about. She was almost overwhelmed by their explanations, but at length she managed to gather something of what they were saying.

"Start a Hobbies Club?" she repeated, as she accepted the chair Gisela was offering her. "Well, I don't know. Whose idea is it?"

"Grizel's!" replied Joey.

"How do you propose to run it, then?" queried Miss Bettany. "What are your aims?"

Grizel looked rather floored over this. Finally, "I—I don't know," she said.

Joey's black eyes flashed. "*I* do, though. You want us to have jolly times together with our c'llections, don't you? An' do proper swopping an' see who can get the best, an' have shows——"

"Yes! And do all kinds of work too!" Grizel knew what she wanted *now*. "Gisela and Bernhilda are awfully keen on embroidery, and some of the others make lace, and some of us wood-carve. *I've* always wanted to do leather-work," she added reflectively.

The Head nodded. "I see! Well, it's a very good idea, and I see no reason why you should not carry it out. You may have definite meetings from four till five one afternoon in the week, and, in bad weather, on Saturday afternoons if you like. I propose that you all choose some handcraft, and work during the winter months——"

"Oh! And have a show at the end of next term!" cried Joey eagerly.

"Oh yes, Madame! We shall all like that!" said Gisela enthusiastically.

Miss Bettany glanced at them. There was no mistaking their feelings. One and all, they were longing to begin. "Very well," she said briskly. "You may do it. We can't do much this term, of course! Exams begin next week, and then we shall break up. But next term you shall begin in real earnest, every one of you, and I hope we shall have a good show!"

"But what can *we* do?" demanded little Amy Stevens.

"You can make scrap-books," replied Miss Bettany without an instant's hesitation. "We'll get raffia as well, and you can learn to make mats and baskets and napkin-rings—oh, there are plenty of things you can do!"

The juniors, who had been hanging on her words, heaved

sighs of satisfaction, and forthwith departed to the other end of the room to discuss their views on the subject. The head-mistress strolled out, and the seniors and the middles gathered together to decide what crafts they should take up.

"Leather-work for me!" declared Grizel. "I'll make bags, and book-marks, and moccasins!"

"I'm going in for fretwork," decided Joey. "I'll cut jigsaw puzzles. It looks easy, and they make jolly presents. What's anyone else going to do?"

There was a variety of ideas. Two or three of the elder girls meant to stick to embroidery; Gertrud Steinbrucke and Vanna di Ricci could both make pillow-lace, and had their pillows with them; some were interested in wood-carving, and others in sketching. Wanda von Eschenau proved to be the most original here, for she decided to take up painting on china.

"I wish there was something one could do with *music*," said Margia Stevens discontentedly, "but there isn't. I shall have to stick to knitting."

"Couldn't you write a song?" suggested Joey, "or, if you like, I've got a *real* musical idea for you."

"Well, what is it?" Margia's curiosity was aroused.

"Why," said Jo, "you just collect pictures of great musicians, and then stick the picture on one page and put down all you can about the man on the other. Like: 'Beethoven. A great German composer. Born at Bonn seventeen and something or other. Went deaf quite young,' and a list of his chief works, and where he died, and so on."

Margia was gazing before her with the eyes of one who sees visions. "Joey! What a *splendacious* idea! It's simply gorgeous! You *are* a brain!"

"I thought you'd like it," replied the originator of the idea as off-handedly as she could.

"Oh, I *do*! I'll make a topping book of it!" Margia's voice died away as she sat visualising her book. She would have brown pastel paper for the picture sides, and the nicest writing-paper she could get for the notes. Miss Bettany would get them for her the next time she was in Innsbruck, she knew. She would make holes through the sheets with a large knitting-needle, and tie them together with brown ribbon. They should have a cover of brown——

"Hi! Margia Stevens! Wake up and take your coffee!" said Grizel's voice in her ear at that moment, and Margia came back to earth with a start, to find that *Kaffee und Kuchen* had been brought in, and Grizel was standing before her and offering her a large cup of coffee, while Bernhilda was just behind with the cakes. They always had it picnic fashion on Saturdays, and no one ever interfered with them. Miss Bettany liked her girls to feel that there was at least one meal in the week which was absolutely theirs. Mademoiselle La Pâttre rather distrusted the idea, but the young head-mistress held to it firmly, and so far there had been nothing to prove it an impossible idea. The girls always behaved nicely, and the prefects kept an eye on the juniors.

Naturally, everyone was full of the new club this afternoon. Gisela had some idea of combining a concert with the "show" at the end of next term, and inviting parents to come. "We could perform some of our new dances," she said. "I have heard Miss Durrant talk of several very pretty ones we might learn when we come back next term, and our parents would enjoy watching, for the English country-dances are so different from those of our own people."

"Our new English songs too," added Bernhilda. "I do like the last one Herr Denny taught us! I like the song so much," said Bernhilda. "It is a folk-song, is it not?"

"Rather! Just as my 'Appalachian Nursery Rhymes' are," replied Jo.

"Why not give a 'folk' entertainment?" suggested Juliet. "Vanna and Luigia and Bianca could dance the Tarantella for us; and some of you Tyrolese could give us one of your Schuhplättler; and the French girls could sing 'Monsieur de Cramoisie', and 'L'Arbre d'Amour'; and the babies could do nursery rhymes of all kinds; and we could *all* show the country-dances."

"We seem to be literally *spurting* with ideas this afternoon!" laughed Jo. "That's a jolly one, Juliet.—Hullo, Robin! What's the trouble?"

The Robin danced forward, curls dancing, cheeks

crimson with excitement. "Me, I will sing 'Ze Red Sarafan' in ze Russian!" she cried, and promptly lifted up a sweet baby voice in the well-known Russian folk-song.

They all clapped her, laughing at the pretty picture she made. She nodded her head at them joyously. Then suddenly the little voice quivered and broke, and she buried her face in her dimpled hands in a perfect storm of tears. *"Maman! Maman!"* she sobbed. *"Oh, je veux toujours Maman!"*

They were round her in an instant, petting her and trying to soothe her; but all their efforts were vain, and she sobbed on. Nearly in tears herself—for there was something so desolate in the baby's little wail—Joey dashed out of the room and into the study, where Miss Bettany was entertaining her staff. At Joey's unceremonious entry they all looked up amazed.

"Jo!" exclaimed her sister severely. "What does this mean?"

"I'm sorry!" gasped Joey incoherently. "It's the Robin —crying! She was singing—'The Red Scavenger', or something like that; and then she wanted her mother! *Do* come!"

Miss Bettany was on her feet in a moment, and across the passage to where the poor mite was still sobbing out her pathetic little appeal, *"Maman! Maman! Viens, je te prie! Maman!"*

Tender arms were round about her; soft dark curls, so like the lost mother's, were against her cheek; then Miss Bettany bore her off to be cuddled back to serenity, while the girls finished their *Kaffee* rather more soberly.

"She is so happy always," said Gisela, "that one forgets how short a time it is since the little mother left her."

"I suppose *she* used to sing that song," added Juliet. "Poor baby!"

Presently they turned back to the subject of the Hobbies Club again, and when a cheered-up and once more placid Robin joined them later on, they were very busy discussing hobbies and collections, and no more was said that night about the concert.

CHAPTER THIRTEEN

The Nativity Play

THE REMAINDER of the term simply flew. Exam week followed the inauguration of the Hobbies Club, and various people wished on different days that they had worked a little harder during the term.

Jo Bettany groaned over every one of the maths papers. "That was a—a—*disgusting* fraction!" she proclaimed to all and sundry after the arithmetic paper.

Margia, who was standing near, opened her eyes widely. "Why Joey, it was easy! It came out to 2/13ths!"

"*What!*" gasped Jo. "I say! I got 67685/107676!"

"Joey! You *couldn't*! What on earth have you done?"

"Goodness knows!" Jo resigned herself to her fate. "I never *could* do maths, and I never shall!"

But if the paper was, as Miss Maynard characterised it, "disgraceful!" her English, French, and German were all excellent, and so were her history and literature, in all of which Margia was only average. Frieda Mensch came out strongly in geography; and of the seniors, Bernhilda headed the mathematics lists, with Grizel a good second, while Gisela and Juliet divided the languages honours between them, and Wanda von Eschenau proved to be an easy first in drawing.

The last afternoon was given up to a concert, which was attended by the people in the valleys round about, Herr Anserl and one or two of his friends from Spärtz, and a few parents, who managed to get up the snowy paths to the Tiern valley. Needless to state, everyone was wild with excitement at the prospect. *Mittagessen* took place at twelve, and by half-past one all the girls were attired in white frocks. They had spent the morning in decorating the big school-room with branches of evergreen. A couple of screens cut off the upper end of the room, and the other part was filled with chairs and forms for the visitors, who began to arrive shortly after two. By half-past the room was full, and then Miss Bettany came forward and announced the first item, a madrigal, "How Fair the Sun". The screens were drawn aside, showing the rows of white-frocked girls, with Mr. Denny in front of them to conduct.

"Plato" might be a freak, as Joey declared, but he certainly knew how to teach singing, and the harmony of fresh voices that filled the room was something to be proud of. Like all Austrians, the Tiernsee people are musical, and they listened in a breathless silence, which told how they enjoyed it.

It was followed by the girls' own favourite, "My Bonny Lass, She Smileth"; and then they sang one of Martini's canons.

Herr Anserl sat looking unusually pleased. "*Herrgott!*" he observed to Miss Bettany, "but he has made something of them, this young man! "

The Head nodded. "They sing well, *nicht wahr*?"

"Excellently well! I must greet him, Herr Denny! "

The singing was followed by a piano solo by Margia, who was some day to surprise the world with her music; and Gisela gave a charming rendering of Martini's *Preghiera* for the violin. Grizel and Frieda played a pianoforte duet, Mendelssohn's "Fingal's Cave", with strict attention to time, and very little to anything else, and then they all sang again—one of the folk-songs this time, "Come, all you valiant Christian men".

After this there was an interval, during which Amy Stevens, Simone Lecoutier, and Maria Marani distributed papers among the audience, on which were written the words of the German carol, *Stille Nacht, Heilige Nacht*, and also the Latin hymn, *Adeste Fideles*. Then Miss Bettany came forward once more and explained: "We are going to give you a little Nativity play," she said. "It is in English, and is called *The Youngest Shepherd*. As you all know, it was to the 'shepherds abiding in the field, keeping watch over their flocks by night' that the angel of the Nativity told the good news of Christ's birth. Our little play is based on that story, and we should like you, when we come to them, to join us in the Christmas songs written on the sheets given you."

Then she vanished, and the screens were drawn, to show an ordinary room with modern children in it. It was Christmas Eve, and the children were talking—quarrelling —till a carol outside made them stop: such a lovely carol —"Good Christian men, rejoice", sung as only Mr. Denny's pupils could sing.

The four children hushed their wrangling then, and spoke instead of the next day, and what it brought to the world. Then the curtains parted, and the Youngest Shepherd stood before them. He told them of the Angel Song, and explained that, as he was the youngest of all the shepherds, he had had to stay behind to look after the sheep, but God had sent an angel down to guard them, so that he, too, might go and worship at the Manger; and he invited the children to go with him. They all sprang to their feet, ready to go. Then they remembered that all who had gone to worship the Baby King had taken Him gifts; so they caught up their own favourite possessions to give. The young shepherd drew aside the curtains, saying, "See! Listen!"

A throng of angels were there, and they were singing the English carol, "In the Fields with their Flocks Abiding".

The children stood listening, till the lights dimmed, and the song died away into the pealing of Christmas-bells, and the screens were swiftly drawn across the stage. The next scene was out of doors. The children came in wearily with the Youngest Shepherd. It was a long way, and they were so tired! A poor Man came by them, and asked where they were going. They told him, and asked him to come with them, but he said kings never gave audience to the poor and needy such as he. For reply, they told him that this was the King of the poor and needy. He laughed at them, and then the Youngest Shepherd, as a final answer, sang the old "Cherry Tree" carol. They had all known that Joey could sing, but no one had quite realised the beauty of her voice before. It was not a very strong voice, but each note was round and pure, with the bell-like quality to be found in some boy-choristers' voices. She was utterly unself-conscious, and had, in fact, forgotten everything but the fact that she must get this Man to realise that the King wanted him too.

There was a low murmur as the last clear note died away, but the audience were too deeply interested in the story to applaud.

Then the Man agreed to come; but, just as they were about to move on, a great Lady, clad in whispering silks with many jewels about her, met them, and asked their destination. They told her they were going to see the King, and she sneered at their mahner of going. Kings, she told them, could only be visited in great pomp. They begged her to come and see, and at first she refused. Then the smallest child held out her hand and said "Do come Oh, do come!" and she gave way and came, and so they passed on.

There was a little silence at that; then suddenly the lovely chorus rang out, "There came three Kings", and the Magi appeared, bearing their gifts of gold, frankincense, and myrrh. Caspar, Melchior, and Balthazar paused in their following of the Star to rest and discuss the meaning of their gifts. Then they too went forward, and the screens were drawn once more.

During the three minutes' interval there came another carol, "When the Crimson Sun had Set", with its wonderful chorus of *Gloria in excelsis Deo*. When it was finished, the stage was revealed once more—the door of the Stable. An archangel stood there, the white lily of peace in his hand. Music stole out into the room, and as one the audience rose, and the old German carol, *Stille Nacht, Heilige Nacht*, was sung with full throats. When it was over, and they were all sitting once more, the Angel-chorus sang again, the "Bird" carol this time. Then silence fell, and the shepherds appeared.

How weary they were—and how eager! At the door they paused. Would the King be pleased to see them? Yes; surely He would. He had sent the angel to tell them. So they passed in, and the chorus sang "The First Nowell".

Next came the Wise Men, and they paused in wonderment before the humble place. *This* was no King's abode But the Star had stopped, so it must be right, and they, too, passed in.

Finally came the Youngest Shepherd and his little group. To the singing of the children's carol, "Come to the Manger in Bethlehem", the children pressed forward into the Stable. The Man and the Lady followed more slowly. Last came the Youngest Shepherd. He had no gift but himself to offer. He was scarcely even a shepherd; just a servant to help the others. But at last he, too, went slowly in, and the screens were drawn back once more across the stage.

The well-known tune of the *Adeste Fideles* sounded, and everyone sang it, so that it rang out as even *Stille Nacht, Heilige Nacht* had not done. Then the screens were taken away for the last time, and the interior of the Stable was shown. They had done the whole thing very simply. As Miss Bettany had said, it would have been in bad taste to have elaborate scenery. An old wooden trough filled with hay stood at the back. Before it was seated the Madonna, Wanda von Eschenau, holding in her arm a bundle to represent the Holy Child. Behind her stood Luigia di Ferrara as Joseph, and at either side stood an archangel with bowed head. Child angels clustered round them, and kneeling at the Madonna's feet, her baby face full of awe and reverence, was a tiny cherub, the Robin. To the right and at the back stood the welcoming Archangel with his lilies.

There was a little silence. Then, once more, music swelled out, and once more Joey's silvery notes stole forth, though Joey herself was behind the scenes. The carol chosen for this was the Breton carol, "Sleep, Holy Babe". The poignant sweetness of the young voice struck home, even to those who could not understand what she was singing, and somehow the scene brought lumps into the throats of the audience.

Then, one by one, the worshippers stole in. The shepherds came first, offering their crooks; then the Wise Men with their symbolical gifts; then the children eagerly laying their treasured possessions before the Holy Child

96

and His Mother. The poor Man had only his old blunt knife, but it was offered and accepted; the Lady tore off all her jewels and piled them at the Madonna's feet. Then the Youngest Shepherd came. He had nothing but himself to give. Humbly he knelt and a sudden strain of music swelled out as the Madonna rose, queenly, to her feet, and held out to him a silver crook. His was the richest gift of all, for he had brought other worshippers.

Then came the final carol, "Brightest and Best of the Sons of the Morning". As it ended, the screens were brought forward, and the lights in the room were turned up. Miss Bettany stood forward. "Thank you," she said in her sweet voice, "for your appreciation of our little play. We wish you all a very happy Christmas!"

A storm of good wishes promptly broke on all sides. Tyroleans are quick to answer emotion, and all were specially sensitive at the moment. The girls' performance, simple as it was, appealed to a people accustomed to giving and witnessing Mystery plays; and for many a day *The Youngest Shepherd* gave the lake people a topic for conversation.

As for the girls, it took them some time to come down to the earth. When they did, there was much chatter about Christmas plans. They were all going home early the next morning. Miss Bettany, Joey, and the Robin would be the only ones left, and they would be leaving the Chalet in the afternoon. The school was to be closed, and Marie and Eigen with Zita and Rufus were going home for Christmas. Jo had begged hard to take Rufus to Innsbruck with her, Bernhilda having assured her that he would be welcomed; but Madge was firm, and would not hear of it. Jo, therefore, had to content herself by giving the faithful Eigen reams of advice about him. "All the same, I know he'll miss me, the darling!" she mourned to Grizel.

"Rubbish!" retorted Grizel. "He'll be all right. Oh, Joey," she went on, "I do wish you were coming with me tomorrow! I hate the idea of being with only Mr. Stevens all the time!"

Mr. Stevens, father of Margia and Amy, was going to London to see the editor of the great daily paper to which he was foreign correspondent, and had offered to take Grizel so far. Her own father would meet her there, and take her to Cornwall.

"Mr. Stevens is awfully nice," said Jo, in answer to her friend's last remark. "And, anyway, you're going to have *weeks* more than the rest of us, so I don't see why you're grumbling! "

"I'm not *grumbling*! But—well—I'd like you and Miss Bettany too," replied Grizel. "I *did* want to be with you for Christmas! "

Jo looked at her curiously. "You'll have Easter with us! "

"I know! But Christmas is such a homey time! 'Tisn't much of a home at *home*! "

Joey was silenced. She knew that Grizel's stepmother had made home anything but happy for her, just as she knew that Grizel loved her life at school. Finally, "We'll miss you! " she jerked out. "Buck up, old thing! "

And with that Grizel had to be satisfied.

CHAPTER FOURTEEN

The Christmas Holidays Begin

"ISN'T IT QUIET?" said Joey suddenly.

It was one o'clock on the following afternoon, and she and her sister and the Robin were finishing a very picnicky meal before finally closing the Chalet and making the journey on foot to Spärtz, where the midday train from Salzburg would carry them off to Innsbruck and the Mensches' flat in the Mariahilfer Strasse at the other side of the Inn. Everyone had been up early, and the last of the girls had gone shortly after ten o'clock. Since then Miss Bettany and the two children had been busy packing their clothes in the light wicker baskets which Eigen and Marie would help to carry down the snow-covered foot-path to the station at Spärtz. It would be easy walking, for the snow was frozen till it was like a rock, and the big nail-studded climbing-boots they all wore would give them a grip on the slippery surface.

"*Don't* you think it's deathly quiet now everyone else has gone?" said Joey.

"Yes; very quiet," agreed her sister. "If you two have finished, we may as well clear these things away so that Marie can clear up. We've a very fair walk before us, and it is dark by four, so I want to get off as quickly as possible. Hurry, children!"

They hurried. One usually did when Miss Bettany spoke in that tone. Marie was busily washing up the few crocks she and Eigen had used, and Joey sped to the *Speisesaal* to fold up and put away the blue-and-white checked table-cloth, and help the Robin to push the chairs into their places. Eigen came in while they were busy, and carefully raked out the remnants of fire left in the big porcelain stove. Like most of the houses along the Tiernsee, the Chalet was built of wood, so the precaution was a necessary one.

Just as he finished, Madge called them to get ready for their walk and the short railway journey, and saw to their wrapping-up herself.

"It's freezing hard outside, and we have a long walk," Madge said. "Run downstairs now, you two, and I'll come in a few minutes."

They clattered off, and ten minutes later Miss Bettany was locking the door, while Marie and Eigen were already trudging ahead, each carrying two of the baskets, while a much smaller one remained for Joey.

"At last!" exclaimed that young lady as her sister dropped the keys into her pocket. "Now we're really off. Oh, Madge, won't it be jolly to see the shops all decorated for Christmas? We've got nearly all our presents to get, you know. Won't it be fun?"

"Splendid," replied Madge. "But you don't want to live in the town always, do you, Joey?"

"Oh *no*! I love the Tiernsee and the mountains. But it's jolly to have a change!"

"What do you think, Robin?"

The Robin lifted a rosy face to the delicate one bent down to hers. "It will be *zolly!* " she said emphatically.

Madge laughed. "So it will! I expect we shall have a splendid Christmas."

"Will the Christ Child put bonbons in our shoes?" asked the Robin eagerly.

"Yes, if He thinks you have been good."

"And then there'll be the Christmas-tree," added Joey. "Frieda says they're going to have an extra nice one 'cos we're going to be there. Her brother's coming too, from Bonn."

"We shall go to the church," the Robin chimed in, "and see the Manger and the little Lord Jesus and His Mother."

"There's tobogganing too, and skating," went on Joey, waving gaily to the hostess of the *Gasthaus* at Seespitz, which they were passing. "Come on, Robin; *this* way now!" And she led off to the right through tall black pines to the narrow winding pathway that ran along the banks of what was usually a very turbulent little stream. Now, Winter held it in his iron grasp, and there was silence where before there had been the music of tossing water. Icicles hung on the boulders in its bed, and fringed the alder boughs that overhung it, and a black pathway of ice was all that showed its usual course.

"Isn't it still?" said Joey in half-awed tones. "Even the sawmill has stopped."

"Of course," said Madge. "It can't go on when the stream is frozen."

"I forgot that! " Joey gave a giggle. "What an ass I am!"

Down, down, they went. The voices of Marie and Eigen floated up to them clearly on the frosty air, and occasionally there was a sharp "crack," as a rotten bough snapped in the woods under its weight of snow. But, except for these sounds, there was silence—a silence that could be felt. Even excitable Joey stopped talking before long, and they went on without speaking.

When they had gone a third of the way, Miss Bettany stopped and picked up the Robin, who was beginning to lag behind.

"Why not take her on your back?" suggested Joey. "I

can give her a boost up, and then you'll be able to see your way better."

"That's a good idea," agreed Madge. "Climb up on that log, Robinette, and Joey will help you up. That's it! Put your arms round my neck, but don't strangle me if you can help it! Comfy?—Come along, then, Joey!"

They set off once more, and this time got on faster. The Robin was a light weight, and Madge, though slightly built, was strong. Joey stepped out manfully, and they made good time down the mountain-side.

Miss Bettany was beginning to feel anxious about Marie and Eigen. They meant to return that night, she knew, and it was growing dusk already under the pines. "Joey," she said presently, "if I send Marie and Eigen back as soon as we reach Spärtz, do you think you and I can manage the Japanese baskets between us? The Robin could carry your little one, I should think."

"Oh, rather!" said Joey enthusiastically. "It isn't far to the station."

"I don't like the idea of those two having to go back up there in the dark. It's clouding in, too, and I'm afraid we shall have more snow. I'll carry the Robin to the bottom, and then she'll be quite fresh. We can take the baskets, and I'll send those two straight back up the path."

"Good scheme!" agreed Joey. "But, I say, Madge, if you get tired, Robin can carry the basket now, and we can give her a queen's-chair."

"Perhaps that would be better," said Madge thoughtfully. "She's very light, but the baskets won't be. We'll stop now, and do as you suggest, Joey baba!"

"But I can walk," declared the Robin as she wriggled down to the ground.

"No, dearie, you will be so tired," replied Madge tenderly. "See, I'm going to tie the little basket to your belt. Then you can sit on our hands, and it will rest on your knees, so that you can hold on to us safely."

The Robin was always obedient. She sat down on their linked hands, settled the basket on her knees, and then put an arm round each neck. "Now I am ready," she said cheerfully.

They hurried on, and another twenty minutes saw them within sight of Spärtz, where already the lights twinkled out merrily.

Marie and Eigen were waiting for them. "Marie," said Miss Bettany, as she and Jo set their burden down, "I am afraid it is going to snow before long, so I want you and Eigen to give us the baskets and go straight back to Briesau at once. We can easily manage as far as the station."

Marie would have argued the matter, but her young mistress gave her no chance. She took the two largest baskets herself, and said firmly, "Jo, take the other baskets. —*Auf wiedersehn, Marie, und fröhliche Weihnachtsfest!*"

Marie curtsied, while Eigen saluted, and both wished the trio *"Fröhliche Weihnachtsfest!"* before they turned and set off on their long walk home.

"Oh, Madge, there's Herr Anserl!"

Herr Anserl, a shaggy-looking monster in his old fur coat, came hurrying across the road.

"Guten Tag, Fräulein," he said to Madge, relieving her of her load. "But where, then, do you go?"

"We are going to Innsbruck for the Christmas holidays," explained Madge in his own language.

" *'Zist gut!"* he said. "I will myself bring you to the *Bahnhof.* Give me one of those basket cases, Fräulein Joey. Yes; I can take it. I will 'see you off,' as you say in England."

Madge was really very thankful for his escort. She was beginning to feel tired, and the baskets *were* heavy after their long trudge through the snow. She took the other one from Joey, who was beginning to look all eyes, an invariable sign of weariness with her, and they all meekly followed in the wake of Herr Anserl, who strode along, shouting greetings, so it seemed, to most of the people they met.

At length they reached the station, and, while Madge went to get the tickets, the somewhat eccentric music-master took the two little girls into the *Restauration* and ordered hot milky coffee for them, with new rolls—"And be sure they are *new!* " he added to the indignant attendant, who tossed her head, but nevertheless produced the coffee and delicious crusty rolls to break into it. When Madge appeared, he insisted that she should have the same.

"There is sufficient time before the train comes," he said. "Yes; eat, *gnädiges, Fräulein!* Here is sugar."

By the time they had finished their meal, the signals were down, and two minutes later the train swept into the station, and Herr Anserl was bundling them into a compartment and wishing them a merry Christmas, beaming widely all the time.

"Isn't he *decent!*" said Joey amazedly, as they steamed out of the station, for Herr Anserl was considerably more feared than loved at the Chalet School. "I'm going to send him a Christmas card."

Madge settled Robin comfortably in her arms, and before they had reached the old town of Schwaz she was far away in dreamland.

Joey turned her attention to the flying landscape. The train had one more stop before they reached Innsbruck—at Hall. Then, presently, came lights, and five minutes later they were on the platform of Innsbruck station, with Frau Mensch taking a very sleepy Robin from Madge's arms, and Frieda and Bernhilda kissing an ungrateful Jo on both cheeks, and welcoming them all very warmly.

"This, then, is all the luggage?" queried Frau Mensch. "We have a *Droschke* ready, and Gottfried will carry the packages. Fräulein, permit me to present my son to you."

She waved forward a tall fair young man, who bowed with his heels well together but said nothing. As he took the baskets, Joey reflected that he seemed to be as shy as his two pretty sisters, who evidently thought him one of the most wonderful beings in the world. Frieda walked beside him, looking up at him almost reverentially. Joey wondered what Dick would have said if she had ever looked at *him* like that. Bernhilda came round to her side, slipping an arm through hers. "It is so nice to have you with us, Joey!" she said. "We have looked forward to it for a long time. Gisela and Maria wished to come with us to meet you, but they live very far away, and there was no one to come with them, so Frau Marani refused permission."

By this time they had reached the *Droschke*. Joey sat silent as they were whirled down the brightly-lighted Landhaus Strasse, into the wide Maria Theresien Strasse, with its big modern shops, all lit up, and its wide pavements, full of merry, jostling crowds, through the much narrower Friedrich Herzog Strasse, where the shops are built under the Arcades, across the fine bridge, and so to the quieter suburb on the left bank of the Inn. They turned to the left from the bridge, and presently drew up before one of the tall narrow houses overlooking the river.

Gottfried jumped down, and helped out his mother and the girls, before he hurried to open the door, to disclose a narrow winding staircase of wood.

"We are on the third floor," said Frau Mensch. "It seems a long way when one is tired, but the air up there is always fresh, and it is a comfortable flat with plenty of room. Come, Fräulein Bettany. I am sure you are weary, and will be glad to rest; and this *Vöglein* should be in bed.—Are you waking up, *mein Liebling*?" for the Robin had opened wide brown eyes to gaze into the kind face above her.

They went upstairs, leaving Gottfried to wrestle with the cabman and the baskets. Frau Mensch stopped before a door on the third floor and unlocked it. "Enter," she said, "and be very welcome!"

She had set the Robin down to find her key, and now she stretched out her hand and drew Madge inside, kissing her heartily before she did the same to Joey.

"These little birds are very weary," she said in her soft voice, which made the guttural German sound musical. "We will have supper, and then they shall go to bed. You will like to see your room, *nicht wahr*?"

It was a typical Tyrolean room in which they stood, with walls and floor of polished pine-wood. There were a couple of mats on the floor, and in one corner was a huge wooden bed, with its big puffy *plumeau*, and pillows in pillow-cases edged with exquisite hand-made lace. Two tiny wooden washstands stood side by side, with the usual baby bowls and pitchers on them; but over the towel-horse hung towels of the finest hand-woven linen. A tall wardrobe, a chest of drawers with a mirror over them, and three chairs made up most of the furniture. At the foot of the bed stood the little cot, and over its head hung a beautiful copy of Guido's "Blue Madonna". The room was warm, but not stuffy, and the white sheets and pillow-cases made Joey long for bed at once.

A tap at the door ushered in a rosy, smiling girl, wearing a full white blouse, short blue skirt, and wonderfully embroidered apron. She was carrying a huge jug of hot water, which she set down by the washstands, beaming all the time.

"Gertlieb is a good girl," said Frau Mensch when Gertlieb had gone. "Now we will leave you to perform the toilet as soon as Gertlieb has carried in your baskets, and Frieda will come to bring you to our *Speisesaal* in ten minutes' time."

At this moment the smiling Gertlieb reappeared with two of their hampers, and a few minutes later she brought the others. Then she withdrew, followed by her mistress, and Madge set herself to "perform the toilets" of her two charges, who ungratefully clamoured for bed.

"I don't want any supper," said Joey, with a wistful look at the big downy pillows. "Oh, Madge, *can't* I just go straight to bed?"

But this, Madge would not allow. She insisted on Joey's changing; made her wash herself thoroughly, and then brushed the short black hair vigorously before she turned her attention to her own toilet, leaving Jo to see to the Robin.

Frieda came presently, looking very fresh and pretty in her dark-blue frock and white pinafore. Her hair hung loosely to her waist, and excitement had deepened the roses in her cheeks. She led them into the *Spiesesaal*, a low, wide room, with flowering plants in one window and a canary's cage, at present covered with a dark cloth, in the other. The long table had the usual blue-and-white checked cloth, and the china was white with a cheerful blue-and-yellow pattern on it. A big book-case, full of books, stood behind the door, and there were chairs set round the table.

As the girls came in, Gertlieb was just placing a big dish of delicious soup before her mistress, who sat at the head of the table. A flat dish piled with crisp little brown sausages stood before Gottfried, and Bernhilda was dispensing rolls.

"Come," said Frau Mensch cheerfully. "Sit down, everyone.—Frieda, *mein Kindchen*, ask *der liebe Gott* for a blessing on our food."

Frieda murmured the pretty Tyrolean grace, and the plates of soup were passed to Gottfried, who ladled a sausage into each before he sent it on to its destination. It was very good; and so were the great *Vanerkuchen* with jam, which formed the next course; but Joey and Robin were almost too tired to eat.

Frau Mensch smiled as she saw the baby's head nodding lower and lower.

"She is too sleepy for supper," she said. "Fräulein, if you will permit, Bernhilda shall take her away and put her to bed."

Bernhilda rose at once, and led the sleepy Robin off to bed, whither both Jo and Frieda were dismissed twenty minutes later.

"It is early yet," said Frau Mensch apologetically to Madge, "but I am old-fashioned, and I like early hours for young people. Also, little Jo is very weary, and should soon be asleep."

"She does not look too strong, Fräulein," said Gottfried gravely.

"She is not strong," replied Madge quietly. "She is much better, however, and Doctor Erckhardt thinks she will outgrow her delicacy."

"Oh, undoubtedly," replied her hostess, as she led the way into the *salon*, another long room, and rather narrow, but bright and cheerful with its pretty mats and blue-covered furniture.

There was the inevitable sofa with its little table before it, but there were no books arranged at mathematical angles, as Madge had expected. Instead, there was a bowl of Roman hyacinths. More flowering plants were in a long wicker stand near one of the windows; a grand piano was at the other end of the room; and in an alcove stood a harp. A beautifully-carved *Brautkasten*, or bridal-chest, was placed near, and on it was Bernhilda's violin. The Tyrolese are an artistic people, and the few pictures on the walls were reproductions of famous paintings, while the ornaments were mainly carved wooden ones, with a few dainty Dresden figures.

"My mother-in-law, who lives with us, thinks our *salon* very modern," said Frau Mensch as she waved Madge to a comfortable chair. "She is very old, you see, and she does not like modern ways. She lives in her own room most of the time, but on festival days she joins us, and then she amuses herself by criticising everything that is not exactly as it was when she was a bride. Well, she is nearly ninety-five now; my husband is her youngest son—and she has not much pleasure in life; so, if she enjoys it, why should we mind? She cannot be with us much longer. Now, *mein Liebling*, it is easy to see that you are tired, so, Bernhilda shall play for us a little, and then you shall go to bed.— Gottfried, will you and Bernhilda make music for us?"

Gottfried and Bernhilda promptly played several things together, he accompanying her violin. Then, at his mother's request, he sang two or three of Schubert's beautiful *Lieder* in a sweet, sympathetic baritone; and at nine o'clock Frau Mensch sent her guest off to bed.

"It is of no use to wait for my husband," she said. "He is always late at Christmas-time. There is much to see to tomorrow, so I will go to see that *Grossmütter* has all she needs, and then Bernhilda and I too will go to our beds."

She walked with Madge to the bedroom door, and then paused. "My child," she said gently, "while you stay with us, may we not treat you as one of ourselves, we older people, and use your pretty Christian name?"

"Oh, please do," replied Madge. "I should like it."

"Thank you! That will be more comfortable I think. Now, *mein Liebling*, good-night, and the angels guard you!"

"How kind!" thought Madge as she undressed as quietly as possible for fear of waking the two children who were sleeping soundly.

When she was ready for bed, she pushed Joey over to her own side, and then slipped in beside her with a sigh of pure pleasure for the relief of stretching her tired body.

"We shall have a splendid Christmas," she thought drowsily.

Three minutes later, Frau Mensch, peeping in, found all her visitors slumbering so profoundly that they never even stirred as she closed the door behind her.

CHAPTER FIFTEEN

A Jolly Day

JOEY WAS THE FIRST to wake up next morning. They all three slept through Gertlieb's brisk sweeping and polishing of the passage-floor, the sounds of Herr Mensch's rising, the tap-tap of the girls' feet as they hurried about helping their mother. But about eight o'clock Jo suddenly opened her eyes wide, and then sat up, fully awake in a moment. She glanced at the cot standing across the foot of the bed, but the Robin never stirred. Then she looked down at her sister, who lay flushed with sleep.

Joey slipped quietly out of bed, and tiptoed to the window. It was impossible to see anything, however, for the window-panes were covered with wonderful frost designs.

A tap at the door sent her flying across the room to open it on Frau Mensch, who exclaimed in horror at seeing her barefoot and without a dressing-gown.

"I've only *just* got out of bed," pleaded Joey in excuse. "Madge and the Robin are both sound asleep still."

"And you would like to get up now?" queried her hostess understandingly. "Will you bring your garments into my room, and you can dress there without fear of disturbing the others. Your sister is very tired, and we will let her and *das Vöglein* sleep as long as they will. Bring your clothes, my child, and you shall dress and breakfast with us."

Joey collected her possessions noiselessly, and then followed Frau Mensch into a room very like the one they had. Early as it was, it was specklessly tidy, and the bed had been made. Frau Mensch explained that they had all been up since six, as there was a great deal to do today. Gertlieb had been at work since half-past five, and already much of the ordinary housework was finished. Then she left Joey, bidding her come to the *Speisesaal* when she was ready. Jo never loitered over her dressing, and twenty minutes later she entered the big, bright dining-room, where Herr Mensch was already seated at the table, consuming coffee and rolls, with Frieda on one side of him and Bernhilda on the other, while his wife dispensed coffee from the other end. She looked up with a smile as Joey entered.

"Come, my child! Here is coffee for you—but, where is your pinafore?"

"I haven't any," explained Joey as she meekly allowed Herr Mensch to pat her head in fatherly fashion, while he asked if she had slept well.

"No pinafore!" Frau Mensch looked horrified. "Run, Frieda, my bird! Fetch Joey one of your pinafores from the drawer in my room.—You will wear it, will you not, *Mädchen*?"

"Yes, of course, if you want me to," replied Joey cheerfully.

Herr Mensch nodded approval. "That is a good, obedient *Mädchen*," he said, as Joey put on the useful black pinafore Frieda had brought her. "It will keep the little dress neat and dainty. Here, with us, all little maidens wear pinafores to save their pretty gowns. Does the baby have them?"

"Oh yes, Robin wears them," said Jo. "Madge packed them in for her."

"What will you do today?" asked Herr Mensch presently, while Joey attacked her coffee and rolls with good appetite.

"We've got Christmas gifts to buy," replied his small guest.

"Ah, then mamma must take you to the shops and the market this morning. And this afternoon, if it does not

109

snow again, Gottfried shall take you to the toboggan run, and you shall see how like flying that feels."

"Perhaps Joey knows that already?" suggested Frau Mensch.

Joey shook her head. "I've never tobogganed in my life! I've read about it, though, and it sounds gorgeous! It would be nice if Herr Gottfried would take us."

Bernhilda laughed. "He will be very glad," she said. "And tonight we will go to church and hear the Christmas singing before we come home to supper and bed."

"I shall not go," said Frau Mensch decidedly. "I shall be busy with the tree. But papa will take you; and Gottfried also. Aunt Luise is coming to help me, so we shall have it finished in time. Remember, children, no one is to go into the *salon* today. Gottfried has gone to get the tree, and I shall lock the door when he has brought it. Frieda, my child, if you have finished, go and feed Minette in the kitchen."

"May I go too, please?" asked Joey. "I love cats."

"Yes; go if you wish," replied the lady, smiling. "Bernhilda, we will leave you to wash up the china and arrange the table again for Fräulein Bettany and the little Robin."

Then she bustled off to see about *Mittagessen*, while Joey and Frieda trotted into the kitchen to feed Minette, who was a magnificent tabby-cat, with a white dicky and white boots. Gertlieb smiled at them—she never seemed to do anything else but smile—but she went on steadily with her work. There was a great deal to do today, for all the mince-pies which would be eaten tomorrow had to be made; and Frau Mensch had suddenly been seized with a fear that there would not be enough sausages, so there were more to be prepared, and Gertlieb must work if she wanted her two hours in the afternoon, when she could go to the market and buy gifts for the little brothers and sisters at home.

When Minette's wants had been satisfied, Joey returned to the bedroom, where she found Madge was still sound asleep, though the Robin had roused and was sitting up in bed with her curls all on end. At sight of Joey she put her finger to her lips.

"Hssh! We must not talk, for Tante Marguérite sleeps yet."

Joey suggested that the Robin should get up.

"*Oui, vraiment!*" agreed the Robin, beaming at the suggestion. She was hungry.

Quietly Joey managed to get the small girl into her clothes, and brushed the short curls. She managed to remember one of the prettily-embroidered pinafores, which the Robin always wore to keep her frocks tidy. Robin never uttered a word till they were safely out of the room. Then she turned wide eyes on her new nurse. "I have not seen you to wear ze pinafore till yet, Zoë," she said curiously. "Why do you wear him now?"

"Frau Mensch told me to," replied Joey, glancing down at herself. "Come on and have *Frühstück*."

Frieda had brought in a little tray with the big cup of milky coffee and rolls and honey all ready for the Robin, who sat down and demolished three rolls with gusto. "I feel more full," she said with a sigh as she finished the last.

Joey smothered a laugh. "You mustn't say things like that, Robin," she said.

"Why?" demanded the Robin, as she rubbed sticky fingers on her bib.

" 'Cos it isn't polite! "

Frau Mensch, who had just taken her third guest's breakfast to her, returned in time to hear this admonition, and smiled broadly, for she understood a little English, though she could not speak it.

"Come," she said in her own language, "we will have no scoldings today. In one little hour Fräulein Bettany will be ready, and we shall go to the shops, and see what they have to offer us for Christmas."

"Oh, is Madge awake?" asked Joey. "May I go to her?"

"Yes, little heart! Go to thy dear sister, by all means! "

Jo darted out of the room, and across to the bedroom, where Madge, wrapped in her pretty yellow jersey, was sitting up in bed, eating her breakfast.

"*You* disgrace! " observed her small sister from the doorway. "You must have slept the clock round! "

"Just about," replied Miss Bettany cheerfully. "I didn't

111

know I was so tired till I got to bed—— Joey Bettany! That's never you in a pinafore! Wonders will never cease!"

"Frau Mensch nearly had a fit 'cos I hadn't any," explained Joey. "I didn't like to say I loathed pinnies when she sent Frieda for it."

"Who dressed the Robin?" asked Madge.

"Me, of course. Do buck up, Madge! I'm simply aching to go out! The sun's shining like anything, and it's a gorgeous day! We're to go shopping this morning; and this afternoon Gottfried is going to take us coasting. I say, what shall I get for Frieda? Bernie wants some hankies, so I'm going to get her some. I've got that fretwork bracket for Frau Mensch, and a pipe-rack for Herr Mensch——"

"Which he won't know what to do with," cut in her sister.

"Well, anyway, I've *got* it," said happy-go-lucky Jo. "We're getting a doll for the Robin, aren't we?"

"Yes. I've made most of the clothes. I don't know what you can get for Frieda. Would you like to join with me and give her a fountain-pen?"

"Madge, you ripper!" Joey gazed at her sister in wide-eyed admiration. "It's just the very thing!"

"More than your language is!" retorted Madge. "Take the tray, Joey; I'm going to get up now, so you can vanish!"

"Not before time—your getting up, I mean!" chuckled Jo as she grabbed the tray and made good her escape.

An hour later they were walking up the Maria Theresien Strasse, all well muffled up, for it was bitterly cold in spite of the bright sunshine which made every place sparkle gaily. All round the town lay the great mountains, ringing it round like kindly giants guarding a great treasure. Under foot the snow crunched as the busy shoppers hurried along. There was no sound of wheels to be heard; but the street rang with the jingle of bells as the horses trotted up and down, drawing *droschkes* and sleighs. The shop windows were brightly decorated and there was a general atmosphere of goodwill and merriment.

Frau Mensch undertook the charge of the Robin for half-an-hour, and a meeting-place was appointed at a café in the Landhaus Strasse, where they would drink chocolate at half-past eleven. Madge and Joey spent a pleasantly exciting time making their money go as far as possible. Joey contrived to slip off by herself for a few minutes, and rejoined her sister with a certain little parcel in the inside pocket of her coat; a beautiful doll was chosen for the Robin, and Frieda's fountain-pen and Bernhilda's handkerchiefs were bought. Madge added an embroidered tobacco-pouch for Herr Mensch, and a dainty little collar for his wife. They had to run to be in time for the others, and arrived flushed and panting with laughter and haste at the café, where the Robin's enormous importance proved that she had been shopping too.

"We must hasten," said Frau Mensch, "for there is much to do; and this afternoon some of us go to ski."

"Ski!" gasped Joey delightedly. "Oh, Frau Mensch, not really?"

Frau Mensch laughed. "But yes, my Joey. Why not?"

"Oh! I never thought we could *ski*!" Joey's voice and face were both filled with rapture at the bare idea. "I thought you had to go to Switzerland or Norway for that!"

"But why not here?" demanded Bernhilda. "We have deep snow, mountain-slopes, and a strong frost; so we ski."

"Well, I think it's gorgeous!" sighed her junior. "Better even than coasting!"

The Austrians laughed good-naturedly at her joy. Madge was hardly less excited at the prospect. The Robin didn't understand what it was all about, but she, too, was thrilled.

"I think," said Joey solemnly, as they gathered up their parcels to go, "that this is going to be the jolliest Christmas we've ever had!"

There was still some more shopping to do; then they hurried home to *Mittagessen*, which the smiling Gertlieb had waiting for them. Joey could hardly bear to sit through the meal, she was so excited, and Frau Mensch half regretted that she had said anything about the ski-ing till later on, as she saw the food left on her plate. Herr Mensch, however, came to the rescue.

"A *Mädchen* who wishes to ski this afternoon," he remarked, "will eat all her meat. Also she will enjoy the

113

little *Kartoffeln* which a gruff old giant gives her." And he ladled on to her plate another heaped spoonful of the little buttery potato-balls.

Joey blushed; but she ate what he gave her, much to Madge's relief.

When the meal was over, there was a rush to get ready, and then Gottfried and Herr Mensch escorted the five girls to the place where ski-ing was going on. It was at their side of the river, only twenty minutes' walk away, and then they were at the foot of the slope which was used for the sport. They stood for a few minutes, admiring the graceful, swallow-like flight of the experts; and then Gottfried suggested that they should all go to a quieter spot where the three novices could make their first attempts.

"It looks fairly easy," observed Jo, as, the quieter spot reached, she allowed the young Tyrolean to strap on her skis, while Herr Mensch performed the same kind office for her sister. "*Is* it, Herr Gottfried?"

"Try for yourself," he suggested, as he rose to his full height. "Keep them straight—that is all."

"Right-ho!" Joey made a tentative step; then another; then a third. "Oh, this is jolly!" she called back over her shoulder. "Quite easy, too—ouf!" In some mysterious manner the points of her skis had rushed to embrace each other, and over she went! Bernhilda fled to the rescue.

"They—they didn't keep apart!" Joey said feebly.

"Never mind," replied Bernhilda consolingly. "That is what one always does in the beginning. Try again."

"Of course! I'm not going to be done by two bits of wood or whatever it is they're made of," returned Joey calmly. "Look at Madge!—I say! Look out, Madge, they're crossing!"

Too late! They crossed with that peculiar malignancy that seems to afflict them when beginners are wearing them, and over Madge went. The Robin fared no better; but, like the other two, she persevered, and by four o'clock, when the city below them was brilliant with lights, and the short winter afternoon was closing in, they could all manage to get along for a fair distance, and Herr Mensch prophesied that in another week's time they would be quite good.

"You like it? Yes?" asked Frau Mensch as she welcomed them to cakes and coffee.

"It's *glorious*!" stated Joey definitely. "I'm aching for another go!"

"I'm aching too—from a different cause!" laughed Madge.

Frau Mensch nodded. "You must have a hot bath tonight, all of you, and I will give you some liniment to rub on, that you may not be too stiff on the morrow. Well, Aunt Luise and I have finished the tree, so we shall be able to come with you to the Christmas Eve singing after all."

"How nice!" said Joey sincerely.

The two ladies looked pleased, and Aunt Luise, a younger and slimmer edition of her sister, said, "But that is kind, *mein Kindchen*."

"When do we go?" asked Madge.

"At eighteen o'clock," replied her hostess. "We go to the Hof-Kirche which lies across the river, so we must not be late. It is in the Burg-Graben, and you have surely seen the wonderful tomb of the Kaiser Maximilian the First? Your own King Arthur stands there."

"Yes; we have seen it," replied Madge.

"It's a *gorgeous* place," put in Joey. "How splendid to hear the Christmas music sung there!"

"But it is all splendid to you, Joey!" laughed Bernhilda as she offered Jo some tempting cakes, all almonds and honey and cream.

"Of course it is!" retorted Joey as she took one. "I'm having a—a *splendacious* time!"

"I am so glad!" replied the elder girl.

Then the conversation turned on to the music, and presently it was time to get ready and set out for the Westminster Abbey of the Tyrol.

CHAPTER SIXTEEN

Christmas in Innsbruck

"MADGE! Wake up, old thing! It's Christmas morning! Merry Christmas to you!"

Madge rolled over and blinked sleepily up at the excited face Joey bent down to hers. She had been dreaming of the wonder-music they had heard in the great Hof-Kirche the night before, when the boys' voices, soaring up and up in almost angelic melody, had brought tears to her eyes with their poignant sweetness. Then had come the walk home through the gay, lamp-lit streets, across the old bridge, beneath which the frozen river lay silent and up the much quieter streets of the suburb. Sometimes, as they passed the lit-up windows of the houses, gusts of melody came out to them. Through one, where the shutters had not been closed, they could catch a glimpse of a Christmas tree, and there floated out to them the sounds of merry voices and gay laughter. By this house stood a little girl, listening to the gay noise with a wistful face. With a vague remembrance of dear Hans Andersen's *Little Match Girl*, Joey the impetuous ran to her, and pressed what was left of her money into the purple hands. "Run!" she cried eagerly. "There are *heaps* of shops open still! Do go and get something to eat *now*!"

Joey spoke in English, but her tones and actions were unmistakable. The child gasped; then caught the kind little fingers pressing the paper into her own, and kissed them. "God bless thee!" she cried, before galloping off at full speed.

The Tyroleans are a simple race. Joey's little action seemed quite natural to the Mensches. Herr Mensch patted the little fur cap with a benevolent smile, and his wife said approvingly, "It was well done, my child! The little Christ Child will not forget!"

All this had got mixed up in Madge's dreams, so that when Jo shook her awake she had to think for a moment before she could realise where she was. Then she sat up, shaking back her hair vigorously as she rubbed her eyes. "Merry Christmas, Joey!" she said, when at length she had got her bearings. "Well, Robinette! Are you awake? Merry Christmas!"

The Robin stood up in her cot. "I give you ze greetings of Noël," she said solemnly. "Zoë, do lift me out, please."

Joey tumbled out of bed and assisted the small person on to the floor. The Robin promptly scrambled up beside Madge, and planted a fervent kiss on to her head-mistress's pretty chin before she trotted over to the stove where the three had put their shoes the night before, so that the Christ Child might fill them. Jo was after her in a minute, and echoed the baby's rapturous cry as she found the little shoe filled with chocolate bonbons and a tiny doll. Joey had chocolates too, and a dear little *Book of Saints and Heroes*, which she had long wanted. "Madge, you *gem!*" she cried, as she opened it, and gazed at the illustrations delightedly. "Oh! Here's *your* shoe!"

"Oh, there'll be nothing in mine!" laughed Madge, as she took it. Then she cried out in surprise. It was she who had filled the children's shoes, and she had tucked a handful of chocolates into her own, but she had expected nothing else. Now, on top of the chocolates was a round flat parcel. She opened it, and there lay a little miniature of Joey, set in a narrow silver frame. "Joey!" she cried. "Where did you get this?"

"Miss Durrant did it," explained Jo through a mouthful of chocolate. "She said I was to give it to you when we were by ourselves; so I thought I'd shove it into your shoe. Do you like it?"

"*Like* it!" Madge's eyes glowed as she looked from Joey of the picture to the pyjamaed figure curled up beside her in bed. "It is just what I most wanted, and exactly like you!"

Jo considered it with her head on one side. "No one on earth could call me beautiful, could they?" she said with unexpected wistfulness in her voice.

117

"No," said Madge truthfully; "they couldn't. You wouldn't be Joey if you were, either; we'd have to call you 'Josephine'!"

"I hate it when you call me 'Josephine'! I always know you're going to rag me about something."

"Exactly!" Madge's tone was dry. "Well now, you're going to get up and get dressed. Hurry up about it, too!"

Joey chuckled and tumbled out of bed. "What frock shall I put on?" she demanded presently, as she stood in her short white petticoat brushing her hair. "My brown velvet?"

"No," replied her sister, who was dressing the Robin. "You'll find your frock over there, on the chair."

"Madge!" Joey made two wild leaps across the floor, and stood enraptured before the little silky frock of soft dull green which lay over the back of the chair. "Oh! What a gorgeous colour! Where did it come from?"

"Dick sent the stuff, ages ago," replied Madge. "Mademoiselle made it for you. Like it?"

"It's beautiful!"

"Put it on," said her sister. "I want to see how it looks."

Joey slipped it on and turned round. The little frock suited her. The soft green brought out the faint flush of colour in her cheeks. It was very simply made, with a short skirt and a round neck, and the silky material fell in graceful folds, which helped to hide her angles.

Madge nodded. "Yes; you'll do," she said. "Now for *your* frock, Robin. Here we are!"

The Robin's frock, of the same silk, was a warm crimson, and had holly leaves embroidered round the hems of skirt, sleeves, and neck in very dark green. Madge had tied up her hair with a big dark-green bow, and with her rosy face and velvety eyes she looked like a Christmas fairy.

"What have you got, Madge?" asked Joey. "*You've* got something pretty too, haven't you?"

Madge nodded and waved her hand to a frock of vivid jade colour. "There you are—I hope it meets with your approval!"

"It's *topping*!" said Joey. "Do buck up and get into it! I think they're gorgeous presents, and Dick's a dear!"

118

"Oh, these are just extras," laughed Madge. "Dick's *real* presents are—but you'll see later!"

"Are what?" Joey pounced on her. "Do tell me, Madge!"

"Not one word! Get out of my way, Joey, or we shall be late for breakfast!"

They filed into the *Speisesaal* just as the bell rang for *Frühstück*, to find Frau Mensch and the girls already there in full Tyrolean dress. Frau Mensch wore the black full skirt gown of the elder women, with soft white lace kerchief knotted under the square-cut neck, and heavily embroidered apron of fine white linen. Bernhilda and Frieda had shorter skirts, and their dresses were dark green. Both wore their long flaxen hair in the double braids typical of the Tyroleans, and both looked as if they had just stepped out of a fairy tale. Jo cried out with delight when she saw them. "Oh, how jolly!" she exclaimed. "What topping dresses!"

"*Fröhliche Weihnachtsfest!*" said Frieda, dancing up to her friend and giving her a hearty kiss. "Do you like our dresses, then? It is to please *Grossmütter* that we wear it. She joins us today, you know. Papa and Gottfried are carrying her into the *salon* now, and we shall go there when we have finished *Frühstück*."

Meanwhile, Frau Mensch had been greeting her other guests, and leading them to their seats at the table. "My sister is with my mother-in-law," she explained; "and here come my husband and Gottfried."

Herr Mensch and his son were also in national costume, with the well-known green knee-breeches, belt with huge filigree silver buckle, full-sleeved white shirt, and green jacket. Their stockings were light fawn, and their shoes had big silver buckles. It was a dress that suited them both, and Joey voiced the feelings of her sister when she said, "It's like Hans Andersen, or Snow White and Rose Red come to life!"

Herr Mensch's deep laughter rumbled through the room at that, but Gottfried looked uncomfortable and shy. He was not accustomed to being likened to fairy-tale heroes. Luckily, Gertlieb brought in the coffee just then, so they sat down to breakfast.

119

When the meal was over, the girls helped to clear away, and then to tidy the room, after which they went into the *salon*.

"No one must go to the part we have hung curtains before," said Frau Mensch. "That will not be looked at till tonight. But we will sing carols, and *Grossmütter* will tell us stories of her youth. This afternoon we will hire a sleigh and go for a long drive into the country, if the snow has ceased; but now it falls heavily."

She was right. It was coming down almost like a blizzard. If it had been a fine morning, Madge had intended taking Joey to the English service held in one of the rooms at the Tiroler Hof Hotel; but it was out of the question now.

"You shall sing to us your English carols," said Herr Mensch, who had guessed at the disappointment the English girls felt. "*Sonntag*, perhaps it will be fine, and then you can worship at your own service."

He led the way into the *salon*, where Tante Luise sat with a little old woman. Very, very old she looked, with a face full of wrinkles, and snow-white hair under her fine muslin mutch; but her eyes were bright, and still blue; and when she smiled, she showed a set of teeth any girl might have envied. She was, indeed, one of the old school. Her granddaughters curtsied to her as they wished her "*Fröhliche Weihnachtsfest*," then Bernhilda took Joey by the hand and led her forward. "This is our English friend, Josephine Bettany, *Grossmütter*," she said.

Something in the old lady's bearing seemed to impel Joey to curtsy.

"She is well-mannered," observed old Frau Mensch—"Exactly as though I couldn't understand!" said Joey indignantly afterwards—"and she has a modest bearing."

Madge nearly choked over this, but Frau Mensch was introducing her, and under the circumstances she felt that she couldn't do better than follow her small sister's example, which pleased the old dame enormously. She patted a chair by her side and said, "You may sit here, *mein Fräulein*, and we will talk."

The autocratic Miss Bettany, head of the Chalet School, meekly took the seat assigned to her, and then it was the

Robin's turn. Old Frau Mensch looked at her with softened eyes. *"Das Engelkind,"* she murmured. Then she turned abruptly to Madge. "I had a little daughter like that once," she said. *"Der Liebe Gott* gave her to me sixty-seven years ago on this very day. Sixty years ago on this very day He took her away to spend Christmas in Paradise. I pray that you, Fräulein, may never know such loss. My sons are good sons; but I can still hear my little Natalie's baby feet, and feel the clasp of her arms as I laid her down when she had wished me *Fröhliche Weihnachtsfest* for the last time."

The Robin came up to the old lady's knee. "Mamma is in Paradise also," she said. "Papa is very far away in Russia; but Tante Marguérite looks after me. Perhaps my mamma is playing with your little girl. "

"It may be so," said old Frau Mensch. "Sit on that little stool, *mein Liebling,* and I will tell thee tales of when I, too, was a little maiden—nearly ninety years ago."

They sat down, and she began. And what tales she told them!

Tales of a little girl who lived in Innsbruck. *Grossmütter* told them, too, of one terrible winter spent in Vienna when the cold was so severe that the wolves came howling round the city walls, and the poor died like flies. "We get no winters like that now," she said. "It was cold—so cold! I was not allowed to go outside for fear I should be frost-bitten, and the great stoves had roaring fires in them day and night. I can remember old Klaus creeping into my room during the night to put more billets of wood into the stove, and coming to pull my *plumeau* closer over me."

"How thrilling! " said Joey. "Are there wolves in Austria still, please?"

"But yes, my child. But it needs very bitter weather to bring them to the towns from the forests. You need not fear."

"And it would be bears at the Tiernsee, not wolves," added Herr Mensch, who was seated on the other side of the stove, smoking his long china-bowled pipe, and listening contentedly to his mother's stories. "Do not weary yourself, *Mamachen,* telling these naughty ones your interesting stories.—Shall we not sing a carol, my children?"

Bernhilda rose at once and went to the piano, and they sang *Stille Nacht, Heilige Nacht*, and *Adeste Fideles*, and several other carols. Then Frau Mensch said, smiling, "And now Joey will sing for us, *nicht wahr*?"

"Rather! if you want me to, that is," replied Joey. "What shall I sing?"

"Sing 'The Little Lord Jesus'," pleaded Frieda. "I love it so much!"

Madge went to the piano, and Joey stood facing them all, and sang with round golden notes, as sweet as any chorister's, Martin Luther's cradle hymn:

"Away in a manger, no crib for a bed,
The little Lord Jesus laid down His sweet head:
The stars in the bright sky looked down where He lay—
The little Lord Jesus asleep on the hay.

The cattle are lowing, the baby awakes,
But little Lord Jesus, no crying He makes;
I love Thee, Lord Jesus! Look down from the sky,
And stay by my cradle till morning is nigh."

When she finished, Frau Mensch wiped her eyes. "It is very beautiful," she said seriously. "Now I must go and see to my goose that it may be cooked properly!" And, with this funny mingling of the artistic and the matter-of-fact, she went off to overlook Gertlieb's attentions to the goose.

"Sing to us again, my child," said Herr Mensch. "There is time for one more song before we are called to *Mittagessen*."

So Joey sang again, "The Seven Joys of Mary," and then, since there was still time, the old Coventry carol, "Lullay, thou little tiny Child," with its quaint little refrain of "By, by, lully, lullay."

A frantic fantasia on the bell by Gertlieb summoned them to the *Speisesaal* after this, and they had a magnificent dinner, even though the English Christmas pudding was wanting. The home-made sausages were far nicer than anything the Bettanys had ever tasted in England, and the goose was a miracle of good cooking. The meal was finished off with raisins, nuts, and grapes; and a big box of crackers, which Madge had shyly offered Frau Mensch the day before.

"Now to get ready for our drive," said Herr Mensch. "The snow has ceased, and it freezes hard; so wrap up warmly, every *Mädchen*."

"Isn't this gorgeous fun?" giggled Joey as she snuggled down between Frieda and Bernhilda, with the Robin wedged in, in front of them, while Herr Mensch and Gottfried tucked in the bearskins round them. "O-o-o-oh! Listen to the bells! Isn't it *topping*!"

"Glorious!" agreed her sister as a loaded sleigh drawn by two horses dashed past, the bells on the harness making silvery music in the snowy world. "Joey, are you *sure* you are warm enough?"

"I'm cooked!" declared Joey. "I couldn't get on another thing if you paid me for it."

"Josephine," said Aunt Luise's voice, "here is my fur-lined cloak for you. We cannot have you ill at Christmas-time."

Joey groaned aloud. "I can't get out," she said.

But Aunt Luise was in the sleigh, fastening the great cloak round her, and tucking its folds well over her. "No," she said, "we cannot run any risk of bad colds. Now you will be safe, I think."

She climbed down, and went back to the house, while Gottfried got into the driver's seat with his father beside him. Frau Mensch and Madge sat facing the girls, and an extra rug or two was tucked into the bottom of the sleigh under the hot bricks which were to keep their feet warm. Aunt Luise was not going, for someone had to stay with old Frau Mensch, and Gertlieb was to have two hours off to go and see her mother, and take her Christmas gifts to her brothers and sisters.

They were going at a fine rate now. The horses were young and in excellent condition, and Gottfried was a good driver. They had left the main streets of the city, and were driving through the suburbs in the direction of the Brenner Road. Other sleighs were going in the same direction, and the usually quiet streets were gay with the jingle of sleigh-bells, the shouting of merry voices, and, here and there, bursts of song, as sleigh-loads of young men went flying along. All round lay the mountains, beautiful and remote in their snow-clad splendour, and over all the grey sky, heavy with snow yet to fall.

Herr Mensch, pointing to it, turned round. "We dare not go far," he shouted. "I had hoped to make the expedition to Berg Isel, but it will not be safe with that sky. We must return when we have reached Wilten. See, Fräulein, that is our University Klinik—where we take the sick. Now we shall turn out of the streets, and it is the country. Over there lies our cemetery, which we shall soon pass; and we return from Wilten by the road that winds out into the country, past the Exercier Platz and along the banks of the river."

Madge nodded. She was enjoying the drive as she had never enjoyed anything. Innsbruck under snow has a loveliness all its own, and out here in the country she felt as though she were living in a story.

"Christmas-card land!" laughed Joey. "This is topping —the jolliest ride I ever had! Just look at those trees!"

All too soon they reached Wilten, and there Gottfried turned the horses' heads to the west, driving towards the river. Just as they reached the Exercier Platz, which lay bare and white under its covering of snow, the first great flakes began to drift slowly down from the skies, and by the time they reached the bridge they were enveloped in a whirling white mist, which made driving difficult. Luckily they had not very far to go, and ten minutes later they drew up before the tall house in the Mariahilfe suburb, where Aunt Luise was standing at the door, looking anxiously out for them.

Herr Mensch and Gottfried carried the younger girls across the snow into the house, and they reached upstairs, thrilling wildly; for now there was coffee, and then—*then* there was the Christmas-tree and their presents. Frieda, Joey, and the Robin were so excited they could hardly eat anything, and Frau Mensch, laughingly remarking that they must make up for it at *Abendessen*, led the way into the *salon*, where the curtains had all been taken down and the Christmas-tree in all its blazing glory of tinsel, glass toys, candles, and frosting stood before them.

"Oh!" gasped Joey. "How *beautiful*!"

Bernhilda laughed. "It is a lovely tree, mamma—the best we have ever had. It is like the tree in the book of Märchen!"

"Come!" cried Frieda. "Come and see which is your table, Joey!"

Then Joey noticed that all the little tables in the house were set in a row, and that each was covered with parcels. A card gave the name of each owner, and Frieda was pulling her towards one marked "Joey," while Herr Mensch had carried the Robin to another, where the doll she and Madge had got the day before sat smiling.

It was thrilling work opening the parcels. Frieda was in raptures over her fountain-pen, and Frau Mensch exclaimed with delight at Madge's collar and Joey's bracket, while her husband regarded the fretwork pipe-rack with rather a puzzled air.

Jo herself found books, perfume, sweets, a kodak, a paint-box, and a fountain-pen like Frieda's. Madge was rejoicing over a copy of *Martin Pippin in the Apple Orchard*, and a string of fine amber beads; and the Robin sat on the floor cuddling her dolly, and alternately admiring a set of doll's furniture and a toy town.

It was nine o'clock before everyone had thoroughly examined everything, and finished exclaiming over it and thanking the giver. By that time supper was ready. When it was over, the Robin was carried off to bed by Madge, nodding like a sleepy fairy, while Jo and Frieda followed, clutching all their new possessions. When midnight came the elders went too. Joey woke up as her sister switched on the light. "Hullo!" she said sleepily. "Hasn't it been a glorious day?"

"Hssh!" said Madge warningly, coming over and sitting down on the bed beside her. "Don't wake the Robin."

But Jo was asleep once more, and Madge hurried up to join her as she lay dreaming of her first Christmas in the Tyrol.

CHAPTER SEVENTEEN

The New Term

"WELL, WE HAD a most glorious time, and the splendidest Christmas I've ever known!" Joey heaved a little sigh, partly for remembrance, partly for pleasure.

"*We* had a splendid time too," declared Margia, who was by no means prepared to allow Joey Bettany to carry off all the honours. "We had the *magnificentest* in Salzburg!"

"Joey, when does Grizel return?" demanded Simone Lecoutier at this moment, interrupting what looked like being a stormy argument.

"Hello, old thing!" Joey spun round to greet her French friend. "When did you come back?"

"I returned with Cousine Elise, of course," replied Simone with dignity. "I have been unpacking for Renée and myself, and then I came across to see *you!*—and y-you have not yet embraced me."

"Oh—bother! Get on with it, then!" And Joey presented her cheek for Simone's kiss, since that young lady sounded tearful.

"But when *does* Grizel return?" persisted the French child. "Will she come soon? Or has she left for always?"

Joey looked at Simone with a funny little smile. "Would that break your heart? No; she hasn't left—only gone to be with her grannie, who's very ill. My sister had a letter the other day, and they're afraid old Mrs. Cochrane won't live much longer. She adores Grizel, and it makes her happier to have her, so she'll just stay as long as she's wanted."

"I am sory for Grizel," said Simone, her black eyes growing very big and soft with sympathy. "She loves her grandmother, and it must be hard to lose those one loves."

"Are there any new girls, Joey?" asked Margia by way of changing the subject.

"Two," said Jo briefly; "one junior and one senior, so they won't trouble *us* very much. The senior will only be a day boarder, too. She lives up the valley in that huge chalet, just beyond the fencing. She was at school in Vienna, but her mother has been ill, so they brought Stéphanie home; but she's only sixteen, so she's coming here for a year."

"Hello, Joey!" cried a fresh voice, and Jo swung round to greet Evadne Lannis, leaving Margia to saunter off towards Frieda Mensch, who was talking at a great rate to Marie von Eschenau, Paula von Rothenfels, and Bianca di Ferrara.

It was the first day of term, and already most of the boarders were back.

Two days after Christmas Day, the whole of the North Tyrol had been swept by a tremendous blizzard, which had raged for nearly three days without ceasing. The snow was followed by such severe cold as no one could remember having known for the past sixty years at least. Reports came from the plains that the wolves were already becoming more daring than had ever been known before, and the mountain regions could say the same thing about the chamois.

New Year's Eve had found the Bettany girls and the Robin staying with the Maranis, where they had a very good time indeed. When the day arrived for them to return to the Chalet, Herr Marani came with them, and saw them comfortably settled in. The short rest had done them all good, and Jo proclaimed herself to be growing *fat*!

Joey said, "I say—Simone! You've had your hair cut again. How's that? I thought you were going to let it grow?"

"Maman says that she prefers I shall have it short while I am at school," replied Simone sedately. "I am very glad, because it is so easy to keep tidy."

"D'you think so?" Joey turned and regarded her reflection in the mirror for a minute or two. "It may be for you; but look at *me*!"

Two or three people, who were standing near, heard, and turned to look. They all shouted with laughter as they did so, for a bigger contrast than Simone's neat little black head like a well-polished boot-button, and Joey's tousled, gollywog locks could not be imagined.

"It certainly isn't tidy for you, Joey," chuckled Juliet. "As for Simone, I couldn't imagine *her* hair ever looking like yours. There's absolutely no comparison!"

"Oh, it is tidy—on occasion," returned Jo casually.

"I should think it *was* 'on occasion'! Pity it isn't that oftener!"

"Oh well; we can't all have the same virtues!"

"No," said Gisela, who had overheard the last part of this conversation, "but neatness is a virtue that one may acquire. Therefore, my Jo, go upstairs and brush your hair, for the bell for *Kaffee* will ring very soon, and it is not polite to Madame that you should appear looking like that."

"Oh, bother!" grumbled Jo. "You Austrians *do* insist on your twopence-halfpenny worth of manners! My sister wouldn't mind first day!"

"No; but I do. Come, Joey! Make haste, or you will be late."

Gisela spoke firmly, and Jo knew better than to disobey her; so she vanished upstairs, grumbling loudly all the time at the bother of having to do her hair. Margia accompanied her.

Joey laid down her brush and regarded her head with approval. "It's heaps better now, but goodness knows how long it'll stay that way. There's the bell! Come on!"

They fled downstairs, Jo with her hands clasped over her head so that she might arrive in the *Speisesaal* reasonably tidy. Unfortunately, she forgot the narrowness of the staircase, and banged her funnybone, which drew a low howl from her.

"What on earth's the matter?" demanded Margia, stopping short.

"Banged my elbow!" was the brief reply.

Margia turned back. "You poor old thing! It's a simply

sickening thing to do, isn't it? Almost as bad as biting your tongue!"

Jo got up from the stair on which she had been sitting. "Come on—we shall be late, and Gisela is sure to say it's rude to Madame!"

Margia wisely held her tongue, and they reached the big dining-room in silence.

By this time everyone had come except Grizel, whose absence seemed to make a huge gap. She was by no means one of the oldest there, but she certainly was one of the leaders. Miss Bettany had not yet made her a prefect, nor given her much responsibility; but there could be little doubt that she was one of the people who counted in their little world.

Gisela Marani voiced the fact for them. "It seems strange without Grizel," she said, as she poured out the last cup of coffee. "I hope she will return soon, Madame."

"I don't know when she will come," replied Miss Bettany. "We must go on with the games without her, Gisela."

"Ah, yes," said Gisela. "We shall have to appoint a new games captain for the time, until she returns."

"There'll be skating too," put in Joey. "The lake is bearing, and they say there will be no more snow for a few days. Marie says that if it's still all right they're going to have an ice carnival on Saturday night. They light up the Seespitz end with torches, and have huge bonfires burning on the banks. One of the Tzigane bands comes up and plays, and there is dancing and feasting and heaps of fun. People come from all round to see it—from the plains, and up the valleys. Doesn't it sound *thrilling*?"

"Yes," replied her sister, "it certainly does.—Mademoiselle, you have no coffee.—Joey, fetch Mademoiselle some more; and Miss Maynard hasn't any cake.—Margia, bring the cakes, dear."

The two did as they were told, but Joey's face wore a mutinous expression which deepened as Madge quietly turned the conversation on to some other subject. Later on in the evening she had to go to the study with some books. Madge was alone, writing letters at her desk.

"Madge," she said.

Miss Bettany looked up. "Well, Joey baba, what is it?"

Jo dropped down beside her. "Madge! Be a gem and say we can go to the carnival," she coaxed. "I want to see it ever so much! "

Madge laid down her pen and leant back in her chair. "Joey, I can't say anything definite till I know more about it. I don't intend for one instant to allow any of you actually to join in. There will be far too many strangers there, and I am sure it will be noisy and rough. But I will go over and see Herr Braun tomorrow, and ask him if it will be all right for you to go to Seespitz and look on. If he says that it will, then you shall go for an hour—all the seniors and middles shall, at least. But if he says *not*, then I'm afraid you'll have to content yourselves with looking on here."

"Oh, Madge! " Joey's voice was full of disappointment. "Nothing could happen to us! Why should it? And I do so want to see it."

"I'm sorry, Jo. I'll let you go if it's possible; but I can't promise."

"If such crowds of people come, p'r'aps they'll want the whole lake," suggested Joey hopefully.

"Then you'll be able to see from the dormitory windows," replied her sister. "Now I'm busy, and you must run away. Will you find the other mistresses and ask them to come and see me in half-an-hour's time? Gisela and Juliet can go over to Le Petit Chalet and take charge there."

Joey left the room and devoted the next ten minutes to delivering her messages. Then she turned back into the little class-room where her own clan were roasting chestnuts.

"Nothing doing," she reported gloomily as she flopped down on the floor between Simone and Margia. "At least, if Herr Braun thinks it'll be all right, we may be allowed to go and watch; but if not, then we mayn't! "

A chorus of groans arose. "Oh, what rotten luck! "— "Would Madame agree if we all went and asked her?" —"*Schrecklich!*"—"*Pfui!*"—"*Tristo!*"—"Oh, Joey! "

130

"It's no use fussing," declared Joey as she accepted the chestnut Frieda dropped into her lap. "Once my sister says a thing, she jolly well sticks to it!"

Finding her chestnut difficult to peel, she put it into her mouth to bite a hole in it. The next moment there was a loud "Pop!" accompanied by yells. The thing had burst in her mouth.

"Ow! Water! Water!" shrieked Joey, whose tongue was badly burnt.

"What on earth is the matter?" demanded Juliet from the doorway. She had been passing at the time of the mishap, and, hearing the noise, hurried to the rescue, quite convinced that someone was badly hurt.

They enlightened her, all talking at once, and she laughed when she understood. "Poor old Joey! No; don't drink cold water! I'll go and get some baking soda from Marie, and that will take the stinging out of it."

She hurried off, and presently returned with the soda, which she put on Jo's tongue.

"It's got a *beastly* taste!" said the patient disgustedly.

"Never mind. It'll help the burning.—The rest of you clear up that mess of shells," said Juliet. "It's nearly eight o'clock, and you can't go to bed and leave the room like that.—Better now, Jo?"

"Yes, thanks," said Joey, who was beginning to recover from her fright.

"Then I must go now. Gisela is waiting for me. Your tongue will be a bit sore tomorrow, I expect, Joey; but it'll soon be all right again. There's the bell. Finish tidying, and then run along to bed.—Frieda and Simone, you'd better come with us."

"And I only had that one chestnut!" mourned Joey as Juliet went off, accompanied by the two middles who slept at Le Petit Chalet.

"Never mind," said Margia consolingly. "There are heaps left, and you can have your share tomorrow."

Then they all trooped off to bed, but that chestnut had helped on something that was beginning to simmer in Joey's brain; and that something was to have direful results.

CHAPTER EIGHTEEN

The Ice Carnival

THE DECISION was made. There was to be no ice carnival for the pupils of the Chalet School. Herr Braun's horror when he heard Madge's queries on the subject had quite settled that.

"But the ice carnival for *die Mädchen!*" he had exclaimed. "Oh no, *gnädiges Fräulein*—it can never be! It is not becoming for young ladies. People come from far and near, and with them they bring beer and *Schnäpse*. That is bad, for they take too much, and there is much roughness and horseplay on the ice. Sometimes there are quarrels, and then we have fighting. Oh no, *mein Fräulein!* But you and *die Mädchen* must lock the doors, and shutter the windows, and go not out at all!"

Madge looked troubled. "Do you think it possible that our part of the lake may be in use?" she asked.

Herr Braun waved his hands in a gesture of helplessness. "I cannot say. It is probable, I think. But I will speak to those who build the bonfires, and ask that one is not placed near the Chalet. That will keep the skaters away. Also, I will have the fencing of the land finished, and we will put very strong padlocks on the gate; but it is all that I can do. At least, *mein Fräulein*, this occurs but once in the year, and it is quite possible that the better people only will come to your side of the lake. The wilder ones will stay at the Seespitz end, where there will be many bonfires and much light."

"You are very good, Herr Braun," said Madge gratefully. "I shall certainly not allow the girls to go outside after nightfall on Saturday, and the fence will be a great protection."

Then she had skated back across the lake to issue her

commands, while Herr Braun sent his men to get on with the fence, with which he was enclosing the Chalet School and its ground. The posts had been driven in before the snow came, and a part of the withe-weaving, which was to build up the fence, had been done. Now the men were set to continue the weaving; and by Friday it was finished; and the Chalet, Le Petit Chalet, the shed, and the cricket-ground and tennis-courts were safely enclosed within a six-foot barrier, which not only shut the school out from curious eyes, but also cut off interesting sights from in-attentive pupils—a rather necessary thing.

Miss Bettany issued her commands; but she omitted to give any reason for them, which was a mistake where one or two of her pupils were concerned. People like her own small sister are usually quite contented to obey orders if a reason is given to them; and Jo had been in many ways treated from a grown-up point of view. Because Madge had chosen to give no explanation of her edict, Joey became restless, irritable, and, finally, downright rebellious.

"It's a mean shame!" she declared to her own special coterie of friends, which consisted of Margia, Simone, Frieda, Marie von Eschenau, and Paula von Rothenfels. "I don't see why we shouldn't go!"

"But it is Madame's desire that we do not," said Marie, who was a law-abiding little soul.

"I don't care," retorted naughty Jo. "I'm going! And I don't care who says what!"

The others gazed at her in awe-stricken silence—all except Margia. *She* flashed a funny little look at the recal-citrant one. Joey flushed pink.

"I mean it," she said defiantly.

"It won't be running away, will it?" queried Margia.

"No; of course not. We're only going for a short while —just to see what it's like—then we'll come back and own up."

"But—will not Madame be very angry?" asked Marie doubtfully.

Up went Jo's head. "Of course, if you're *afraid!*" she said scornfully.

Marie was; but she had her fair share of pride, so she

133

retorted, "I have *not* fear! But Madame will be very angry, and she will also be hurt, and that I do not like!"

If Jo's tongue had been all right, the chances are that the last part of Marie's final remark might have carried weight. Instead of yielding, she merely snapped, "Don't come, then! We can manage without you!" Then she faced on to the others. "Any more funks here?"

"But I am *not* a funk." Marie was nearly in tears. "I will come with you, Joey, *of course!*"

The "of course" slightly mollified Jo, and, as the others all agreed without further argument, she calmed down considerably.

"Right! Then we'll fix up our plans and go. It can't do any harm just to be on the ice for an hour or so; and we'll own up the minute we get back, so it'll be straight enough."

It *was* straight—up to a point. What Joey wouldn't and the others didn't see was that it wasn't straight right through. It was all very well to say it was a "sporting" thing to do—this was one of Jo's arguments—but they all felt more or less uncomfortable about it.

Meanwhile Madge, having given her commands, imagined that there was no further need to worry, and plunged whole-heartedly into the term's work. The English and German of the school showed a tremendous all-round improvement; but the French of some of the juniors was appalling. Also, at the request of several parents, she had decided to have Italian classes for the seniors. The Chalet School must of necessity specialise in languages, and Miss Bettany had decided that it should have an excellent showing in them.

To these classes Jo, Paula, Marie, and Margia were admitted, although they were two years younger than most of the seniors. The Gräfin von Rothenfels had specially asked that Paula might join them, and had also mentioned that Frau von Eschenau would wish Marie to learn; while Jo and Margia both knew a certain amount already, and would profit by the regular work.

There were time-tables to arrange and rearrange; new stationery and one or two new text-books to give out; one or two kitchen details to see to; and the games to settle. It was hardly surprising that during all the bustle of the first week the mutiny of certain middles should be overlooked.

A fresh fall of snow on the Friday made it impossible for the girls to go out; so when games time came round, the big class-room was cleared, pretty Miss Durrant came over from Le Petit Chalet, where she had been teaching the juniors how to make raffia baskets with beautiful designs of chequers and triangles, and the girls worked off their superfluous energy in "Picking Up Sticks", "Jenny Pluck Pears", "Mage on a Cree", "Butterfly", and other country-dances. Then, when they were all sitting round the wall, breathless and laughing, Mademoiselle played a tune none of them had ever heard before, and Miss Durrant danced for them a morris-jig, which drove them all wild with delight.

"Oh, what is it?" cried Joey, her rebellion forgotten for the moment. "What *is* it, Miss Durrant? It's simply lovely —the jolliest thing I've ever seen!"

Miss Durrant, who was flushed and panting with the exercise, laughed at her enthusiasm. "It's one of the morris-jigs—you people are going to start morris this term —'Jockie to the Fair' it's called."

"It's simply top—er—*glorious*!" proclaimed Joey. "I just *love* it. When can we begin?"

"Jigs? Oh, I'd advise you to learn the steps first," said Miss Durrant demurely. "You surely don't want to start on jigs straight-away?"

"I don't care what we start on so long as we start on something," declared Joey. "Will you teach us the step today?"

Miss Durrant shook her head. "No. You've all been working fairly hard, and morris isn't easy. You must be fresh to do it well. We'll learn a new country-dance, though, and you shall begin your morris tomorrow morning. Form into sets of eight. I'm going to teach you 'Oaken Leaves'."

They ran to do her bidding, and were soon busily learning "Oaken Leaves", with its pretty figures, which was quite new to them. Joey, deeply enthralled by the work,

135

forgot all about her plans for Saturday, and danced hard, all her zest showing in her face. If other people had been contented to let things be, the chances are that she would have forgotten all about the carnival till it was too late to make arrangements. Unfortunately, Simone was rather bored by the dancing, and before going upstairs to change from their tunics, she pulled Joey into a quiet corner and said eagerly, "And for tomorrow, Jo! Where do we meet, and when?"

"Oh, bother tomorrow! I'd forgotten all about it," replied Jo, frowning.

Simone had not been particularly keen on the escapade. However, once she had screwed up her courage sufficiently to enable her to agree to doing it, she did not wish to give up the idea. A wicked little imp inspired her to make the one remark that would bring Joey up to the scratch.

"Have you, then, fear?" she asked.

That settled it. The blood rushed to Jo's face in a crimson tide. "No," she said shortly. "I'll tell you about arrangements before we go to bed tonight." Then she turned and ran off, all the joy and zest gone from her face, and only a heavy frown on her brow. Madge met her, and stopped her to ask what was the matter.

"Jo! What's wrong with you, child? Has anything happened?"

"I'm all right," mumbled Joey, scarlet to the tips of her ears.

Madge concluded that she had quarrelled with one of her friends, and let her go. She could hardly push the question any further at the moment; and next day a letter arrived from her twin-brother, which put everything else out of her head; for Dick had written to tell her that he was engaged to his chief's youngest girl, and that they hoped to be married very soon. There was a note from the lady herself, which showed her to be a jolly, rather schoolgirlish, person, who evidently took life as a huge joke. She sent her love to her two sisters-to-be, and added that she enclosed some snapshots of herself, so that they could see what she was like. On the outside of the note was scrawled, "Can't find the beastly things. Sending them later." Madge giggled over this, and decided that Miss Mollie Avery was the right person for Dick to marry. She meant to tell Joey about it, but that young woman studiously avoided her, and then Marie contrived to upset a kettle of boiling water over herself, and was rather badly scalded. By the time things were righted, and poor weeping Marie was lying in bed with her own small sister to look after her while Eigen assisted Miss Bettany to do his sister's work in the kitchen, the entire school was playing net-ball, and Joey, at Centre, was unget-at-able.

In the afternoon she and the rest of the middles vanished into the shed, where Rufus, now a handsome fellow, with fine head and great massive body, spent the day with his mother. The Head had said that the girls were not to go outside of the fence today, and, unfortunately, this meant depriving the dogs of their usual walk, so she was glad to hear the sounds of romping that came from the big shed. Marie's accident made a good deal of difference, and Miss Bettany was kept busy till after the girls had had their coffee. As they came out of the *Speisesaal* to go and change for the evening, she contrived to catch Jo, and draw her into the sudy. "Jo, I've had a letter from India," she began.

"When?" demanded Jo.

"This morning, of course—— My dear Joey, what *is* the matter?"

Jo faced on her. "You've had a letter from Dick all day, and never told me about it till *now*!" she gasped.

"But, Joey baba, I've had no time!"

Jo made no answer. She simply stood there, very white, and with angry eyes. Madge looked at her, amazed.

"Why, Joey! What *is* the matter with you? Aren't you well?"

"I'm all right. Don't *fuss*, Madge."

Madge began to get angry now. "You ungrateful child! You don't deserve that anyone should fuss over you!" Then, as the memory of the tremendous news she had just received came to her, she softened. "Joey, don't be so cross with me; I am awfully sorry it's got delayed—the more so because of the wonderful news I have for you. What do you think? Dick is engaged!"

"What as?"

"Engaged to be married. We shall have a new sister before long."

"Rats! I don't believe you!" returned Joey rudely.

Madge was dumbfounded. She simply could not understand this attitude. She never once dreamed of connecting it with her refusal to allow the girls to go to the carnival, and she could not think that it was the result of not giving Joey the letter sooner.

"Joey! Do you realise how rude you are being?" she said quietly. "I have told you that I am sorry that I didn't show you the letter sooner. I see you are very angry with me, but I couldn't help it. Here is the letter; will you take it away and read it for yourself, please? And I don't want to see you until you have come to your senses."

Joey almost snatched the letter from her, and left the room. She *was* cross about not having had it sooner, but the principal trouble was the deep sense of shame she had. She had often been tiresome before this; but she had always been straight. What made it worse was the fact that she was dragging other people into it. She took the letter upstairs and tucked it into her drawer; she didn't feel like reading it just now.

When she got downstairs she found that the others had nearly finished their coffee, and through the unshuttered windows came flickering light from the bonfires which were being lighted. Snatches of music drifted across to them from the lake, accompanied by an increasing chatter of voices as the revellers began to turn up in full force. The carnival was beginning.

Miss Bettany had arranged that the girls were to go upstairs to the dormitories that overlooked the lake, and watch the fun from the windows; so, after *Kaffee*, the girls streamed upstairs, while Eigen closed the shutters of the downstairs windows. This was the chance of the naughty middles. They slipped into the dark cloak-room, and hid among the coats while the others settled themselves in the darkened dormitories. The staff went with the school; Marie was in bed; and Eigen had permission to go to the carnival for two hours.

It seemed ages to the six, standing as motionless as possible in the little cloak-room, before silence settled down on the lower part of the house, though, as a matter of fact, it was barely half-an-hour. When, finally, they felt safe, they closed the cloak-room door very quietly, and switched on the light. Then they dressed as quickly as possible in woollen jerseys, big coats, thick boots, woolly caps and scarves and gloves; lifted their skates carefully lest the jingling should betray them, and stole along the passage and out of the side-door, which had been made for the convenience of the day-girls. It was not till they were outside that they realised just how difficult it was going to be to get down to the lake without being seen.

"What *shall* we do?" asked Margia. "If they see us they'll come after us, and we shall have all the fuss for nothing."

Joey, however, was a resourceful young person. "Go round the back," she said. "Then we can cut across the cricket-ground, and climb over the fence, and go down by the side."

It was the only thing to do. They crept along, keeping well in the shadow of the house until they reached the cricket-field, across which they fled at full speed till they came to the fence. This had to be climbed, but they were all active enough, and even Simone, with a good "boost," was got over it in safety. When they were all at the other side they looked at each other. The excitement was doing its work. Even Joey had forgotten her conscience pains, and they caught hands and ran gaily down to the edge of the lake, where they sat down to put on their skates.

Joey got to her feet. Then she looked round. It was a wild picturesque scene. Overhead was a stormy sky, with a young moon gazing down on the white-clad mountains, remote and silent, even now. Against the snow the pine-woods stood out in black masses, and the ice-bound lake lay like a pool of midnight in its sparkling frame. Great bonfires flared up to the distant stars, casting a lurid light on the snow, and linkmen glided about the lake carrying flaming torches. Already the Seespitz end was crowded with figures, but just where they were it was quiet. On the frosty air the music from the great Tzigane band, playing like possessed creatures near one of the bonfires, came clearly to them. It was a wonderful picture.

The six little girls kept pretty close together. Frieda, Marie, Margia, and Paula were excellent skaters for their age, and Joey, during her fortnight's holiday, had learnt to be fairly safe, though she was by no means as good as she thought she was. Simone was wobbly to the last degree, but Frieda and Marie took her between them, and Paula caught Joey's hands, and they enjoyed themselves enormously for the first half-hour or so.

Then Paula took Marie's place with Simone, and Marie, anxious to prove her skill, began cutting a figure of eight on the ice. Joey watched her with keen interest—so keen, in fact, that she paid little heed to where she was going, encountered the dead branch of a tree which some one had flung on the ice, staggered, tried to recover her balance, and fell headlong, her hands above her head, directly in the path of a skater who was coming along at full speed!

He was going too quickly to swerve, and to the horrified children it seemed as though he must go clear across Joey's fingers. They set up a wild shriek, and as for Joey, she fainted, just as the skater flung himself wildly to one side and fell with a crash on top of her.

It was at this moment that Miss Bettany, hunting through the cloak-room, discovered that her missing pupils had vanished, and dashed upstairs to her room to scramble into her outdoor garments and snatch up her skates before she hurried out to reclaim them.

To say that Madge was angry, is to put it very mildly. She was *furious*. It was bad enough that the other children should have gone; but that her own sister should have set her at defiance like this was unbearable. She shut the door firmly behind her and hastened down to the lake.

A little cavalcade met her as she opened the gate. First came Simone, crying heart-brokenly with Frieda trying to comfort her; then came Marie and Paula, both crying too; lastly, Margia walked sobbing beside a tall man, who carried in his arms a limp burden that lay very still.

Madge said afterwards that she felt her heart stop beating as she saw them. Then she sprang forward. "Joey!" she said.

The stranger spoke in a reassuring tone. "She's only fainted—and she'll be a bit stunned too. I expect she's badly bruised, but that will be all. Let me carry her to the house for you."

The voice was vaguely familiar, but Madge could only think of Joey.

"Bring her in," she said, and led the way up to the Chalet and into the study, where she switched on the light. The stranger laid Joey on the couch, and as he did so she opened her eyes.

"Hullo," she said. "I say! Aren't you the man who helped us in that train accident last term?"

Before anyone could reply, Simone had flung herself down by the couch. "Joey—Joey!" she sobbed.

Then Joey remembered. "My fingers!" she gasped. "Oh, are they still on?" She tried to move, but the action was agony, and she screamed.

"There! Steady!" said the man, who had been stripping off his coat and scarf. "You'll be black and blue all over, I expect. Your fingers are all there; I fell on you instead." Then he turned to Madge. "I'm a doctor—James Russell's my name; you may remember me. If you will permit me, I will examine her."

Madge gave thankful permission, and while Miss Maynard, who had joined them by this time, removed the other children, she helped him to undress Joey and examine her. It was as he had said. Jo was badly bruised. In addition, she had sprained her ankle when she fell, but there was no serious damage.

When things had all been explained, Dr. Russell looked down at his small patient—now safely in bed—with a smile. "You've punished yourself," he said. "You won't be able to move comfortably for a week or more, and that sprain will keep you in bed for longer than that. Oh, I'm not going to rub it in; but you've asked for trouble—and you've got it!"

Then he said, "Good-night," and left her.

Madge came back presently, to find a thoroughly peni-
tent Jo awaiting her. "Joey!" she said.

"I'm a *beast!*" declared Jo. "I'm awfully sorry, Madge;
and it was my fault. Don't blame the others, please!"

Madge—fresh from an interview with Simone, who had
declared it to be *her* fault because she had taunted Joey
with being afraid; and another from the other four, who
had insisted that it was *theirs* for not opposing Joey's plan
more firmly—nearly smiled. She just stopped herself in
time.

"I'm not going to say anything about it," she said
gravely. "I know you are sorry, and won't do it again, so
we'll leave it at that. Now I'm going to give you some hot
milk, and read you Dick's letter, and then you must go
to sleep."

"Shake," said Joey, moving her right arm gingerly.

Madge took the bandaged hand in hers, and then, bending down, kissed her small sister as final token of
forgiveness.

"I *hate* ice carnivals!" said Jo viciously; "and you're a
dear."

CHAPTER NINETEEN

Jo Writes an "Elsie" Book

Dr. Russell had been quite right when he said that Jo
had made her own punishment. She had! For more than a
week she was stiff and aching from her bruises and her
sprained ankle, while any movement was a sheer agony
for the first two or three days. Like most excitable children,
she developed a temperature very easily, and during those
first nights she was quite light-headed, which might have
alarmed her sister seriously had she not been accustomed
to Jo. Then, when the worst of the bruises began to heal,
and the throbbing in her ankle grew less, the young rebel
became decidedly bored with life.

Very little had been said to any of them about the ice carnival affair. Bernhilda, it is true, had scolded Frieda roundly, and Wanda had followed her example with Marie and Paula; but the Head had merely informed them that their behaviour had showed that they were unworthy of the trust she had given them, and said that, for the present at any rate, they were to be treated like the juniors and always have someone in authority with them.

This hurt; and the five left the study, weeping bitterly. Miss Bettany had said very little, but what she said was impressive, and they all wished that they had never heard of such things as ice carnivals.

As for Joey, the leader in it all, there was, of course, no need to watch her. She was tied to her bed; the other girls were not allowed to visit her except at very long intervals, and she was thoroughly bored.

"I wish there were some fresh books to read!" she sighed one day.

The doctor happened to be with her at the time. "Find it dull?" he asked.

"Duller than dull! I wouldn't mind so much if I'd only something to read; but I haven't! I've read all the books in the library, and I'm tired of them. Dr. Jem, can't *you* lend me something?"

Dr. Jem—he had told her to call him this—chuckled. "As a matter of fact, I can," he said. "Ever read the Elsie books?"

"No; but I've often heard of them," replied Jo. "Aren't they about an awfully good little girl; and aren't there dozens of them?"

"But how in the world do *you* know anything about the Elsie books?" demanded Madge, who was sitting beside Joey.

"I picked 'em up cheap in an all-sorts shop," explained the doctor. "There are six or seven, I believe. I'd heard one of my aunts talking about them once, and lamenting the loss of her copies, so I thought she'd appreciate them. Anyway, I'll fetch them along sometime. At least they'll be fresh."

"Jolly!" said Jo. "It is decent of you, Dr. Jem."

He was as good as his word. During the afternoon Marie trotted up the stairs with a parcel of books which she gave the delighted Jo, who spread them all out on the bed in front of her and feasted her eyes on them. There were six of them—*Elsie Dinsmore, Elsie's Holidays, Elsie's Girlhood, Elsie's Womanhood, Elsie's Motherhood*, and *Elsie's Children*. Madge, coming upstairs an hour later, found her fathoms deep in the first, and felt thankful.

For the rest of the week Joey revelled in the deeply pious atmosphere of "Elsie" and her companions. The wild adventures with the Ku Klux Klan awoke a desire in her to know more about American history, and she nearly drove Madge crazy with her questions.

At length the sorely-tried sister struck, and vowed she would answer no more. "Read up your history if you want to know!" she cried.

"Well, get me some more books, then, please," replied Joey. "I'd like one all about the War of Independence, and the Pilgrim Fathers, and the Civil War. Oh, and an atlas to find the places! Where's Fort Sumter, and why did its fall start the war? And——"

Madge flew before the storm, and Joey was left with a half-finished question on her tongue; but presently Frieda trotted in with two or three books of general history, and a big atlas. "Madame sends these," she announced. "Do you require anything else, Joey? for I will bring it."

Joey considered. "Yes; you can bring me some paper—reams of it; and some blotchy—oh, and my fountain-pen. D'you mind, Frieda? You *are* a sport!"

Frieda brought her what she wanted, and when Miss Bettany came up in the afternoon she found Joey propped up against her pillows, and a pile of sheets, covered with her irregular writing, on the bed beside her.

"Well," said the elder girl, "what are you busy with now?"

Joey raised an excited face to hers. "Oh, Madge, I'm writing an Elsie book!"

"What! Morals, texts, and all?" inquired Madge, choking back a laugh—she had glanced through one of the books, and knew their type.

"No-o-o!" said Jo reluctantly. "I don't know enough texts."

"I see! How much have you done, Joey?"

"Just the first three chapters," replied Joey. "I'm calling it *Elsie's Boys*, and it's all about the boys—Eddie, and Harold, and Herbert."

"Don't start writing again. It's getting too dark to see, and you'll strain your eyes if you go on."

"Well, can't I have the light on, then?" pleaded Joey.

Madge shook her head. "No; not yet. Lie still and rest. You'll overtire yourself if you don't, and then you won't be able to get up tomorrow."

"Get up? Am I going to get up? Oh, how *gorgeous*!"

"Dr. Russell is coming to carry you down to my study in the morning, and you are to lie on the couch there. Herr Anserl, who will be here for the day, will bring you back here at the end of the afternoon."

"Mag—nificent!" pronounced Jo with a sigh. "I was getting *sick* of this room."

"It's your own fault you're here," replied Madge. "I'm *not* going to lecture now. You've had your punishment, and a fairly severe one. Past things are past. But I do want you to realise that it isn't playing the game to grumble at consequences." Then she changed the subject, and that was all Joey heard about her escapade.

The next day, as soon as Dr. Jem had left her, comfortably arranged on the couch, so that she could see out of the window into the garden, she demanded her "book" and went on with undiminished ardour.

As long as it was advisable to keep her quiet, Madge was thankful that she could employ herself so happily. But Monday of the next week found her back in the schoolroom, settled in an invalid chair, manufactured out of an ordinary one and some wood, so that she could keep her sprained ankle up. She was glad enough to be back with the others, but it was a fearful nuisance not to be able to go on with her writing. Every spare moment she had she devoted to it, and the pile of exercise paper containing the doings of the Travilla boys grew daily larger. Even so, however, she found it difficult to get on as quickly as she would have liked. Then came doubts about it. It was sure to be full of mistakes. It was stupid.

At this juncture Madge unconsciously came to the rescue. "When are you going to let me see that story of yours?" she demanded one day. "Isn't it finished yet?"

"No—not exactly," faltered Joey.

Her sister looked at her amazedly. "May I see it, Joey?" she asked.

Joey mutely held out the bundle, and her sister gasped at its size. "Why, Jo, it's quite a book!" she cried.

Madge went off to her own den with the manuscript. It was some hours before she could get time to look at it.

Jo's writing was not her strong point, and parts of the "book" were almost illegible. Her punctuation was shaky, and her spelling frequently verged on the phonetic. But, for all that, the story was surprisingly good. The characters in it were *alive*, and the young authoress showed a decided gift for description. Dr. Jem, dropping in casually as he often did now, demanded that a chapter should be read to him. So, after some deliberation, Madge selected her chapter and began to read.

"Madge!" Joey stood before them. "*Oh!* How mean of you! How *could* you!"

Madge lifted amazed eyes to the flushed face above her. "Why, Jo——" she began.

The doctor stopped her. "Joey, it was *my* fault. I very much wanted to see what you had made of it, so I asked Miss Bettany to read it to me. I am the one for you to be angry with—but I hope you aren't going to be angry."

The flush died out of Jo's face; she looked at him in a puzzled way. "I don't see why you want to read it," she said slowly. "Madge is different—she's Madge! Why *did* you want to see it?"

"Because," said the doctor, "I had read your fairy-tale in the *Chaletian*. It was very pretty, Joey; but any ordinarily clever girl might have imagined it—though she would not have expressed it in quite your way; that, I grant you. This is a totally different thing, and I wanted to see how you would tackle it. Even the little I have heard has told me what I wanted to know. You can vary your style to suit your subject, and that is a very great thing in story-writing. It's early to prophesy—you are only, how old? Thirteen, is it?"

Joey nodded. She had never taken her eyes off his face once, and Madge was listening with the same tense eagerness.

The doctor looked at them. "You are very young, Joey; but I'm going to take it upon myself to prophesy after all. If you go on as you have begun, and work hard at grammar and literature, and all your other lessons, then, one day, you will write something really worth while."

Joey's eyes widened, and the slow colour flushed her face. "Do—do you really mean that?" she asked in a breathless sort of way. "*Really?*"

"Yes; I mean it. It will be hard work, Joey, and hard work all the time; but if you go on you will do it."

There was a little silence in the room. Then Jo, the undemonstrative, suddenly flung her arms round the doctor's neck, and gave him a vigorous hug. "Oh—oh! Dr. Jem! I love you!" she gasped.—"Madge, I *will* work—I'll be an angel of goodness at my lessons!" She released the doctor and collapsed into her sister's arms. "Madge!"

"You silly child!" Madge scolded her gently. "You mustn't get so excited, Joey baba.—Yes? Come in!" as a tap sounded at the door.

Gisela Marani appeared. "Excuse me, Madame, but Miss Maynard wished to know if Joey had told you that papa is here, as he has to hurry back, and would be glad to see you if you can spare him the time."

Madge looked at Jo speechlessly.

"I quite forgot!" said the future authoress.

CHAPTER TWENTY

Joey and Rufus to the Rescue

JANUARY had faded into February before Grizel returned
to school. She was a somewhat subdued Grizel, for her
grandmother had died only the week before she came back,
and the long days spent in the old lady's room had helped
to soften a certain hardness in her character.

She had also come back full of the Girl Guide movement. A company had been begun in the High School
which she and Joey and Rosalie had attended when living
in England, and most of the members of their old form
had joined. Grizel, always interested in anything new, had
learned all she could about the Guides, and she was very
keen for Madge to start one in the Chalet School.

Mr. Cochrane had bought his small daughter two of the
handbooks, *Girl Guiding*, and *Girl Guide Badges and
How to Win Them*, as well as half-a-dozen story-books on
the same subject, and she lent them all round among the
seniors and middles in her desire to make the others keen.
Many of the badges appealed to them. Living in a moun-
tainous district where ropes were in constant use, they saw
the value of learning the various knots. The making of fires
in the open, as well as the cooking and housewifery knowledge demanded for many of the tests, seemed matter-of-
course to girls whose mothers did a great deal of the house-
keeping and house-caring themselves. The Nursing tests
did not appeal to them quite so much; but the Arts and
Crafts they hailed with joy. Wanda wanted to take Artist's
Badge; Gisela felt a yearning for Basket-Worker's and
Embroiderer's; Joey plumped for Book-Lover and
Authoress.

The upshot of all this was that, finally, a deputation
waited on the Head in her study and begged that she would
let them start a Guide company.

148

Miss Bettany surveyed them consideringly. "Why?" she asked.

"It's such a fine thing, Madame," said Grizel eagerly. "It bucks you up and makes you smart!"

"Also, I like the idea of learning to do many useful things," added Gisela. "It appears to me that to be a Guide makes one also capable of much."

"And it will make for oneness," put in Juliet. "That is a big thing."

Miss Bettany nodded. "Yes, Juliet; you are right. A sense of unity is one of the biggest things in life. So is all-roundness and smartness. But the Guide movement seems to me to hold even more than that—it gives you a big outlook, and strengthens one's ideas of playing the game and being straight. And those are very big things indeed."

"Will you help us, then, Madame?" asked Grizel. "May we have a company?"

"Yes," replied the Head. "I had intended speaking to you about it before we broke up—which we do in three weeks' time—so it is only anticipating things a little. We cannot do anything much about it this term, I'm afraid. You must all work up for your Tenderfoot badge, and you can begin to learn Morse for your Second-Class. Next term we will begin in real earnest."

There was a little pause. Madge could see that the girls wanted to ask her something else, but that they felt shy about it. "What else?" she said, looking straight at Gisela.

"Will—will you be our captain, Madame?" said the head girl in response to the look. "We would wish it if you would."

Miss Bettany flushed with pleasure. "I should like to be your captain," she said quietly. "Joey and I are going home to England for these holidays, and I hope to be able to go to an instruction course for Guiders while we are there. It will be difficult for me to get training otherwise, I am afraid. By the way, Jo does not know of my arrangements. Will you please say nothing to her till I give you permission. I would not have told you, but, you see, you have rather forced my hand."

She smiled at them, and then dismissed them to go and tell the others that it was all right, and they were going to have their Guide company.

"But what about *us*?" demanded Amy Stevens. "*We* can't be Guides, 'cos we're not eleven yet."

"You can be Brownies—if Madame can get someone to be your Brown Owl," replied Grizel, finishing rather doubtfully.

"Probably Miss Maynard or Miss Durrant will do that," suggested Juliet.—"I say! It's half-past five and we ought to be at prep."

Silence presently reigned over the big school-room, where thirteen people sat struggling with algebra, and French essay, and history; with Juliet, the duty prefect, sitting with them, and striving to prove something complicated in conic sections. Joey Bettany, taking a peculiar attempt at a simultaneous equation up to her for explanation, thanked goodness that *she* hadn't such awful things to work out. She hated mathematics, and considered equations of all kinds an ingenious form of girl-torture.

Juliet, who *was* mathematically inclined, was rather horrified at the muddle Joey had made, and set to work painstakingly to help her to unravel it. Jo listened to her explanations with about half an ear, and then, having said she understood, went back to her seat, and proceeded to make confusion worse confounded, which resulted in her work being returned next day, so that she was kept in after *Mittagessen* to have an algebra lesson to herself while the others went out for a romp along the edge of the lake.

Before the younger Miss Bettany fully understood what she was supposed to have done, both she and Miss Maynard were hot and weary; and finally the pupil remarked that she loathed maths.

"Because you can't do them—or, rather, won't try," replied Miss Maynard scathingly. "Take your book back to your desk and work out that example and the next *correctly*."

Joey took her untidy exercise-book back to her desk, and flounced down on her chair with a scowl that said what she daren't speak aloud. Miss Maynard ignored her little exhibition of temper, and went on with her corrections.

It was a glorious March day. Outside the sun was shining brightly, and a fresh wind was blowing the cobwebs away.

There was no hope of being let off; Joey knew that very well. She heaved a deep sigh and returned to *x* and *y*.

"Finished?" asked Miss Maynard, looking up for a moment.

"Not quite," said Joey truthfully.

"Hurry up, then! Ten minutes steady work will do it!"

Jo heaved another sigh, and then suddenly gave up the struggle, and went at it. Twenty minutes later she was racing along the lake-path like a mad thing, her coat flying open, and her hair tossing wildly in the wind. Grizel joined her just opposite the Kronprinz Karl, where already there were signs of activity in preparation for the coming season.

"O-o-oh! Isn't it a *gorgeous* day!" Joey gazed round her rapturously. "I loved the winter here; but it's been deadly dull since the snow melted. I must say I think thaws are the most boring things imaginable. Let's join the others over there, shall we?"

They walked along towards the little rivulet which acted as the outlet for the mountain streams. In the summer it was rarely more than a trickle of clear water bubbling over the pebbly bed. There was nothing of the trickle about it today. The snows on the lower slopes of the mountains were melting rapidly, and a perfect torrent of grey, rushing water fought its way between the narrow banks to the lake, whence the ice had melted for the most part, though blocks of it still floated here and there.

"If that river rises much more, it'll flood," said Grizel, as they stood watching it for a moment. "Look at those alders, Joey. They're nearly washed out!"

"Not quite, though! Madge says they root pretty firmly," replied Jo. "I s'pose they *have* to or they wouldn't be able to grow by the sides of rivers. What a noise the water makes, doesn't it?"

"Come on! Let's cross," said Grizel. "Miss Durrant must be talking of something awfully jolly, to judge by the row they're all making! Let's go and see what it is." They hurried down the path to the light plank bridge which crossed the stream. Grizel danced over without a thought, but Joey shut her eyes as she made the crossing.

"Why on earth——" gasped her friend. "Joey! Why do you do that?"

"The water makes me so giddy," explained Joey. "I love the *sound* of it; but I do loathe to see it rushing along like that. It makes me feel all queer and funny."

"Silly flop!" said Grizel, a little contempt flavouring her tone.

"I can't help it!" Joey flushed scarlet. "It always does! It looks so—so *cruel*; as though it didn't care for anybody or anything! Ow!" She concluded with a wild yell as Rufus leapt up against her. He was growing up into a handsome dog; very big, with enormous paws, and a fine head. Several pounds of excitable St. Bernard puppy flung against her proved too much for Jo, and she sat down violently on the wet grass, Rufus rolling madly beside her, frantic with joy.

"Get *up*, Joey!" began Grizel. Then she stopped as a scream of terror cut across her speech.

There was a splash. Then a little grunt from Joey, and the next minute she was tearing over the ground like a possessed creature, while Miss Durrant, who had seen what had occurred, raced after her.

The Robin and two or three of the other juniors had been playing together with the paper dolls which had been Simone's hobby during the previous term.

Robin had brought them out with her today, and had been playing with them quite happily on some big stones a little way on past the bridge. A sudden breeze had lifted one and drifted it slowly across the grass towards the water. The Robin had run to catch it, and had forgotten to look where she was going and fallen headlong into the icy torrent that was raging down to the lake.

It all happened so quickly that no one could reach her in time to save her, and it seemed as if she must be whirled down to the lake before any of them could prevent it. Mercifully, her coat caught for a moment on one of the

152

alder-trees swept by the water, and this just gave Joey time to clamber down a little in front of her. Then the coat gave and she was swept onwards. The current drove her into the bushes where Jo was waiting, and, clinging to them with one hand, she stretched out and caught the baby's shoulder with the other. Then she set her teeth and held on.

The racing water was frightfully near, and she was sick and giddy, partly from terror, partly from watching that swirling torrent. But any idea of giving up was very far from her. She clung with might and main to the little shoulder and the bushes, wondering dully how long it would be before the alders would give under the strain and send them down with that wicked grey water that seemed to be coming higher and higher.

It seemed hours to Joey, though actually it was barely two minutes before there was a crash and a splash, and Miss Durrant was standing beside her, waist-deep in the water, and lifting the Robin with one arm comfortably round her, while with the other hand she too held on to the bushes, for the force of the snow-fed torrent nearly took her off her feet, strong, big woman as she was. "Hold on, Joey!" she said. "Here come the others! Hold on!"

Then Gisela and Bernhilda bent down from the bank, and between them took the unconscious Robin from the young mistress. Miss Durrant promptly transferred her support to Joey, who found things fast becoming misty and unreal to her. Then there came fresh help, as a huge tawny body plunged in, and Rufus caught his little mistress's skirt between his strong young teeth! It was an easy matter after that for Miss Durrant to scramble up the bank, still holding Joey with one hand, lest even Rufus's strength should prove unequal to the strain. After that the world grew black, and Joey never knew what happened next. Of Miss Durrant's lying down on her face and lifting her by degrees from the water, while Rufus tugged and scrambled up beside her; of the sudden appearance of Dr. Jem on the scene, and his picking her up and racing back to the Chalet with her; of the stripping off of her wet clothes, and the plunging of her into a hot bath, she remembered nothing. She came back to the world with a hot stinging taste on her tongue—a nasty taste—and the rough hairy feeling of blankets next her skin.

"Hallo!" she remarked. "I say! What's up?"

"All right, old lady! Lie still," said Dr. Jem's voice. "Drink this like a good girl!"

Jo obediently swallowed it, and spluttered. "Ugh! What *filthy* stuff!" Then she remembered. "The Robin!" She gave a sharp cry.

"Quite safe," replied the doctor. "Snug in bed and fast asleep!"

"Sure?" Jo was growing drowsy.

"Certain. She's had a bit of a shock, of course, but she'll soon get over it. Now we're going to pack you off to bed. Come along."

Joey felt him lift her, but she was too sleepy to think of anything. Her head dropped on to his shoulder, and by the time he and an agitated Miss Maynard had her snugly tucked up in bed with hot bottles all round her she was lost to the world.

"She ought to be all right," murmured the doctor. "We've been so quick, I'm in hopes that she may even escape a cold."

"And the Robin?" queried Miss Maynard.

"She ought to do all right too. She struck her head as she fell, so she was a bit stunned and didn't take in the full horror of it. There *may* be a little concussion—I can't say yet! But otherwise, there's no need for alarm, I hope. You said Miss Bettany and Mademoiselle had had to go to Spärtz?"

Miss Maynard nodded. "They went to get some things we needed."

"I see. Well, I'll go and meet them and break the news gently. Don't leave these two alone—you can send up that sensible head girl of yours."

So it happened that half-an-hour later Madge Bettany and Mademoiselle la Pattre, climbing up the last bit of the mountain-path, were met with the story of the latest doings of the Chalet girls. They were horrified, but the doctor managed to calm their fears. He walked back with them before going off to the Post, where he had been staying ever since the night of the ice carnival, and, as he had predicted, neither Joey nor the Robin was much the worse for their adventure. Joey woke with a bad headache, the result of the neat brandy he had made her swallow to stave off a cold; and the Robin had a lump the size of a pigeon's egg on the top of her head, and was inclined to be miserable and fractious for a day or two, but otherwise they were both all right.

The girls were tremendously thrilled over having a heroine in the school; and Rufus was in a fair way to be spoilt for his share in the business.

The most discontented person in the school was Grizel. "It's too bad!" she moaned. "If only our Guide company had been formed, Joey would have been a Guide, and then she might have had the Silver Cross for saving life at the risk of her own. It's hard luck!"

CHAPTER TWENTY-ONE

An Unpleasant Problem

THANKS to the doctor's rapidity of treatment, and also to the treatment itself, nobody was much the worse for the ducking so far as bodily comfort went. But there was a certain amount of unpleasantness over it. For one thing, the juniors were forbidden ever to play near the brook again, no matter *who* was with them. For another, it was requested that, for the remainder of the term, walks should avoid that side of the valley, and should be taken either up to the Bärenbad Alpe or in the Seespitz direction.

Hitherto, no one had minded much where the walks went; but it only needed this prohibition to fill all the middles, at any rate, with a deep desire to go in the Geisalm direction. Even Frieda, the law-abiding, was overheard to say that she wished Madame had not made that rule. As for Grizel, she was nearly speechless with indignation. Nearly; but not quite. She managed to rake up enough breath from somewhere to voice her disgust. "It's too bad," she wailed. "The water from the dripping rock will be simply *shooting* down! I did want to see it in full swing!"

Thus reminded of the rock which overhung part of the way to Geisalm, and over which water trickled from a spring at the top on to the footpath, making it necessary to rush past at full speed—a proceeding not unattended by danger, since the path had broken away here, and the lake was deep at this point—everyone was seized with a deep desire to see what it would be like now. "I expect it's a regular waterfall," said Joey mournfully. "Oh, I *should* like to see it!"

"I also," put in Simone, who was standing at her elbow as usual. It was significant that no one suggested going to the Head and asking her to remove her embargo. They had learnt by this time that when Miss Bettany *said* "No," she *meant* "No."

"It's all your fault, Simone!" cried Margia unexpectedly. "Yes it is!" as Simone bristled up furiously. "If you'd never played with those idiotic paper dolls of yours, we wouldn't have had them! If you hadn't had them, you wouldn't have got tired of them. If you hadn't got tired of them, you wouldn't have given them—some of them, anyway—to the Robin. "If——"

"Oh, choke her off, somebody, do!" groaned Grizel. "It's worse than the house that Jack built!—Dry up, Margia, and give someone else a chance to talk! The amount you do, it's impossible to get a word in edgeways! Madame has said we're not to go there, so we *can't* go there, and that's an end of it! Now shut up and talk about something else!"

"Shut up yourself!" Margia was beginning heatedly, when Miss Bettany appeared on the scene.

"Grizel! Margia! Is that the way you talk when you are by yourselves? I think I had better send someone to sit with you children during your free time if that is the case. Clear away those books at once, and put this room tidy; it's more like a pig-sty than a form-room in a school!

And please don't let me hear *any* of you talking like little hooligans again!"

She walked off, leaving them all angry and rather afraid that she might carry out her threat and send them someone to sit with them while they played.

"It'll be Grizel's fault if we do," said Joey, who was feeling the effects of the spring weather, and was cross and out of sorts. She wandered over to the window and stared dismally out at the high fence of withes which cut off the view of the lake. There was little else to see, although in a week or a fortnight's time the ground would be green with the young grass.

"What are you staring at?" demanded Margia unamiably. "You might come and lend a hand instead of gawping out of the window like that at nothing."

"'Gawping' is slang," pointed out Joey, somewhat priggishly, it must be confessed. "You're breaking the rules."

"You're so particular yourself!" fumed Margia, who felt that this was adding insult to injury, and resented it accordingly.

"You've *never* heard *me* say 'gawp'!" mentioned Joey self-righteously.

"I've heard you say a dozen worse things!" retorted Margia.—"Oh, *Simone!*"

For Simone had burst into tears. "You are so un—kind!" she sobbed. "Always it is me who must do the work—but always!"

"Oh, for goodness' sake, stop it!" groaned Jo.

Almost on the words the door opened, and Mademoiselle came in. "Simone, why do you then cr-r-r-y?" she asked dramatically.

"*Je n'en sais rien!*" sobbed Simone.

"In English, if you please."

Simone gulped noisily, and then wailed, "I do not know!"

"It's the spring," said Miss Durrant, who had been standing behind her, an interested spectator of all this. "She ought to have some sulphur or something, to cool her down a little."

At this lively prospect Simone literally howled, bringing

157

Miss Bettany to the spot. She gave the French child short shrift. "Off to bed with you!" she said. "A dose of salts will put you right.—Come here, you others. Joey, let me see your tongue."

Joey obligingly hung it out as far as it would go, and Margia followed her example. Miss Bettany promptly decided to dose them all round, and went off to superintend the mixing of a big jorum of sulphur, lemon juice, tartaric acid, and one or two other items. At seven o'clock the next morning she made the round of the dormitories, and saw to it herself that every girl took her dose.

The next day "Mrs. Squeers," as naughty Jo promptly christened her sister, appeared again with her medicine. All swallowed their doses in silence.

Work, that day, proceeded as usual. The only thing that was *not* usual was the behaviour of the dogs. Usually quite happy with their freedom of the enclosure and the long walk they always had with the girls in the afternoon, today they were restless and unhappy. Zita prowled up and down the fence nearest the Kronprinz Karl and the torrent, every now and then sitting back on her haunches and baying mournfully—an example faithfully imitated by her son, who yelped loudly.

"I can't think what has happened to those dogs," said Miss Bettany during the half-past ten break as she stood by the gate, talking to Miss Maynard and watching the girls, who were wandering about in twos and threes. "I never knew Zita to behave like this before!"

"You know the old idea that a dog howls at the approach of death?" said Miss Maynard.

"Marie has been wailing about it whenever we've met," replied Miss Bettany. "She's convinced that something awful is about to happen. But you aren't superstitious, surely?"

Miss Maynard laughed half-ashamedly. "I'm not, as a general rule. But there's certainly something wrong, and Zita knows it. Animals always sense coming disaster, I think—dogs and cats especially."

"She may be feeling unwell," suggested Madge. "Let's go and examine her."

They strolled across to where Zita stood with Rufus nuzzling against her, and Joey petting them both, the ever-faithful Simone beside her. She looked up as the two came near.

"I can't think *what's* the matter with Zita," she said seriously. "I've loved her and talked to her, and she only howls. Oh, do you think she's ill?"

"Let me see," said her sister, bending over the big dog.

Zita turned mournful eyes on her young mistress, then she lifted her nose to the sky and gave utterance to her long howl. Miss Bettany patted her head and felt her nose. "Poor old Zita! I wish you could tell us why you are so unhappy! What is it, my dear? Have you hurt your paw? Let me see."

Zita allowed them to examine her feet one by one, but there was nothing wrong there.

"Is she going to die?" asked Joey almost tearfully.

"Nonsense, Joey!" replied his sister sharply. "I don't know what can be the matter, but she's well enough in herself."

"Perhaps she wants a long walk," suggested Miss Maynard. "She seems terribly restless. Look at her!" For Zita was once more pacing along the fence.

Miss Bettany looked after the dog, and then glanced round. "I've a good mind to send the girls for their walk now, and let them have their lessons this afternoon. Look at that sky! There's a storm threatening in the near future."

Miss Maynard nodded. "You're quite right; there is! Isn't this Mr. Denny's afternoon, though? There won't be much time for lessons!"

"*Kaffee* can be half-an-hour later for once, and Mr. Denny has them in three classes, so we'll cut the middles' sewing, and they can have my history instead; I don't suppose *they* will object! There's the bell. Send Gisela round to the various forms to tell them to get ready, and ask Miss Durrant if she will take the middles and the seniors. Juliet and Gisela can take the juniors. They are to walk round the lake to Buchau and back.—The little ones had better go no farther than Seespitz. This is very tiring weather."

"It's horribly oppressive," agreed Miss Maynard as she set off on her errand.

Needless to state, the girls were charmed at the idea, and ten minutes later were all ready. Then a queer thing happened. Joey went, as usual, to fetch the dogs. Rufus came eagerly enough, but Zita merely looked at her pathetically, and bayed again. She simply refused to stir from where she was.

"What a queer thing!" said Madge when she heard Joey's report. "I do hope she's all right. Leave her, Jo, if she won't come, but take Rufus."

However, when she saw the two long files of girls marching down to the gate, Zita reluctantly left her post and followed them, although she kept looking back at the three mistresses who were left behind.

"I simply don't understand it," said Miss Bettany. "Zita has never behaved like this before."

"It is the spring, perhaps," suggested Mademoiselle. "It is affecting the younger girls, and why not the dog too?"

"That must be it," agreed Madge. "Well, shall we go for a stroll in the other direction? We might go out of the pine-woods gate, and walk down by the river and along the lake-path home. What do you say?"

"I have much to do, *chérie*," said Mademoiselle. "If you will forgive me, I will stay behind and finish my work."

"You need a walk, really," said her Head. "However, if you want to work——"

"I ought to stay too," laughed Miss Maynard. "I have a pile of algebra books to correct. But they can come later on, and I'll come with you now."

They set off across the enclosure to the gate which opened on to the pasture, close by the pine-woods at the base of the slopes of the Bärenbad Alpe. There was no wind today, and the woods were very still. The only sound they could hear was the roaring of the torrent as it thundered down the valley to the lake.

"What a noise the water makes!" exclaimed Miss Maynard as they neared it.

A sudden turn in the road had brought them in full view of the stream, and a magnificent sight it was: the grey foaming water, tossing and boiling between its narrow rocky banks, fighting every inch of its way to the Tiernsee. It was a bare six inches below the summit of its banks, and it looked to Madge Bettany as if it must, ere long, overtop them and fling itself across the valley. She remembered it as it had looked on that hot day in the summer when they had gone dry-shod over the pebbles on their way to the Mondscheinspitze for her birthday picnic. She recalled, too, how Bernhilda had told her that three bridges had been swept away by the winter floods, so that now there was only a log across it. She glanced down to where she knew the log to be and felt a little wave of thankfulness to see it still there.

"Here's Herr Braun," said Miss Maynard suddenly.

Madge looked up, and saw the good-natured hotel-keeper coming to meet them. His face was very grave, and all the cheeriness seemed to have fled from it.

"*Grüss Gott, Fräulein,*" he said as he reached them.

"*Grüss Gott, Herr Braun,*" replied Madge; then she added, "the stream is very full, *nicht wahr?*"

"Too full, *mein Fräulein*, too full!" he said.

"How do you mean—too full?" asked Madge, paling slightly.

He explained. "As you can see, gracious lady, the banks are narrow. There is a great deal of snow still melting. That means that there is much water still to come down. If it should occur that the water was dammed higher up, then, when the dam broke—as assuredly it must—there would be little or no room for the flood to pass to the lake, and it would overflow and flood the valley."

"Has it happened before?" asked Miss Maynard.

"Twice within my recollection. Once, the village up yonder," he pointed up the valley, "was completely overwhelmed, and there were many lives lost. That is why all the houses are now built on the higher ground, while many are raised off the ground altogether. The other time it was

161

not so serious, but still much of the valley was several inches under water for two days, and there were many goats drowned."

"And do you think there will be a flood now?" demanded Madge.

He shook his head. *"Der liebe Gott* knows, and He only. At least, *mein Fräulein*, you are safe, and the little ones; for the Chalet stands high. Nevertheless, if you will permit that I advise you, I would suggest that you take food with you tonight upstairs. If there should be a storm, it might chance that the water will rise high enough to make it unpleasant for you to eat in the lower rooms. It would soon drain away to the lake; but it is always well to be prepared." By this time, they had reached the Kronprinz Karl, and he bade them farewell, repeating his advice about the food. Then he left them and they walked home along the lake-path.

"What shall you do?" asked Miss Maynard of her Head.

"I wish I knew!" Miss Bettany looked worried. "If I thought there really would be a flood, as he suggests, I should take the girls to Seespitz, and ask them to take us at the Gasthof for the next few days until the water goes down. But I don't want to do that unless it is absolutely necessary." She paused; then, "What do you think yourself?" she asked.

Miss Maynard frowned. "I really don't know. It's fearfully difficult to decide."

Mademoiselle, tackled on the same subject, held the view that doubtless Herr Braun was exaggerating the danger. She also pointed out that the Kronprinz Karl lay much nearer the stream, and also that it lay at a lower level than the Chalet, and therefore might quite possibly be damaged by a flood while the school stood high and dry. The ringing of the bell for *Mittagessen* put an end to the discussion, and nothing more was said. After dinner, the afternoon's engagements were explained to the girls. The juniors would have their singing as usual at half-past one, while the middles had history, and the seniors mathematics. Then the middles would have their singing lesson, and the juniors would make up the French they had missed in the morning. It would then be the turn of the seniors for singing, and the middles and juniors would do English literature and German dictation respectively. Finally, all the school were to have half-an-hour's folk-songs at the end of the afternoon instead of the beginning. Then Miss Bettany made the announcement which set everyone gasping with surprise. "After we leave the table," she said, "everyone will go over to Le Petit Chalet. The juniors will bring their night things, brushes and combs, and washing paraphernalia, over here. The elder girls will bring the bedding, and we will make up your beds over here for once. Grace!"

She said grace, and then marshalled them out of the room, and saw them over to Le Petit Chalet, where the prefects took charge. Then she turned back to the *Speisesaal*, where the excited mistresses awaited her.

"So that is your solution of the problem?" cried Miss Maynard. "I congratulate you, Madame! It's quite the best you could have made!"

"But why? I don't understand," said Miss Durrant plaintively. "Is anything wrong that you are doing this?"

"Herr Braun is afraid the river may flood, and flood badly. I don't suppose we are in any real danger, but it's best to be on the safe side, and Le Petit Chalet lies lower than the Chalet itself; so I decided to bring the babies over here. Now come with me, all of you, and let us decide how we can best manage."

They went upstairs, and an exciting time followed while they pushed beds together and fitted in mattresses for the juniors. When half-past one came Miss Bettany and Miss Maynard went off to take their various classes, leaving Mademoiselle and Miss Durrant to wrestle with the problem of fitting thirteen extra people into the upstairs rooms.

Downstairs, in the big class-room, "Plato" struggled with the excited juniors. He wondered vaguely why they were all so much upset; but he lived largely in a fairy world of his own, and as long as they did not sing out of tune he did not worry about them particularly. It was worse when the middles came, for Miss Bettany had felt it would be wiser to give them some explanation of the state of affairs, and they were deeply thrilled. They simply couldn't give their singing-master any attention, and, finally, even "Plato" the gentle was roused.

Flinging down his baton he clenched his fists and hammered on the music desk, effectually awaking their interest at once. "This is terrible!" he shouted. "Nay, more! It is blasphemous! You debase the divine Apollo! You wrong the celestial Euterpe! It is not to be borne!"

The middles looked at him with gasping surprise—not at his invocation of Apollo and Euterpe. They knew all that he could teach them about those divinities by this time. No: what startled them was his anger. During the whole of the two terms during which he had taken them for singing they had never once seen him in a temper, and had, indeed, decided that he didn't possess one. Now, with his eyes blazing, the colour coming and going in his cheeks, and his lips set in a thin, hard line, they suddenly realised that "Plato" was, for once, in a thorough-paced rage, and that they must be careful.

For a moment no one quite knew what to say. Then, suddenly, the decision was taken out of their hands. A vivid flash of lightning leapt across the sky, tearing the sullen greyness apart; there was an awful silence; then a terrific crash of thunder, and at the same moment the rain came.

CHAPTER TWENTY-TWO

The Flood

"PLATO'S" WILD OUTBURST had brought Miss Bettany from her study. She never got any very clear idea of what had happened to upset the master, for the suddenness and awfulness of the storm brought "Plato" to his senses. He was thoroughly ashamed of having lost his temper; and when Miss Bettany, shouting to be heard above the noise of the rain and the thunder, asked what had happened, he stammered out something about "the little maidens are excited—upset by the approach of the storm."

He got no further, for Simone flung herself on the young head-mistress, crying hysterically, "Oh, is it the flood? Is it the flood?"

Madge shook the child. "Stop crying *at once, Simone!*" she thundered. And Simone promptly stopped.

"Plato" had heard the question in open-mouthed amazement. "But, Sweeting," he cried, "there will not be a flood as in the days of Noah! There cannot be! Our dear Lord has given us His promise!"

Madge's eyes dared the girls to laugh, while she explained rapidly what they feared. "Plato's" face was grave when she had finished. "I must go at once, Madame. My sister is at the hotel, and it stands even lower than the Kronprinz Karl, for it lies in the little dip near the fence. If, in truth, there is danger of the flood here, how much more there!"

"Bring your sister here," suggested the young head-mistress. "It will be safer, and, if there *should* be a flood, we might need a man."

He bowed sweepingly to her. "You are kind, Madame.

We will come with pleasure. My dearest Sarah has a great dread of water, and she will be happier here with you. I go; I will return swiftly."

They saw him crossing the enclosure with great bounding steps before he was lost in the grey mist of rain that beat down as though the skies were attempting to swamp the earth.

Miss Bettany no longer doubted that the torrent would flood—it most certainly would. But she hoped that the fact of the Chalet being raised above the rest of that part of the valley would tell in its favour and save them. There was quite a deep dip between them and the river, and this would help to carry off some of the waters.

"Will the whole valley be flooded?" demanded Jo suddenly.

"No; I don't expect it for an instant. I think the river will overflow its banks a little, but I don't suppose it goes much farther than just the pasture round," replied Madge. —"Put those desks straight, girls. Take out all your books and carry them to the stationery cupboard. I don't suppose the flood will touch us, but we'll run no risks."

She hurried off to give the same commands to the other girls, and for the next hour they were busy packing away all spoilable things, while the mistresses, Marie, and Eigen provisioned the dormitories as if they expected a siege of weeks. If only it had once stopped raining, Madge would have rushed the girls along to Seespitz. But she dared not risk it in that awful downpour, and it continued all the afternoon and evening in a steady, relentless torrent.

"Plato" duly returned with his sister, who, rejoicing in the name of "Sarah", had been christened "Sally-go-round-the-moon" by naughty Jo—"Sally" for short. Sally was short, sturdy, and plain, with a pair of twinkling brown eyes, which went far to reconciling the girls to her lack of beauty. Usually she was most matter-of-fact and full of common-sense. But her brother's remark that she was terrified of water was no more than true. The twinkle had faded out of her eyes, and she was very white and shaking when she entered the Head's study.

"My dear, I can't thank you enough!" she jerked out.

"I am a perfect fool where anything in the nature of a flood or running water is concerned."

"But I question if there will be a flood," put in her brother. "The river appeared to me to be lower than it was. Mayhap the snow has ceased to melt, or the water has found another outlet."

"I hope so, indeed," said Madge absently.

She left her guests to themselves in the study and went off to superintend matters. Later on Miss Denny made herself useful by helping to put the juniors to bed; while her brother moved desks and heavy furniture, and carried loads of fuel upstairs in case it should be needed. By eleven o'clock at night everything was finished, and the girls were all safely in bed and sound asleep.

Before she went up to her own room, where Joey and the Robin were already tucked in, Miss Bettany opened the jalousies at the study window and looked out. The rain had ceased to fall, and the full-moon was struggling out from behind the ragged clouds that were chasing each other across the sky. The wind was rising, and howling in melancholy fashion among the black pine-woods at the back of the house. In the distance the steady roar of the torrent could be heard, and Madge noted that the sound seemed less than it had been early in the day. Clearly the river was falling, and therefore the danger was past. A heavy "pad-pad" of feet behind startled her as she leaned against the window looking out, and she turned swiftly, to find Zita beside her, looking at her with anxious eyes.

"How you startled me, Zita!" she said, with a little laugh at her own silliness. "Poor old thing! What is the matter with you? And where is Rufus?"

Zita whined softly. Her dog instinct had sensed coming danger, and she was doing her best to warn her young mistress.

Madge closed the jalousies again, glanced round the room to see that everything was right, and then went out, switching off the light, and followed by Zita, who kept closely to her. The Head bolted the front door and locked it safely. Mademoiselle had made the round of the form-rooms earlier in the evening, and made sure that all the windows were shut so Miss Bettany left them alone, and went to the kitchen to take Zita to her own quarters. At the door she paused. She didn't think there was any likelihood of a flood now; still, perhaps, the two dogs would be happier on one of the upper landings. She went into the kitchen, called Rufus, who was curled up in a huge woolly ball, and went upstairs, accompanied by both animals. In her own room Joey and Robin lay together in her bed profoundly asleep. Anxious not to wake them, Madge began to undress by moonlight. It was a glorious night after the storm. The clouds were vanishing, and the dark lake reflected the light of the moon in its tumbled waters. Madge opened the window and leaned out, revelling in the beauty that lay around her. Suddenly the expression of her face changed as a dull, thundering sound came to her. Louder and louder it grew. The dogs outside began to bay loudly; there were startled cries from the wakening girls. But Madge Bettany paid no heed to these. Her eyes were turned towards the valley where, coming with a swift, relentless sweep, a wall of water, fully six feet high, raced across the pasturage to the lake.

In a flash she realised what had happened. The torrent had been choked somewhere up in the mountains. This accounted for the river's falling. Then the barrier, whatever it was, had given way, and the great mass of the water had been literally hurled down to the valley below.

Even as the thought passed through her mind the wall broke around the Kronprinz Karl, which for a few moments was smothered in the foam. Then it raced, lower, but still horrible to watch, right across the valley to the Chalet.

There was a minor crash as it encountered the six-foot fence. But it was not to be expected that anything so light should prove a barrier, and the next second it broke round them, and the Chalet groaned and shuddered under the force of the blow. It all happened so quickly, that to Madge it seemed as if no time had elapsed between the moment when she had first seen that horrible grey, white-crested wall of water rushing down the valley and the moment when it broke against the school. The horror of it stunned her for a moment.

Then a voice from the bed roused her:

> "The foot had scarcely time to flee
> Before it brake against the knee,
> And all the world was in the sea.

"It *is* the flood, isn't it? I say! *That* was a whanger! "

"Stay where you are, Joey," cried his sister as she hurriedly pulled her dressing-gown round her. "I'm going down to the others.—It's all right, Robin, darling! " as the baby turned a scared white face to hers. "Joey will stay with you, and I will come back soon." Then she vanished, and the two little girls were left alone together.

Joey's first reaction was to tumble out of bed and race over to the window. She gasped at the sight she saw. All round there was nothing but water, which seemed to be becoming momentarily deeper. Already it was well up to the first sash of the ground-floor windows, and it seemed to be rising in surges.

After the first two or three washes there were no more waves; but it was quite alarming enough to see the water rising, creeping foot by foot up the side of the house. Joey could see the Kronprinz Karl, which, as it stood at a much lower level, was heavily awash to the first-floor windows. From downstairs came cries and sobs. Then there was the patter of feet as the girls climbed up to the next storey.

The door opened, and Madge came in. "Get up and dress," she said quietly. "Joey, you must help the Robin. I must go to Miss Denny."

"I wish Dr. Jem were here! " sighed Jo. "I can't think why he should be at Innsbruck just when we need him most! "

"Be quick, child," said her sister gently. "Help Robin, and dress yourself."

"But *don't* you wish he was here, Madge?" persisted Joey as she began to put on the Robin's stockings.

Madge blushed, and shook her head. "I must go," she said; and left them to dress.

When they were ready, Jo looked out of the window once more. The water was up to the top of the ground-floor windows, but, as far as she could tell, was not rising now. The trouble lay in the fact of the narrowness of the valley, and the unusual fullness of the lake. It would drain off by way of the Tiern; but it looked like being a fairly long business.

"*What* a mess things will be in downstairs!" observed Jo. "I should think the place will be about knee-deep in mud. It'll take weeks to clean!"

Zita, who was near her, pushed a big sable head under her arm in search of petting. The dog knew that things were not right, and she was frightened. Joey stood pulling her ears absently, while the Robin hugged Rufus, who had followed his mother into the room. Here Miss Bettany found them, when she came along later to bring them some hot cocoa and biscuits, and to see that all was well with them.

"I'm sending Juliet up with Simone and Frieda," said the Head. "You are to stay here until I send for you. The others are quite safe with Miss Maynard and Miss Durrant to look after them, and Mademoiselle is taking care of Miss Denny, who isn't well. There isn't room for everyone in the other rooms, so I want you to stay here. I shall be in and out all the time, and you are quite safe. They will be bringing the boats along presently; and then you shall all go over to Seespitz until the waters go down again."

"And *that* won't be long," remarked Joey, who was hanging out of the window once more. "I b'lieve it's going down already. Look, Madge!"

Madge came and looked. "I believe you are right, Joey," she said. "It would drain away fairly quickly, of course; and the wind will help it."

"What about Le Petit Chalet?" asked Joey.

"Well, it isn't on the same level, of course, and it's a much lower house; but I don't think it has really suffered much more than this," replied Madge. "Now I must go."

"*Must* we stay here?" pleaded Joey, catching at her sister's arm.

"Let me go, Joey! Yes; of course you must!"

Madge went off to send up Juliet with the other two, and to help Mademoiselle to calm the fears of the more excitable of the girls. One or two of them were completely hysterical, and it was to prevent the impressionable children from seeing this that she kept them away from the others. Vanna di Ricci and Luigia di Ferrara in particular were very bad. Both were highly-strung excitable girls, and they had completely lost control. As far as possible, they had peen isolated from the others, and were in Miss Maynard's little room with Bernhilda the placid, and Gisela, strong and calm, with them. The others were crowded into the big green dormitory and the little blue one, so that they were all on the top floor or the second one.

As the Head went upstairs to send Juliet with the other two down to her room, she was confronted by "Plato". "Pardon, Madame," he said with his old-world courtesy, "will you permit that I offer a suggestion?"

"Yes, of course," replied Madge. "What is it?"

"It is that our little damsels should sing," he replied. "Music acts as a soporific to disordered nerves; song is a drug to calm fears. Let us gather on the stairs, and all carol gaily."

Madge agreed that his idea was a good one.

There was a little silence when the singing was finished and Miss Bettany came out of the blue dormitory. "The water is falling," she said quietly. "I think it would be as well for you all to go and lie down. The danger is past, we hope; and you are all very tired. But, before we go, let us thank God, Who has kept us safe in the midst of so many and great dangers." She dropped on her knees as she spoke, and the girls followed her example. There was no thought of differences of creed in that moment as the school followed her through the General Thanksgiving and the well-known "Our Father". The Fatherhood of God came very near many of the elder girls then.

They were all so worn-out with excitement and loss of sleep that even the discomfort of their unusually close quarters could not worry them. When Madge went the round half-an-hour later, it was to find nearly everyone asleep already. Gisela was waking, and thrilled to the few words of thanks and praise her head-mistress bestowed on her. But the only other girl awake was Joey, who was cuddling the Robin, so soundly asleep that she scarcely moved when Miss Bettany gently lifted her out of the other child's arms and laid her down on the pillow.

"I couldn't help it, Madge," said Joey. "She's so wee—and I wanted something to hold; *badly*, I did!"

"I know!" Madge sat down beside her. "It's all right now, Joey." She took the hot sticky little paw Jo thrust at her in her cool grasp. "Go to sleep, Joey baba. All's well now!"

"You won't leave us?" pleaded Jo. "You'll stay with us now?"

"No. Don't worry, darling; I won't leave you."

Joey's eyes were growing heavy. Her long lashes fell on to her cheeks. "Madge, dearest," she murmured drowsily, "oh, I *do* so love you! I hope—I—hope—Dr. Jem——"

There was no more. She was asleep.

CHAPTER TWENTY-THREE

Joey's Bath

FOR LONG HOURS the Chalet School lay sleeping. They were all worn out with excitement and want of sleep during the early hours of the night, and most of the other inhabitants of the valley were up and out and hard at work before one of the girls stirred.

Joey was the first to open her eyes. For a moment she wondered where the yellow cubicle curtains had vanished, and why the Robin was snuggled down beside her. Then she remembered. With a low exclamation she scrambled out of bed and ran to the window, which stood wide to the sun and the breezes, and poked out a ruffled head. It was a curious scene of desolation which lay before her eyes. The ground immediately round the Chalet was clear of water; but there was a thick layer of grey mud all over it. In the dip beyond there was a small pond, and the Kronprinz Karl was still surrounded, while the lake was tossing madly under the whip of the north-west wind upon its swollen waters. All around, wherever the ground was low, water was standing, and bushes and trees rose from lakes and pools all over. A haystack which had been swept down by the flood was entangled in some wild barberry bushes; and as for the six-foot fence, it was a thing of the past. Here and there a stake rose forlornly from the ground; but the withes were scattered all over, and it was quite obvious that the work must be done over again.

Jo had just taken this all in, when a little stir from the couch brought her in, and she turned round to find that her sister was looking at her with startled eyes. "Hello!" she said gaily. "It's gone down."

"What has? Where?" asked Madge foggily, for she was only half-awake.

"The water, silly! Mean to say you've forgotten about it? You can't be well!"

Madge sat up, fully awake by now. "No; I haven't forgotten, of course. Only I was so sleepy. Gone down, has it? That's a blessing!"

"Not everywhere," said Jo, who was hanging out of the window once more. "The hollow is swimming still, and it's all round the Kronprinz Karl, but we're clear. There's oceans of mud everywhere, though."

Madge threw back the bed-clothes, and got out of bed. "Let me see, Joey. What a mess! I wonder what the downstairs rooms are like."

"Awful, I should think. Are we going to get up now?"

"Yes. It must be fearfully late! Just look at the sun! I wonder Marie isn't about. Where are the dogs?"

"Outside, I suppose," replied Jo. "I say, what an adventure we've had!"

"More of an adventure than I like, thank you!" retorted Madge. "I hope to goodness we're going to have a little peace after this. We've done nothing but have excitements ever since we came to Austria. I don't want any more adventures for a long time to come!"

Jo considered her sister with her head on one side. Her remark appeared to have nothing to do with the subject. "I wonder when Dr. Jem will get up from Innsbruck," she observed.

Madge turned to the mirror, and began to brush her pretty hair with much vigour, and without saying one word.

"He's sure to dash up when he hears," pursued Jo.

"Do talk quietly, Joey!" exclaimed Madge. "You'll wake up the Robin, and I want her to have her sleep out, but she won't if you go on yelling at the top of your voice like that."

Jo moderated her voice, but she was far too excited to stop talking. Madge was dressed and downstairs before she had begun to brush the thick mop of her hair; and sundry sounds told that the other members of the Chalet School were waking up.

The damage done *in* the school was not very extensive. The rooms were muddy, of course, and far too damp to be used for two or three days. One or two books which had been overlooked in the hurried clearing-up of the night before could never be the same again; and one or two of the chairs stood in need of repair.

Miss Bettany collected all this information, and then turned to the rest of the staff. "What do you think?" she asked. "This is the twelfth of March, and we break up on April the second—that's exactly three weeks. Shall I break up now, and bring the girls back earlier? Or shall we just carry on as best we can until the proper date?"

"Oh, carry on, I should think," said Miss Maynard. "For today, of course, we can't do much. The rooms must be cleared and dried first. But it's Thursday, luckily. I should let the juniors have lessons in one of the big dormitories, and the middles in the other. The seniors might help to sweep the mud out of doors. Then Marie and Eigen can scrub the floors and get the stoves on. Set all the doors and windows open, and I should imagine the place will be comparatively dry by tomorrow. Then, if we can manage again tomorrow, we shall have the week-end, and everything ought to be all right again by that time. If you can start Marie straight away after breakfast, I'll clear away the breakfast things and wash up. I don't teach the first period, luckily!"

"Then," added Mademoiselle, "I will attend to the cooking during the next period. I could not scrub a floor, I! But I can cook!"

"I'll clean furniture when I'm free," decided Miss Durrant. "I'm a dab at cleaning windows too," she added, laughing.

"And I'll do odd jobs," agreed the Head. "Well, at *this* rate, I see no reason for breaking up early. I must wire the parents that we are all quite safe, and then, I think, we might get to work."

The staff were very pleased with the arrangements, but the girls were *not*. They had looked forward to a thrilling time of spring-cleaning, and the news that the younger ones, at any rate, would have lessons as usual completely upset their calculations.

Meals and lessons were a good deal of a scramble that day. The seniors and the mistresses worked hard to get the place into something like order. Eigen and Marie produced brooms, and the seniors swept the grey mud out of doors, where the sun and the strong wind were already drying up the sodden earth as quickly as possible. Herr Pfeifen, the father of the two servants, came along to see if his children were quite safe, and to let them know that all was well at Wald Villa, their home. He insisted on lending a hand, with the result that soon Marie was hard at work, scrubbing the floors, while Eigen lit huge fires in all the stoves, and stoked them assiduously. Shortly after noon, Herr Braun came round from the Kronprinz Karl, to see how it fared with the school. The hotel was much worse off, for, standing at a lower level, and almost on the bank of the river, it had received the first fury of the torrent, and the wooden verandah had been badly smashed, while the water had covered the first two floors. "And I have just had all painted and polished!" he groaned. "Now it will all be to do over again, and the season is at hand!"

"Perhaps it will scrub clean," said Madge comfortingly. "How is Frau Braun?"

"She is working hard," he replied. "Ah well! The good

God sent the flood, and doubtless He had some great purpose behind it. We can only bow to His Will!" With which truly pious remark he said good-bye, and left them.

By the evening the Chalet was clean once more, and it was drying rapidly. Miss Bettany looked round, pleased with the result of her labours. "Tomorrow we must attend to Le Petit Chalet," she said. "It is smaller than this, of course; but, unfortunately, it lies in the hollow, and the flood washed higher. I see the water is draining away from the dips, so I suppose it will be clear by Monday. The Seespitz path is fairly dry now, and I am going for a walk up there. If anyone likes to get into thick shoes, and coat and tammy, she can come with me."

There was a shout of joy, for the girls had been indoors all day, and were longing to get outside. The next moment the air was full of confused shouts and exclamations as they all fled to get ready. Ten minutes later, the whole thirty odd of them were walking demurely down to the path which had been cleared of mud earlier in the day, and the four mistresses came behind them.

Once they were past the white-painted fence, which showed by a mark half-way up where the water had reached, they broke rank, and the juniors ran, laughing, and chasing each other gaily up the lake road, while the middles wandered along in clumps, and the seniors, talking very seriously, paraded along by the edge of the lake. The staff, with one eye on the younger girls in case of accident, were busily discussing the next term's arrangements. There would be a good deal to see to, for Miss Bettany had several new pupils in prospect, and one of her reasons for going home to England for the holidays was to engage another mistress and a matron. "I shall get an English mistress," she said. "Now that we are growing so quickly, I really need more time, and as long as I have to teach all the English subjects to the seniors, and history and literature to the middles, I simply can't *make* the time!"

"We shall be very big next term?" queried Mademoiselle.

"Between forty and fifty, at least. It is quite possible that we shall be more, because we may get a few day-girls from the summer visitors. Of course the Maranis, the Mensches, and one or two others cease to be boarders; and next term is the last for Gisela and Bernhilda. Still, we are doing very well. We need a matron too. We've managed quite well, so far; but it will be far better to have someone— Good heavens! What's that?" as a splash and several shrieks rang out simultaneously. With one accord the staff threw its dignity to the winds and tore down the road, to find Amy Stevens, the Robin, and Simone Lecoutier scrambling out of the ditch at the side of the road. It was full of water and mud, and anything more disgraceful than the three dripping objects that Gisela, Bernhilda and Juliet hauled forth on to the road it would have been hard to discover.

"Girls!" gasped Miss Bettany. "What *were* you doing? Back to school at once, you three.—Miss Maynard, will you take them, please? Hot baths, hot drinks, and bed at once.—Joey, come back on to the path! How on earth did you get there?"

She might well ask! The ditch which lay between the roadway and the mountain slope at this point was, normally, two feet wide at the most. Since the night before it had increased to four feet in width, and its waters washed up against a steep bank covered with young heather and curly fronds of bracken. How Jo had managed to get across without falling in was a mystery. How she was going to get back seemed likely to prove another.

Jo evidently thought so herself. "I can't!" she said agitatedly. "It was a fearful scrum to get here. I can't get back, 'cos it's too steep."

Miss Bettany measured the distance with her eye. "You'll have to jump," she said. "Come down as far as you can, and then jump hard so that you clear the ditch. I'll catch you."

"No, don't! *Please* don't!" begged Joey. "Honest Injun, I'd rather you didn't! I can jump it all right—*really* I can!"

"I'm afraid you may hurt yourself," began her sister, but Jo waved her aside.

"I won't! I truly won't! Please let me alone!"

Realising that the child was working herself up to a

violent pitch of excitement, Madge yielded, much against her better judgment, and stood back, motioning the others to do the same. They obeyed at once, and stood watching a rather frantic Jo, who crept down as far as she dared, and then cautiously straightened herself. "I'm coming!" she cried, as she braced herself for the spring. "One—two —three—*O-o-ow*!" As she finished counting, she gave a mighty leap downwards. She cleared the ditch; she cleared the path—it was narrow just here—she went clean over, into the lake, and, with a terrific splash that quite outdid anything the others had accomplished in that line, she vanished under the water.

She was at the surface again in a second, and was swimming frantically for the bank. As a general rule, the water was not shoulder-deep here; but, then, you couldn't go by general rules today, as Miss Maynard remarked later when she heard the full story. Miss Bettany was leaning over and catching her wrists as she clawed at the bank. Miss Durrant joined her, and between them they lifted Jo out just as Dr. Jem appeared on the scene and took in the situation at a glance. "Hurry her home," he cried, not attempting to greet anyone. "Don't let her stand for a moment! Here, I'll take one side. Miss Durrant and Mademoiselle will look after the girls—and you, Miss Bettany, grab this awful infant with me. Now then, young lady, just buckle your stumps a bit!"

It was, of course, the end of the walk. Jo was raced home as hard as they could go, and obliged to share the fate of the other three. Mademoiselle, certain that the lake-path was charged with accidents today, and convinced in her own mind that it was tempting Providence to go any farther along it, marshalled the girls into "croc," and, with Miss Durrant at the head and herself at the tail, marched them back to school, uttering exclamations and ejaculations.

"Just as though she were a sky-rocket!" said Grizel. And was promptly embroiled in an attempt to explain to Luigia di Ferrara just wherein the likeness lay.

"What on earth made you do that?" demanded Dr. Jem of Joey later on when she was safely tucked up in bed.

"Hadn't you had enough of water for once in your life without pitching into it like that?"

"Well, I never *meant* to do it," argued Jo. "It was Madge's fault, really."

"My fault! How was it *my* fault?" demanded her sister indignantly. "It was your own stupidity! If you'd let me catch you as I wanted——"

"We'd both have gone in," Joey finished for her. "My weight would have sent you flying! O-o-oh! Wouldn't it have been priceless! You wouldn't have looked very dignified, my dear, pitching into the lake with me on top of you!"

Madge shrugged her shoulders. Then she laughed. "That's true for you, Joey, my child! But I don't for one moment believe your weight could upset me to *that* extent."

"I was jumping," Jo reminded her. "I jumped for all I was worth."

"I rather think you did!" laughed the doctor. "Well, 'All's well that ends well'; and it's high time you were off to sleep. You four must all stay in bed tomorrow till I have seen you. I don't, for an instant, expect there will be anything wrong with you, but it's just as well to be careful! Now, go to sleep. If you are very good, I may have something to tell you in the morning!"

"Oh, what?" Joey started up in bed.

He promptly laid her flat again, and tucked the clothes firmly round her. "You don't hear till the morning; and only *then* if you've been good.—Miss Bettany, you shall report to me."

"I think you're mean!" grumbled Jo as she settled down. "Oh, all right, I'm *going* to sleep! Good-night!"

"Good-night," replied the doctor. "Pleasant dreams!"

But Jo was buried in oblivion, and gave him no reply.

CHAPTER TWENTY-FOUR

Joey's Future Career is Settled

As MIGHT have been expected, the first person to wake that next morning was Joey. It was barely six o'clock when she stirred, opened her eyes to their fullest extent, and then sat up, wide awake. As Le Petit Chalet was far from fit for them to be in it, the juniors were still sleeping over in the Chalet, and were likely to remain there for two or three nights longer, so sleeping arrangements were, as Grizel had remarked the night before, rather on the crowded side. Joey stretched herself luxuriously, and then glanced down at the Robin, who lay in the profoundest slumber, her dark curls all rumpled, her lovely little face flushed with sleep. "Darling!" murmured the elder child. "I hope we can keep her for ages! It's just like having a wee sister of my own! She is a pet!" It was not in Jo Bettany, however, to spend time over thoughts like these. She had a horror of anything approaching sentimentality, and, except when she was well off her guard, never voiced her affection for other people. Now she slipped cautiously out of bed, and hunted for her dressing-gown and bedroom slippers. She wriggled into them with an eye on the couch where her elder sister lay sleeping as peacefully as the baby, and then, catching up her towels and her clothes, made for the bathroom. Ten minutes later she returned, dressed as far as her knickers, and proceeded to give her golliwog mop a good hard brushing till it shone glossily. Then she got into her gym top and tunic, caught up her slippers from beside the bed, and tiptoed cautiously from the room, leaving the other two blissfully unconscious of her disobedience to Dr. Jem's orders of the night before.

Downstairs Marie was moving about already, intent on getting most of the day's work finished, so that she might go over to Le Petit Chalet and help to set it to rights. Eigen was busily stoking the stoves in the form-rooms and Miss Bettany's study, with Rufus accompanying him— apparently to see that he did his work properly. Marie looked up from her rolls with a cheerful, *"Grüss Gott,"* as Joey dashed into the kitchen demanding something to eat; but Eigen was far too busy to pay attention to anyone.

Marie rose to the occasion with a roll and some cheese, and Joey wandered forth into the fresh spring air, munching happily. She was wildly curious about Dr. Jem's remarks of the night before, and spent her time in wondering what it was he had to tell her. Of his hint that she should hear only if she had been good—which, she supposed, meant if she had obeyed his orders—she took no notice. As a matter of fact she had forgotten it, and she only remembered when she went in to seek a coat, as the morning air was sharp. "Goodness!" she gasped; and collapsed on to the lowest stair where she had been standing. Then, "Oh, but he *couldn't* be such a mean! He just wouldn't!"

A little doubt as to whether the doctor would really keep his word crept into her mind. Finally, she put her coat away again, took off her slippers, and stole upstairs in her stockinged feet. A minute later, Madge was rudely awakened from a thrilling dream by a scarlet-faced Jo shaking her.

"Made! Madge! Wake up, do!"

Madge sat up in bed, pushing back her hair from a startled face. "Joey, what is it? Are you ill?" She stretched out her hand and felt Joey's.

"Oh *no!*" said Jo promptly, as if she and illness of any kind were utter strangers. "I'm not ill in the least! Only I got up, after Dr. Jem said I wasn't to until he came, and now perhaps he won't tell me what he said he would!"

"Hush-sh-sh!" warned Madge, glancing across at the bed where the Robin was sleeping. "Don't wake Robin! Here, sit down on the edge here! You are an idiot, you

181

know, Joey. You seem all right; but I do think you might have remembered! "

"I'll go back to bed if you like," suggested Joey in very subdued tones.

Madge considered the idea for a moment. "No; I don't think you need this time, as you are fully dressed. You certainly *look* as though there was nothing wrong with you! "

"I've just eaten a roll and cheese," said Jo, as if this were a guarantee of her all-rightness.

The elder girl relaxed, and bit her lips to stop herself from laughing. "You really are *awful*, Joey baba! All right! I'll tell the doctor I said you might."

"Madge! You gem! " Joey hugged her sister vigorously. "Then he will tell me what he was going to tell me! I do wonder what it is! "

"Well, it's no use asking me, for I haven't the least idea. He hasn't said a word to me about it," declared Madge as she threw back the *plumeau* and got out of bed.

"Reach my slippers over, Joey, there's a good child. Thanks! " She put them on, and then went across to the bed and bent over the Robin. News from Russia was very scarce, and Madge could not forget the pretty Polish mother who had died in decline. She was almost more careful of her youngest pupil than she was of her delicate sister. Luckily, the Robin was sleeping healthily, and they had been very quick in getting her home.

"She's all right, isn't she?" queried Jo.

"Yes; I think so. Now you can trot. I'm going to dress; then I'm going round to see the others. Put on your big coat if you want to go out. Tell Marie I shall be down presently, will you?"

Jo nodded, and left the room. Going downstairs she started whistling the Nonesuch air, and was promptly caught by Miss Maynard, and fined. Whistling was forbidden in school, and Jo had simply asked for trouble, as the mistress reminded her in somewhat caustic language.

Jo had nothing to say for herself, and listened meekly to Miss Maynard's strictures on her behaviour, shooting away downstairs as soon as she was free, and giving

Madge's message very briefly to Marie, before calling to Rufus and Zita to follow her out of doors.

Through the gaps where the fence had been she could see the Kronprinz Karl, the Post, the Zeidler, and the other hotels. The little valley was full of people working to repair the damage done by the flood. Already workmen were busy rebuilding the verandah of the Kronprinz Karl. The Villa Adalbert was receiving a fresh coat of paint. And along the banks of the stream were men busily engaged in deepening the bed.

Jo was so interested in what was going on that she paid no attention to footsteps behind her, and was considerably startled when a strong arm swung her round and she found herself facing Dr. Jem.

"Now then, young woman," he said sternly, "what did I say about bed?"

"Madge said I might——" began Joey. Then she stopped. She knew, better than anyone else, that if she had not been up and dressed before her sister woke up she would have been kept in bed until the doctor's arrival. Jo was nothing if not honest. "I mean—I was up, and she said I might stay up," she finished.

Dr. Jem scowled at her portentously. "Mutiny in the ranks, eh? Why can't you be obedient, you scaramouche? How do *you* know you're not sickening for something awful?"

"Like—like thrush?" said Jo unexpectedly.

"Well—er—no; not quite that. Still, that's not the point."

"I know it isn't! I forgot, you see. I *did* offer to go back."

"A lot of use that will be now! Let's have a look at you."

Joey promptly put out her tongue and offered him her wrist. He laughed.

"You monkey! Well! There's nothing wrong with you so far as I can see. All right! Passed with a clean bill of health!"

"Oh! Then *will* you tell me what you said you would last night?" pleaded Jo, clinging to his arm. "I'm *aching* to know!"

"I'm coming in to see your sister about ten o'clock," he replied. "I'll tell you then."

"But I'll be having lessons then—geometry," protested Jo.

"Then you can come out of your class for once," he replied. "I want to tell you when your sister is there——"

"Madge is up now. Oh, *do* come *now* and tell us!" Jo put forth all her coaxing powers into both voice and face as she spoke, but he was adamant.

"It can wait till ten o'clock. I mean what I say, kiddy," he added gravely. "It won't do you any harm to wait. Now I must go. Tell your sister from me to keep the other infants in bed till I come, and you keep out of draughts." He was hurrying off, when he suddenly turned and called the child to him. "Joey! Come here, please! Don't you have a singing-lesson today?"

"Yes! Why?" demanded Joey, staring at him wide-eyed.

"Mr. Denny is ill," explained the doctor. "I am just going to him."

"Oh, *poor* 'Plato'! D'you want me to tell Madge for you?"

"Yes, please. Will you say that I am afraid he will be ill for a while. And, look here, just keep it to yourself for a bit!"

"All right," nodded Jo. "I'll tell Madge, but no one else."

"Good girl!" he said. "You'll get your reward all right —at ten o'clock!"

This time he really did depart, and Joey was left to return to the house, where she encountered her sister, who asked where she had been.

"'Plato's' ill," said Jo in reply.

"Do you mean you have been to the Adalbert?" demanded Madge.

"No; I met Dr. Jem, and he told me to tell you. Oh, and he's coming to see you and me at ten o'clock. He's going to tell me then!"

"Joey! Talk sense!" cried her sister in exasperated tones. "Tell you *what*?"

"What he said he would. The others are to stay in bed, by the way, till he comes. I say, Madge, I think 'Plato' must be awfully bad. The doctor said he'd be ill for a while. Will that mean no singing-lessons?"

"I don't know." Madge looked worried. "Don't say anything to the others, Jo. Mr. Denny is not strong, you know."

"He behaved like a brick the other night," replied Joey. "No; I shan't say anything—Dr. Jem told me not to. Is breakfast nearly ready?"

During breakfast it was noticeable that Joey Bettany was unusually quiet.

This state of affairs lasted right through the bed-making period, and when Frieda asked her to come for a run by the lake before school she was startled by the answer she received, "Sorry, but I can't. Too busy!"

"But you do nothing!" protested Frieda.

"I'm doing a lot; I'm thinking," replied Jo with dignity.

"Mind you don't hurt your brain, then!" jeered Grizel, who was passing and had heard.

Jo said promptly, "All right, Frieda; I'll come after all, I think. Race you there!" And she set off at top speed, followed by Frieda, who was waking up, and was a very different person from the shy junior who had come to the Chalet School three terms before, although she still was much quieter than many of the others.

Rufus, who had been ambling along beside his young mistress, uttered a wild yelp and flung himself after her. They tore madly down the path, nearly fell over a group of the prefects who were busily discussing the examinations, which lay only a week ahead, and wound up their wild career by collapsing in a heap at Miss Durrant's feet.

"Get up!" she said severely when she had recovered her breath. "Get up *at once*, both of you!—Frieda, I am surprised at you!—Jo, what does this behaviour mean? Take that dog back to his proper place, and please don't race about in that mad way again!"

They got meekly to their feet, and Jo, calling Rufus to order—he was rolling wildly in the grass—led him off to his own quarters. Then, as the first bell rang just then, she made her way to the form-room to get her books out for the first lesson.

185

It is to be feared that very little sense was to be got out of the younger Miss Bettany during that period. She listened blandly to Miss Durrant on the subject of similes and metaphors, and when invited to show how much she had learnt by explaining what a simile was, absently murmured something about "a cake eaten in Lent in Yorkshire"—an answer that created quite a sensation.

Miss Durrant was righteously indignant, but much of what she had to say passed harmlessly over Jo's head, for at that moment she caught sight of the doctor walking up the path, and was at once lost to the world. Fifteen minutes later Maria Marani came to ask if Joey Bettany might please go to Madame in the study. Joey scarcely waited for permission to go.

She scampered down the passage, and literally fell into the study. The doctor was there, with Miss Bettany sitting opposite him, her eyes bright, and her cheeks vivid with excitement. As her little sister came in she held out a hand to her. "Come here, Joey baba! I am proud of you!"

Jo went to her sister's side. "Proud of me? Why, Madge!"

"Listen to what Dr. Russell has to say to you," replied Madge, slipping her arm round the slender waist.

Joey turned big black eyes, gleaming with excitement, on the doctor.

"Do you remember writing your 'Elsie' book, Joey?" he asked.

Joey nodded dumbly. She couldn't speak.

"Someone showed me your story in the *Chaletian*," he went on. "I liked it. It is good, you know, Joey. You have told the tale simply and freshly, and your people live, which is a big thing. I heard of a competition for children. Ten pounds was offered as a prize for the best short story written by a boy or girl under eighteen. There was a second prize of five pounds, and another of one pound. I thought your little tale might have a chance, so I copied it out and sent it. Yesterday I had a letter from the judges—a registered letter. Here it is!"

He handed it over, and Jo took it with hands which literally trembled. It was addressed to

186

but she had no time for that at present. She tore it open, and a typewritten note with a crackly piece of paper wrapped in it fell out. Madge picked it up for her, and Joey unfolded it. For a moment the printing danced before her eyes. Then the words settled themselves, and she was able to read it.

There was a long silence. Then she turned to her sister. "Madge! They—they've given me the second prize! The five pounds prize is mine! Here it is!"

She held the five-pound note out to her sister. Not knowing what else to do, Madge took it, and then pulled the child down to her level. "Joey baba! I'm so glad!"

Then Jo disgraced herself for once in her life. Burying her head on her sister's shoulder she burst into tears, and cried as she had not done for ages. Madge held her close, petting and soothing her, till the outburst was over.

Then Jo suddenly sat up. Her eyes were swollen and red, and so was her nose, but this in no way detracted from her sudden sense of importance. "This settles it," she announced, with a hiccough. "I'm going to start in right now and be AN AUTHORESS!"

CHAPTER TWENTY-FIVE

The End of Term

"GOOD-BYE, Wanda; good-bye, Marie! Sure you've got everything? Good-bye, Paula! I hope you will all have very happy holidays."

"*Auf wiedersehen, Madame!* We wish you the same! We'll send you post-cards from Prague, if we may."

"Please do! Good-bye, Thrya and Inga! Enjoy your-selves in Cologne! Ready, Margia? Good-bye, then! Re-member me to your mother."

The last of the "early" people scrambled into the little mountain-train, which was running once more. They waved their hands excitedly out of the windows; there was a puff and a jerk; they were off!

Madge Bettany, standing on the path with her small sister and the Robin, waved to them, and then turned back with a sigh of relief.

"Let's get back to *Frühstück*," observed Joey, tucking her arm through her sister's. "I'm panting with hunger!"

"You look it," laughed Madge. "All right; come along. —Tired, Robin?"

The Robin shook her curly head. "No, t'ank you! But I s'*ould* like some milk!"

"You shall have it when we get back. Marie is sure to have it ready, because the Mensches, the Maranis, and the Steinbrückes are going by the next train; and Miss Durrant is taking Evadne, Juliet, Grizel, and Rosalie to Euhrbach by the ten o'clock bus."

"We *shall* be empty!" sighed Jo.

"Yes; but only till midday. Then we and Miss Maynard go off in the Paris-Wien express, and we shall be in Eng-land on Saturday."

"Why didn't Mademoiselle wait and go with us?" asked Joey.

"Because Signora di Ricci wanted Vanna home as soon as possible, and she had to change at Innsbruck. It was easier for all the Italian girls to go together, and for Mademoiselle to take the French girls and look after them all."

"I see," said Jo thoughtfully. "And Miss Maynard is at Spärtz to put the early people on to the proper trains, I suppose?"

Madge nodded. "Yes. Now you know all about it."

"Yes, I know *that*; and I know we're going to stay with Miss Maynard in the New Forest, which is gorgeous! But isn't there something else?"

"How do you mean—something else?"

"I don't know. Only there's a sat-on sort of feeling, as if something *thrilling* were going to happen!"

"In a way you're right. I hope to go to the big Guiders' Camp to train for a week while we are in England."

"When?" demanded Joey excitedly. "Oh, Madge! *Are* we starting Guides for certain sure next term?"

"We are, indeed! As for when, I think it's the second week of the holidays. You and Robin will be with the Maynards by yourselves. You know we are going to London to stay with the aunts for the first week, don't you?"

"Yes; and I jolly well wish we weren't!"

"Hush, Jo! You are not to say things like that! They want us; and we couldn't possibly be in England and not go to see them! They would never forgive us if we did that!"

"Well, I know it's jolly decent of them, and all that; but they bore me!" declared Jo. "They will talk about taking care; and say I'm delicate; and fuss, *fuss*, FUSS till I want to shy things round!"

Miss Bettany laughed. "Poor old thing! What an awful state of mind! However, you needn't worry! I don't think they'll fuss over you this time! The Tyrol has certainly made a big difference to you. You don't look like the same girl!"

"I know I'm fatter! And I've grown heaps! That frock I had this time last year won't go near me! Well, what do we do after London?"

"You two go down to Winchester on the Monday, where Miss Maynard will meet you and take you to her home. I shall come the following Monday. We leave England on the twenty-fifth, and get back here about the twenty-ninth. School begins on May the second. Now you know all our holiday plans, and I hope you're both satisfied."

"Razzer!" said the Robin emphatically.

But Jo looked doubtful. Madge shot a glance at her. There *was* more to tell, but she felt that she would rather keep it until they were by themselves, and she could explain things thoroughly. However, they reached the school just then, and there was no time for more, for Marie was ringing for *Frühstück*, and they had to hurry to get to the table in time.

It was a festive meal. All rules were in abeyance, and the people left chattered all at once, and in a wild mingling of English and German, which made the Chalet *Speisesaal* sound more like the monkey-house at the Zoo than anything else. When it was over, there was a scramble to finish up the oddments and see to the locking-up of cupboards. The Chalet was to be closed for three weeks, during which Marie and Eigen would be at home, taking Rufus with them. Zita had gone back to her owners, who had been almost hysterically grateful to Miss Bettany for her care of the great dog during the winter.

Herr Braun had undertaken to keep an eye on the place, and also to have the new fence put up while Miss Bettany was away. He had one or two schemes of his own, which related to the rolling of the cricket-pitches and the tennis-courts, the planting of a flower-garden, and so on. Of these, however, he said nothing as yet.

Nine o'clock brought Herr Mensch up to Briesau to escort the Innsbruck girls back to their own city, and to offer Miss Bettany a basket of little cakes from Frau Marani and his wife, "to be eaten on the journey, *mein Kind*. And here is chocolate for *die Mädchen* from *Grossmütter*."

When he had gone off with his charges, Miss Durrant was taken down to the steamer with hers. They were to catch the bus at Scholastika, and go by it to the nearest town, just over the border, into Germany. Then they would take train to Euhrbach, in the Black Forest. It was a roundabout journey, but all the people concerned had plumped for it, declaring that would be far more fun than going *viâ* Innsbruck and Munich.

At last the Bettanys and the Robin were alone; and, as they walked slowly round the lake to Seespitz to catch the mountain-train to Spärtz, Madge told her news to the two little girls.

"Do you remember how ill poor Mr. Denny has been?" she began.

"Yes," said Joey soberly. "But he's better now."

190

"Yes; he is better now," agreed her sister. "Dr. Jem says that so long as he remains up here in the mountain air he will be fairly all right. But he is to go still higher. Do you remember the day we climbed the Sonnencheinspitze last summer?"

"*I* wasn't zere," said the Robin reproachfully.

Madge smiled at her. "No; I know you weren't. But Joey remembers."

"Rather!" said that young lady. "Is he going up there?"

"Yes. They are building a huge place—a sanatorium—up there in the little village on the Sonnalpe, and Dr. Jem is going to take charge of it. He won't live there: he's going to have a chalet built above the village, where he will live."

"Coo! Won't he be lonely?" queried Jo with interest.

A little smile edged Madge's lips. "At first he may. But it won't be for long. You see, he's going to be married."

Joey stood stock-still in the middle of the path. "*Married!* Who to? Oh! How absolutely *rotten* of him!"

"Joey!" Madge fairly gasped.

"Well, it is! Oh, he *is* a mean! I just hate him!" And Joey turned and walked on, frowning heavily.

"Joey!" Madge's voice was sharp with dismay. "Why, I thought you liked him so much!"

"I *did*! I don't now! I think he's a pig! I'll never speak to him again!"

"But, Joey, why?" Madge was so much upset that she forgot to scold Jo for unparliamentary language.

"To go and get *married*! To a beastly stranger!"

The elder girl's face relaxed. "*Oh!* But—but—it *isn't* a stranger, Joey dear!"

Jo looked up sharply. Then the slow colour flushed her face. "Madge!"

"Yes, Joey!" Madge's eyes were starry, and she looked lovely as she smiled at her little sister. "You won't hate him, Joey dear, when he is—your brother!"

Joey's answer was to fling her arms round her sister, nearly upsetting the pair of them into the lake, and hug her vehemently. "Oh, Madge! Really, truly? Oh, I *am*

191

so glad! I've wanted it for ages! He's such a dear—nearly nice enough for you!"

The whistle of the engine interrupted them then, and they had to tear across to the train, and only just got in in time. There were very few passengers, and no one but themselves in their carriage, so Madge finished her story on the way down.

"We shan't be married for a year at least, Joey. Probably it will be two years. I want to see the school well begun, and he has to establish his sanatorium. And I'm young yet; so I shall be Head of the Chalet School for some time yet. When we are married, you and the Robin will live with us till you have homes of your own; for, Robin, your father is leaving Russia, and coming to be Jem's secretary up here. Isn't that splendid?"

The Robin snuggled closer. "I am so glad, Tante Marguerite! And *Monsieur le docteur*, he will be my Oncle Zem, *n'est-ce pas*? And Papa and Zoë, too?—Zoë, you shall call my papa 'Oncle,' too! Oh, it will be nice!"

"Nice!" Joey repeated her words rapturously. "It'll be gorgeous!—Oh, Madge, it's just the very nicest and splendidest of all our adventures!"

Madge looked down at the slender ring on her left hand, where a sapphire glowed in the sunshine, blue as the waters of the Tiernsee under summer skies, and smiled softly to herself. "I think so, too!" she said.

THE END